Relative Strangers

Relative Strangers

Joyce Lamb

Five Star • Waterville, Maine

Five Star First Edition Romance Series

Published in 2002 in conjunction with Kidde Hoyt & Picard Literary Agency.

Set in 11 pt. Plantin by Elena Picard.

Printed in the United States on permanent paper.

Library of Congress Cataloging-in-Publication Data

Lamb, Joyce, 1965–
    Relative strangers / Joyce Lamb.
       p. cm.—(Five Star first edition romance series)
    ISBN 0-7862-3730-9 (hc : alk. paper)
    1. Women journalists—Fiction. 2. Mistaken identity—
Fiction. 3. Jewel thieves—Fiction. 4. Billionaires—
Fiction. 5. Florida—Fiction. I. Series.
PS3612.A546 R45 2002
813'.6—dc21   2001054329

To Mom and Dad, for believing in me and offering encouragement from the very start.

Prologue

Twin headlights thrust aside the darkness as Margot Rhinehart steered the black Lexus into the long, winding driveway. The air conditioner was on full blast to combat both the unusual humidity of the October night and the nerves that made her palms damp against the steering wheel. She had directed the vent right at her face minutes ago, hoping the steady stream of artificial breeze would help clear her head. The weight of her hair lay heavily against the back of her neck, and she pushed the thick length back. Southwest Florida was too humid to have such long hair. If Beau hadn't liked it so much, she would have lopped it all off in an instant.

Thinking of him churned her stomach, and she gripped the steering wheel as the car rounded the last curve in the tree-lined drive and the house loomed out of the darkness. Jagged lightning flashed behind it, and the thunder that followed seemed to shake the car. Rain had yet to fall, but it would be only a matter of minutes.

As the car rolled to a stop, Margot studied the tall white columns, marble steps and floor-to-ceiling windows. It looked different, and she knew her perspective had changed. She was not the same woman she'd been when she'd first seen Beau Kama's estate.

7

But that wasn't it. The house wasn't supposed to be dark. She checked her watch. After nine. The lights should have been blazing by now, emphasizing the home's best features while discouraging burglars.

Her heart hammered as she shut off the car and rummaged through the glove box for a flashlight. Her hands began to shake, and she told herself to calm down. The storm had evidently knocked out the power. That was all. She remembered the many times she had huddled in Beau's arms on the second-floor balcony, watching as an afternoon thunderstorm raged above the Gulf of Mexico, a frightening yet spectacular show. But she'd been with Beau—protected. Now, he wasn't here, and she couldn't help but feel jittery.

Margot wiped a damp palm down one jean-clad leg before stepping from the car into the heavy, wet air. A strong breeze blew the hair back from her face and rattled the palm fronds overhead. In the distance, she heard forceful waves breaking on the beach.

Her steps faltered when the lights blinked on, outside and inside. She glanced up at the corner of the porch and saw the red eye of a surveillance camera blinking at her. Switching off the flashlight, she stepped through the front door. Every light in the house seemed to be on.

"Beau?" she called. "Are you here?"

Silence.

She checked the living room, taking in the masculine, black leather furniture and glass-topped tables that screamed for a feminine touch. One of these days, she would take care of that. When we're married, she thought. The one thing she wouldn't change was the framed photograph on one wall, taken several years before by Beau's brother. A child of war with striking, sad, blue eyes, clutching a ragged teddy bear to her dirty dress, gazed straight into the camera. There was

8

something about the photo that clutched at Margot's heart every time she saw it. She avoided glancing at it now as she headed for Beau's office.

There, she saw that his computer and all the gadgets attached to it were off. The large square picture of a Florida beach scene that hid the wall safe was just as she had left it that afternoon—a tiny bit crooked. She considered returning what she had stolen earlier but didn't know whether Beau was home. It would be better to wait until she was certain he was asleep or gone. Then he would never have to know.

Passing through the dining room, she flinched as lightning flashed beyond the windows. During the day, the windows provided a view of the beach and the beautiful expanse of the Gulf. Now, there was just darkness occasionally vanquished by lightning.

She mounted the carpeted steps that led upstairs, tapping the flashlight against her thigh. Thunder boomed, and she jolted again. "Beau?"

She told herself to relax. He was probably just playing with her as part of the surprise he had promised her that morning. Her birthday surprise.

At the top of the carpeted steps, she paused. The master bedroom appeared to be the only room in the house that was dark. "Beau? Come on, stop teasing."

No response.

She hit the light switch. Nothing happened.

"Damn it, Beau. This isn't funny."

She forgot the flashlight and stepped into the room, muscles tense, expecting him to jump out at her. "Beau?" She tried to sound pathetic to let him know he was getting to her.

Her foot encountered something soft but heavy. Lightning flared, and she saw a bulky shape on the floor. A person. Her breath caught, her fingers clumsy as she fumbled for the button on the flashlight and pushed it. Thunder cracked.

She screamed and backed out of the room too fast, dropping the flashlight. It hit the floor and winked out. Her back struck the wall across from the bedroom, and she slid down it, clamping a hand over her mouth.

She could smell the blood, coppery and metallic. Bile surged into her throat. She choked it back. Maybe he was still alive.

Maybe it wasn't Beau.

She pushed herself up and staggered toward the dark bedroom. Light. She needed light. Picking up the flashlight, she shook it, but it was dead.

The bathroom light. Taking a deep breath, she plunged into the room, careful to steer clear of the body. When she stumbled over an object that clinked, she dropped to her knees and ran her hands over the smooth, cool surface of a lamp base. The cord flopped in her hand. It was unplugged.

She crawled toward the wall, where she knew there was an outlet next to the bureau. It took her several tries to align the prongs with the outlet and plug it in. Without its shade, the light was blinding. Still on her knees, she turned.

It was Beau.

A neat, black hole between his eyes.

Blood everywhere.

Margot couldn't move. His eyes were open, and there was no mistaking the blankness of that stare.

Compelled by the need to be sure, she reached forward and pressed trembling fingers to the place in his neck where there should have been a pulse. Nothing. Just blood that wet her fingers.

He was still warm.

She gagged, crabbing back on all fours. The heavy dresser halted her retreat, and she used it to pull herself to her feet.

Gasping, she snatched up the bedside phone and called nine-one-one.

A woman answered.

"I need help," Margot said.

"What is the nature of your emergency?" the woman asked.

Margot heard the tap-tap of computer keys. She swung around to look at Beau in the unnatural light cast by the shadeless lamp on the floor. The shadows made his eye sockets look empty. Her chest convulsed with a dry sob.

"I'm dispatching emergency vehicles to your address right now. Please tell me the nature of the emergency so they can be prepared to help quickly," the woman said.

Margot forced herself to look away from Beau and froze.

Blood on the mirror.

Scrawled words.

Happy Birthday! Love, Slater.

She saw her image reflected through the blood; her dark hair was wild, and her green eyes wide with shock. And she saw the snapshot of her and Beau that he had pressed between the mirror and the frame a week ago.

"Oh, God." Her knees buckled, and the phone clunked to the floor.

"No," she whimpered, her fingers curling into the carpet. "You son of a bitch. Son of a bitch."

Sirens drove her to her feet. With another hoarse denial, she smeared the words on the mirror, erasing the message, then stumbled out of the bedroom. She skidded halfway down the stairs, her feet almost sliding out from under her in the tiled entryway.

Sirens wailed closer as Margot leapt down the porch steps and raced for the Lexus. Her fingers slipped on the door handle, and she realized why as she wiped them on her jeans.

They were coated with Beau's blood.

Moaning, she yanked the door open and dove into the car, fumbling for the keys in her front pocket. The jeans were tight, the way Beau liked, and she had to arch her back, straightening her body in the confines of the driver's seat, to cram her fingers into the pocket.

Her hands trembled violently, but she managed to get the key into the ignition on the first try as fat raindrops began to splat against the windshield. When she jammed it into gear, the car jumped forward.

Hurry, damn it, hurry.

She didn't ease up on the accelerator even as she rounded the first curve of the driveway and banked too high. Tires bit into the lawn, spun for a second, churning up grass and dirt, then caught on the edge of the asphalt. At the end of the drive, she jerked the steering wheel to the left, leaving mud and tread marks in her wake.

Flashing red lights appeared behind her, and she pressed the accelerator to the floor, tears burning her eyes.

The vent blew icy air at her face, but Margot barely noticed as her brain began to decipher what had happened.

Happy Birthday!

Love, Slater.

Chapter 1

Three Months Later . . .

Meg Grant rolled down the car window and propped her elbow on it, unable to tame the smile of satisfaction that curved her lips. It was January tenth. Seventy-five degrees. Not a cloud in the dazzling blue sky. Life was good. Damned good.

In twenty minutes, she would be at Southwest Florida International Airport to pick up Dayle, her first visitor since she'd moved to Florida. Meg was looking forward to sharing with her closest friend the excitement of a new city. She had lived in Fort Myers a month and was just learning the courthouse beat at the newspaper. Although it was all very new and thrilling, she missed home. Not the cold, of course. Christmas had seemed odd without snow, but that hadn't been the only strangeness this year—it had been her first Christmas since her parents had died.

With a slight shake of her head, Meg turned on the CD player. Nothing like a Melissa Etheridge tune to steer her mind away from depressing thoughts.

She made it to the airport with minutes to spare and marveled at how convenient it was to zoom into a parking space just yards from the terminal. No parking garages, no confusing signs, no impatient drivers and rude hand gestures. Fort Myers was blessedly laidback compared with the harried pace of the Chicago suburbs. She had yet to regret the move, had yet to miss the smog and sub-zero temperatures.

In the terminal, Meg boarded the escalator, grinning at the three papier-mâché manatees suspended from the ceiling. At the second level, she checked the overhead monitors. Dayle's flight would be arriving any moment.

Meg hurried to the gate, imagining her friend on the plane, cramming legal pads and her PalmPilot into her black leather briefcase. Dayle, even though this was supposed to be her vacation, had probably not left her work at home. Meg couldn't blame her. She was the same, dragging a laptop with her pretty much wherever she went. You never knew when a Pulitzer Prize–winning news story would break right in front of you.

Pausing in front of the windows, Meg saw airport personnel preparing to unload the plane's cargo. The first passengers were trickling through the gate when a black limousine glided to a stop on the tarmac. Curious, she watched as the back door opened and a man stepped out.

A businessman, she assumed. A well-paid businessman, by the cut of his suit. He wore sunglasses and shoes as shiny black as the car.

Standing next to the limo, a breeze blowing tangles of dark hair across his forehead, he reminded her of a model in an advertisement for men's cologne. He had the body—broad shoulders suggested that muscles rippled under that tailored jacket, and a lean waist spoke of regular workouts and skipped desserts. His jaw was angular and clenched as if in perpetual anger, his chin nearly square, with a cleft.

Yes, he definitely had the "I'm-a-great-smelling-guy" look. All he needed was a blond, too-thin goddess in a form-fitting red dress clinging to his arm.

He removed his sunglasses, and Meg realized with a jolt that he did it to see *her* better. The blazing Florida sun made him narrow his eyes, and she resisted the urge to shift under the probe of his gaze. She wanted to glance away but couldn't, as if the stare-down had become a dare to see who would buckle first.

A reflection in the window caught her eye, and Meg pivoted, grinning at the woman she'd known since they were both gangly, looking-for-trouble kids living on the same block. The man and his limo were instantly forgotten.

Dayle dropped her carry-on, and they hugged.

"God, it's great to see you," Meg said.

Dayle, a small woman with blond hair, brown eyes, and a shrewd gaze, drew back to look her friend up and down. "Jesus, you're even more stunning than usual. What is that? A tan?"

Meg's smile grew at the compliment. She didn't think of herself as beautiful. Her slimness was more athletic than willowy. Her dark brown hair—auburn-streaked now that she had spent some time in the sun—was long, curly and in her face if she didn't tie it back into a loose ponytail. A former lover had said her green eyes reminded him of the ocean off the shores of Jamaica, a more-green-than-blue shade that hid the undercurrents of her emotions too well.

She wore simple clothes by necessity—slacks and flat, comfortable shoes—because chasing after defense attorneys and prosecutors for quotes wasn't practical or comfortable in a fancy dress and heels. Dayle had once kept a tally of her male lawyer acquaintances, who, knowing the women were friends, had pumped her for information about Meg. Although Meg assumed that Dayle exaggerated, the compliments never failed to give her confidence a boost.

"Yes, believe it or not, I have a tan line," Meg said. "First one since high school. But then, I live on the Gulf. What's a girl to do in her free time but hang out at the beach?"

"Yeah, right. I can see you lounging on a towel, computer planted on your lap." Dayle glanced around. "I'm starving."

Meg laughed as she scooped up Dayle's carry-on. "You're always starving. First, your luggage. Follow me."

They took their time walking to the baggage claim, discussing Dayle's flight and the frigid air she had left behind. On the escalator, Meg slipped an arm around her waist and gave her another hug. "I've missed you."

"I wish you could have made it home for the holidays. My family was asking about you," Dayle said.

"Someone had to cover the news."

"I felt bad that you spent Christmas by yourself."

"I was too busy to notice."

Dayle took the cue that Meg wasn't ready to talk about her first Christmas since she'd lost her parents almost six months ago. "Well, the Midwest isn't the same without you," Dayle said.

"Still cold, though, I presume?"

Dayle grinned. "As hell. Good God, what are those?"

Meg glanced up at the papier-mâché sea cows dangling over the escalator and laughed. "Manatees. They're endangered."

"Uh-huh."

"They're so ugly they're cute. You can buy license plates with a manatee on them, and the extra money goes to a wildlife fund. You can even swim with them."

After the escalator deposited them on the first level, Dayle made her way to a baggage carousel that had yet to start. Meg hovered at the edge of the crowd of newly arrived vacationers

16

and took the moment to check in with her editor at the newspaper.

She had just turned off her cell phone when a hand grasped her upper arm. "We have to talk," a man said near her ear.

Startled as she was, Meg felt no real fear. People often mistook her for someone they knew—she had one of those faces. But when she turned toward him, recognition stole the words from her lips. He was even more gorgeous up close, taller than she had guessed, and he did indeed smell good, like soap and wind. His jaw was set, muscles bunching into knots at his temples. Sunglasses were perched on his head.

His fingers dug into her flesh as he herded her toward a short hallway that branched off the baggage claim area.

"I'm afraid you—"

"Shut up and come on."

His rudeness erased her courtesy. "Look, pal—"

"I'm not your pal. Walk."

She saw that the area where he was steering her was deserted and relatively secluded. Suddenly afraid, she dropped Dayle's bag and whacked his forearm with her phone. "Let go."

His grip loosened, then tightened. "You're making a scene."

"No shit. Let me go." She whacked him again, more startled by his nerve than his strength. "Help!"

The clatter of a baggage carousel as it started up swallowed her cry. Catching her wrist, he twisted her arm behind her back and forced her toward the hallway. Any effort to jerk away increased the pressure he put on her arm and her certainty that he would not hesitate to break it.

"You're making a big—"

"Save your breath and walk."

They were at the mouth of the hall when Meg rammed her

head back into his jaw. Stars burst before her eyes, and she heard him grunt before she was free. She whirled. A wild punch snapped his head back, sent his sunglasses flying and pain singing up her arm into her shoulder.

Unfazed, he shoved her back against the wall. She opened her mouth to scream, but his lips muffled the sound. She pushed at his chest until he pinned her wrists to the wall on either side of her head, deepening the kiss even while she tried to wrench her head to one side.

Meg clamped her teeth together, narrowly missing the tip of his tongue. When he eased back, she hitched in a breath.

"Don't scream," he said. "Or I'll do that again to shut you up."

"Let me go." She struggled against him, alarmed to discover how intimately his body had trapped hers. Evidently, he didn't trust her to keep her knees to herself.

Fear shuddered through her. She was at his mercy unless someone entered the small hallway. Even then, with him pressed against her, they no doubt looked like just-reunited lovers stealing a passionate embrace.

She drew another quick breath, but he crooked a finger across her lips. "Don't."

He didn't appear to be a man who would need to assault a woman to get what he wanted from her. He was wearing an Armani suit, for God's sake, and he smelled as good as he looked. "What the hell are you doing?" she demanded, twisting her hands in his grasp.

"Stop fighting. You're only going to end up with more bruises."

Meg almost laughed. "Give me a break."

"All I want is to talk. But not here."

"Yeah, okay. Just let me go, and I'll follow you right to

your limo." She jerked her hands just to see if he was on guard. He was.

"Are you finished?"

"Did you think I was going to stand here quietly while you attacked me?"

"If you would stop struggling—"

"Sorry," she snapped. "I have this thing about self-preservation."

He yanked her forward until their noses nearly touched. "Just shut up and talk to me," he snarled.

The contradiction of what he'd said seemed lost on him, but the look in his eyes—rage tinged with desperation—reined her in. Meg swallowed. If he was telling the truth, and he just wanted to talk, then she only had to ride out the moment. An airport full of people was just beyond the wall at her back. The chances of him causing her significant harm without drawing attention were slight, and it was obvious he was not going to let go until she complied. "Fine. Talk."

"Tell me what happened three months ago."

Meg's mind raced. *October.* She'd been living in Arlington Heights, working night and day to avoid dealing with the aftermath of a late-night car accident that had claimed the lives of her parents a few months before. She couldn't imagine that that was what this man wanted to know about.

When she hesitated, he shook her by the wrists. "Don't tell me you don't remember."

"But I don't . . . what—"

"Don't lie to me, lady."

"I'm not lying," she said.

"Beau is dead, and you were there. I want to know what happened. What the hell happened?"

"Who's Beau?" Her voice rose with fear. "I don't know anyone named Beau."

"He was my brother."

"I don't know him." She winced as he leaned into her, her ribs protesting under his weight. "You're hurting me."

"Meg? Hey!" Dayle was beside them, pushing him away from Meg even as he released her. "Are you all right?"

"This isn't over," he said, backing out of the hallway.

Meg and Dayle watched him edge around the corner, as if afraid one of them would draw a gun and shoot if he turned his back.

"What the hell was that about?" Dayle asked.

Meg rubbed a bruised wrist. "I don't know."

"Do you know that guy?"

"No."

"Jesus, if I hadn't been looking for the bathroom . . ." Dayle stopped, her gaze on Meg's face. "Should I call the police? Maybe they can grab him in the parking lot."

Meg shook her head. "I just want to get out of here."

"Are you sure? He really shook you up."

"I'm okay. Let's just go."

As they walked to the car, Meg scanned the area, spotting a black limo parked at the curb. His?

"Hey, slow down. I can't keep up," Dayle said.

"Sorry." She slowed her pace, replaying the scene in her head. Obviously, he had mistaken her for someone else. He must have realized his mistake by now.

At the car, she glanced sideways at her friend. "Welcome to Florida."

"Want to tell me what happened?" Dayle asked. "You're white as a sheet."

"My tan's fading already?"

"I'm serious, Meg."

She shrugged it off. "I guess he thought I was someone else. End of drama. Hey, you're on vacation. How does pizza and a walk on the beach sound?" She was sure she sounded as awkward as she felt.

"Perhaps a walk on the beach and a drink."

Meg laughed as she unlocked the car. "Make mine a double."

In the back of the limousine, Ryan Kama poured himself a drink. His hands were shaking, and Absolut dribbled over his knuckles. Putting the glass aside, he took several deep breaths, conscious of how his heart knocked against his ribs.

It was her, damn it. It had to be.

"Downtown, Mr. Kama?"

He glanced up at the driver. "I'm sorry?"

"The benefit, sir?"

Remembering the reason he had flown into Fort Myers instead of Naples as usual, he checked his watch. A photo exhibit featuring his work and benefiting a local children's clinic would start in half an hour.

He glanced out the window and saw her getting into a silver Honda. He had never met her before, but he'd seen a picture. And he was certain this was the woman his brother had told him about. She had the same dark hair with auburn highlights, the same striking features, the same stunning green eyes.

He was perplexed by her reappearance in southwest Florida. Why had she returned? Did she think enough time had passed and she was safe? Did the feds even know she was back?

Ryan shook his head. It didn't matter why she was here. What mattered was that she knew what had happened to his brother and why. He had spent three long months trying to figure it out. The police had been of little help, parceling out tiny pieces of information just to find out what *he* knew.

Which was nothing. All he had was the one picture.

Once the FBI took over, Ryan had found himself almost completely shut out of the investigation. His one source of information had proved minimal so far. The helplessness, the questions, the need for justice—they were driving him crazy.

"Follow her," he said, reaching for the vodka he had poured.

"Sir?"

"The silver Honda."

"But the benefit—"

"The photos will sell even if I'm not there. Go."

Chapter 2

Dayle dropped her bag on Meg's living room floor and looked around. "This is nice."

Leaving her purse and unopened mail on the desk by the door, Meg retrieved a liter of tonic water from the refrigerator and an almost full bottle of gin from the cupboard above the refrigerator.

"Don't waste any time breaking out the booze," Dayle said, laughing.

Meg's hands trembled as she dropped ice cubes into a rocks glass and added a liberal amount of alcohol. She topped it off with tonic and drained it in two gulps, grimacing as the alcohol burned its way down her throat.

Dayle watched with an arched eyebrow. "You okay?"

Meg nodded. "Better. Thanks."

She made a drink for each of them, taking an extra minute this time to slice small wedges of lime and drop them in. Her hand was steadier as she handed a glass to her friend.

Dayle wandered over to the dollhouse perched on an antique table. It had been freshly painted. "You're finishing it."

"Mother never had time."

"She loved it because you gave it to her."

"Whatever."

Kneeling, Dayle checked out the gray, wooden crate under the table. MOMS KRAFT BOCKS had been stenciled in black on the weathered wood. "I always thought this box was so cool. And you left the spelling alone all these years. How unlike you."

"She wouldn't let me fix it." Meg sipped her drink this time, conscious of Dayle watching her as they plopped down on the sofa.

"Have you had any luck?"

Meg knew what she was referring to and was surprised that Dayle had waited so long to ask. "I haven't found my biological parents yet, no."

"Oh." Dayle's shoulders sagged. "I'm sorry."

"It'll take time, but I'm prepared for that. It's why I moved here."

"Not entirely."

Meg smiled. "You don't let me get away with anything, do you?"

Dayle smiled back, and her eyes were warm with affection. "Why should I?"

Meg pushed herself off the sofa and strode to the sliding door that led to a balcony. Drawing the vertical blinds aside, she slid the door open and stepped out. Even at night in January, it wasn't cold—just cool and slightly humid. Heavy clouds hung low in the sky, and a haze had settled over the Gulf, its waves crashing onto white sand only yards from the balcony. She leaned on the railing and gazed out at the darkness.

The beach house had been a lucky find. She'd been driving by when the owner was pounding the "For Rent" sign into the front yard. She wouldn't mind trying to buy it in the future but knew she wouldn't be able to afford the coveted beach property on a reporter's salary. Securing a mortgage wouldn't be that difficult, though. Her parents had left behind a hefty sum when they died, though the money was in a trust fund that she couldn't touch until she married and had a child.

It was yet another way that her father had used money to try to control her, his last-ditch effort to regain the control he'd lost when, as a college student, she'd changed her major from business to journalism without consulting him. It probably hadn't helped that she informed him over the phone after drinking a couple of beers to boost her flagging courage.

"I'm paying for your college education," he'd thundered at her. "And you'll get the education that I choose for you."

"I'm paying for it, so you'll do as I say." It was his stock response, and it never failed to make her feel angry and helpless. He had a plan for her life, had it all mapped out what she would do for a living, when she would marry, when she would bear his grandchildren, and never once had he consulted her. The resentment, building for years, boiled over, and she told him to go to hell, that she didn't want or need his goddamned money.

She would never forget the stony silence that followed before her mother's voice came on the line, a tremor in it that Meg had never heard before. Later, she chastised herself for losing her cool, but she wasn't sorry for fighting for her freedom. Her mother had begged Meg to apologize to her father, to accept his generous offer to work for him at a ridiculously huge salary once she finished a business degree. All would be forgiven. As if her insisting on making her own choices had been something she'd done to hurt her father.

Her mother's attitude was just as frustrating as her father's. Both made her feel as though she were a bad child because she wanted to live her life the way she chose.

In spite of their objections, she had done quite well as a

journalist and looked forward to a promising career. But, according to her parents, success could be measured only in dollars and cents. The size of her paycheck was a pittance compared with the one waiting for her at her father's investment banking firm. She was a failure in their eyes.

Over the years, Meg had remained stubborn. She was civil to her parents, spent holidays with them, and exchanged mostly pleasant phone calls at least once a month with her mother. She loved them. They were her parents, her family. They were all she had. But she'd often wondered what life would have been like if her father had had no money or had never equated money with power.

Of course, she'd never know. Her parents had died in the accident, and she had inherited their money. Every last penny, certificate of deposit, bond, mutual fund and stock. Except her father took one last stab at trying to force her to live the life he'd planned for her: no money until you're married and have a kid. Take that, you ungrateful brat.

Dayle joined her at the balcony's railing. "Did it help to move more than a thousand miles away from the memories?" she asked.

Meg nodded. "A little. I didn't like who I was there."

"Are you different here?"

Meg laughed softly. "Not yet. It's only been a month."

"So there's still time."

"Yeah." She tipped her glass to capture an ice cube and crushed it between her teeth.

Dayle turned and braced her elbows on the railing so she could see Meg's face. "Where are you in the search for your biological parents?"

Meg held up her empty glass. "I need a refill. How about you?"

"No, thanks."

Meg went inside to mix herself another drink. "Mother didn't leave me a hell of a lot to go on. Just the letter in the safe-deposit box that said I was adopted from a Fort Myers couple." The alcohol in her system made her feel clumsy, but the shaking had subsided.

Dayle leaned a shoulder against the door. "Have you turned up anything yet?"

"I have no idea where I was adopted, in what county or state, so I haven't gotten very far. My parents' lawyer is still trying to track down the paperwork." She swirled the alcohol in her glass. "How about that pizza? There's a place not far up the beach. Want the usual?"

"Double everything. I might waste away."

Meg laughed as she picked up the phone to place the order. When she was done, Dayle was holding up an ashtray that she'd found on the balcony. "What the hell is this?"

Meg chastised herself for not getting rid of it. "What's it look like?"

"Since when do you smoke?"

"I tried it briefly," Meg said.

"Why?"

Meg shrugged. "It was something different. I was bored."

Dayle gave her an incredulous look. "That's messed up, Meg."

Taking the ashtray from her, Meg dumped it in the trash in the kitchen. "Don't worry about it, Dayle. I did it for a week and couldn't stand it. It's a filthy habit. Okay?"

"What other filthy habits have you been trying on for size?"

"Nothing. It was stupid. Where were we?"

Dayle paused, her gaze searching Meg's face. Apparently satisfied by what she saw, she said, "We were talking about your mom's letter."

Meg nodded, remembering that that subject wasn't necessarily attractive either. "Right."

"What else did she say in it?" Dayle asked.

"Standard stuff. 'We always thought of you as our own. We wanted to tell you, but we didn't want you to be hurt.' Blah blah blah."

"They must have had reasons that seemed like good ones at the time, Meg."

"Guess I'll never know, will I?" She choked up but forced the emotion back. She shouldn't have had so much alcohol so fast. Her feelings were much harder to control when her guard wasn't solid.

"It's okay to be upset," Dayle said.

Meg dumped the rest of her drink in the sink and rinsed the glass. "They denied me the right to know whether someone else out there belongs to me, Dayle. Now that they're gone, now that no one is left . . ." She trailed off, swallowed. "I'm alone now. Truly alone."

"You're not alone," Dayle said.

Meg looked up and smiled. Dayle was one of her few real friends. She loved Dayle's whole family, seeing in their closeness what she had longed for in her own. Those qualities had drawn her to the Richmonds when she and Dayle had been kids: warmth, caring, and laughter. The chaos of their home—Dayle had four brothers and two sisters—had been a welcome respite from the silent chill at her own house. The Richmonds had made a fine surrogate family, and Meg sometimes wondered what kind of person she would have become had they not been there for her.

Dayle said, "I understand your need to make a connection with someone after what happened with your parents. But do you think this hunt for the people who gave you away twenty-eight years ago is the answer? I hope you're not expecting to find an instant family to replace the one that let you down."

"Hell, I don't know what I'm looking for. An anchor, I guess. A connection of some kind. Distraction maybe. I have to do something besides work and think about how they died before my father and I could resolve our issues."

"You resolved them as much as possible, Meg. I know it wasn't to your satisfaction, but you did what you could. He wasn't willing to accept your choices, and that's not your fault. You tried to make him understand. He should have been proud of you, and I think he was."

"Why would he have been?"

"Why not?" Dayle demanded. "Your life will calm down eventually. Give it time." She blew out a breath. "God, I know how trite that sounds."

Meg smiled, loving her for being everything she could have asked for in a friend. "Don't worry about it. You're a good listener, and that's exactly what I needed. I'm going to change out of these work clothes before I go pick up the pizza." At Dayle's questioning look, she gave a rueful shrug. "Carry-out's cheaper, and it's a short walk."

Dayle laughed. "Think you'll be so frugal when that trust fund kicks in?"

"Like it ever will."

"Optimism, Meg. I'll introduce you to it sometime."

In the bedroom, Meg pulled on faded blue jeans, a white tank top, and a black sweatshirt that she left unzipped. She put on her favorite pair of ragged Nikes. On her way to the door, she slipped some money and her keys into a pocket. "Make yourself comfortable. I'll only be a few minutes."

"Want some company? I'd feel better if we went together," Dayle said. "Considering."

Meg thought of Mr. Armani. "Okay."

★ ★ ★ ★ ★

The beach was dark. Clouds hung low overhead, muting the scuffing of their shoes as they walked along the water's edge where the sand was packed and easier to navigate.

"It's so peaceful," Dayle said. "Listen to the waves."

For thirty nights, the rhythmic beat of the waves had soothed Meg to sleep. The immensity of the Gulf awed her, making her feel vulnerable and content at once. On a bad day, its vastness had a way of snapping life back into perspective. She'd needed that, depended on it.

Dayle glanced over her shoulder.

"What is it?" Meg asked.

"I thought I heard something."

"Probably tourists." She turned and saw the dark outlines of two men about ten yards behind them. They were casual, unhurried. One of them was smoking, and she heard laughter.

The scrape of shoes on sand-covered rock drew Meg's gaze to a low cobblestone wall that separated the beach from a vacant lot. Another dark outline, also a man, was less casual, somewhat furtive.

"What the hell?" Dayle said under her breath.

"They're tourists," Meg said, but she wasn't as certain as she sounded. In the past month, she had taken many solitary walks along this stretch of beach and had not once felt uneasy. If it had not been for the bizarre encounter at the airport, she wouldn't have thought twice about sharing the beach with strangers tonight.

"Just keep walking," she said. "The pizza place isn't that far. There'll be people all over."

A minute later, Meg glanced back. The men were less than twenty feet away. No longer casual. No longer laughing. The one with the cigarette flicked it away, and she heard the sizzle when it hit the water.

Fear made her breathing shallow. She and Dayle were pretty much surrounded, with the Gulf to their left, the two behind them and the other one on the wall who seemed to be guarding the quickest route to public places and safety.

"Dayle," Meg hissed.

"Yeah?"

"I think we're in trouble."

"Shit," Dayle muttered.

"Our best bet might be to make a run for it."

"Shit."

"The pizza place is straight ahead. There's a red neon palm tree on the side of the building," Meg said.

"Where are you going?"

Meg heard the alarm in her friend's voice and glanced at her. She was paper white. "Just telling you in case we get separated."

"Damn it, Meg."

"Don't look back. It'll slow you down."

"Meg—"

"Go!"

They broke into a flat run. Behind them, someone swore, and two pairs of heavy feet pounded the sand.

A grunt sounded from the right, and Meg saw the man from the wall scrambling up from where he had sprawled in the sand. He charged toward her and Dayle like a greyhound after a mechanical rabbit.

Dayle sprinted ahead of Meg and looked back.

Meg waved her on. "Go, go, go!" she yelled.

A high-rise towered several yards ahead, just beyond the low wall that was no longer being guarded. She was ahead of the third man now, having gained precious yardage when he'd fallen. Veering across the beach toward the wall, she prayed they would follow her and not Dayle and that she would be able to outrun them. The drier sand slowed her down, made the muscles in her calves cramp as the toes of her shoes sought purchase in the shifting granules. She heard Dayle call her name, a frantic warning.

Shit shit shit.

She was within feet of the wall, mere steps away, when a hand landed forcefully between her shoulder blades and shoved. She had just enough time to raise her hands as she crashed into the cobblestone wall. Pain exploded through her right shoulder—the point of impact—and her right knee, which took the rest of the brunt of the fall. She didn't have a chance to roll, play dead or scream before fingers caught in the back of her sweatshirt and tried to jerk her up. She wriggled out of the sleeves, found freedom and tried to scramble away before a hand landed hard on her shoulder and spun her around.

A scream from the beach—*Dayle!*—choked off.

Meg tried to fall back from the man who'd grabbed her, saw over his shoulder the third man racing toward them. He had something in his hand. A gun?

A fist smashed into her jaw, and Meg hit the sand, her head striking the ground with a dull thud. Grit crunched in her teeth as she lay still, stunned.

Fingers curled into the front of her shirt and hauled her into a sitting position. Battling a wave of dizziness, she tried to focus on the face thrust near her own.

"Slater's gonna be happy to see you, Margot."

Meg fought the tide of blackness that welled behind her eyes. And lost.

"Let her go!" Ryan aimed the gun at the guy's leathery face. His hand was shaking, his dark hair in his eyes. The mad dash from the wall, where he'd been following the women at a discreet distance, had left him out of breath. He'd noticed the two men behind them, had watched, incredulous, when they'd made their move. He hadn't thought after that, just reacted.

Now, one of the women, the blond one, was slung over the shoulder of the other man, who stood several feet away, silent and wary.

The woman Ryan was interested in was unconscious, her assailant's fingers still curled into the front of her tank top, her head lolling on her shoulder. Blood trickled from the corner of her mouth. Her attacker glared at Ryan. "This isn't any of your business, mister."

Ryan cocked the gun, not quite believing that he was threatening someone with the weapon he'd bought after his brother was murdered, a safeguard until Beau's killers were caught. When he'd left the car to follow the women, he'd stuffed it into the waistband of his jeans, feeling ridiculous but at least protected if something went wrong.

"I'm making it my business," Ryan said. "Let her go and keep your hands where I can see them."

The guy released her, letting her fall back into the sand, and raised his hands in a placating gesture. "You don't want to do this, man. Believe me."

"Too late."

"My boss is going to be really pissed if you don't back off," the man said. "You don't want this guy pissed at you." He nodded at the woman on the ground. "Ask her."

Ryan glanced at her, saw her chest rise and fall, then focused on her attacker. "So you're working for someone. You and your friend aren't just out here looking for a little fun."

"Right. We're on a job." His weathered skin wrinkled as he smirked. "Retrieving the one that got away."

"Well, I'm not backing off."

"Maybe we can work something out."

"Seems to me I'm the one holding the cards here," Ryan said, gesturing with his gun.

"My friend back there, he's got one of those, too. I'm pretty sure he could get to it faster than you could shoot."

Ryan narrowed his gray eyes at the other man and clenched his square jaw, trying to look menacing but fearing they saw a guy who didn't know what the hell he was doing. "Go for it."

No one moved, and Ryan's lips formed a satisfied smile even as his stomach constricted. "The deal is this: I want to meet with your boss. All I want are answers. He tells me what I want to know, he can have her. If he fails to show, I turn her over to the feds and she can give *them* the answers they're looking for."

"You're nuts, man. You don't know what you're dealing with."

"Then I'm about to find out, aren't I?"

Chapter 3

Throwing back the heavy layer of covers tangled around her body, Margot Rhinehart sat on the edge of the bed. The clock read seven-thirty a.m. She had slept fifteen hours.

Running a hand through her hair, she was surprised by its shortness, still not used to it. She hadn't gotten used to a lot of changes.

Fending off the threatening despair, she went to the sliding glass door that looked out on a frozen Lake Michigan and slid it open. The frigid Wisconsin breeze rushed into the room, and she shivered, missing the heat of Florida.

Getting here had been remarkably easy. She had driven Beau's Lexus to the Florida–Georgia state line, where she had cut her hair and dyed it black. Next, she'd abandoned the Lexus and paid cash for a used Cavalier, tapping her backup bank account and the new identity she'd been setting up for a while. She'd considered going home before realizing the futility of returning to a family she had not seen since she'd been a troubled teenager. She didn't even know where they were or if they were still living.

She'd nearly let the grief and the panic overwhelm her. Where could she go? Who could she turn to? There was no one.

She'd chosen to go north, thinking that Canada might offer a fresh start. But in Wisconsin, she couldn't stand driving anymore and went instead to Door County, a jut of land that extended into Lake Michigan. It reminded her of Captiva Island, only frozen, and she had stopped, almost undone by the memories of the tiny barrier island off Florida's Gulf Coast where she and Beau had often escaped.

For once, luck had been with her. She had found a secluded lodge halfway between Baileys Harbor and Sister Bay, a private resort with a golf course, tennis courts, and sandy beaches. Its isolation had caught Margot's eye. Small, intimate cabins were tucked behind a thick grove of trees, invisible to passing traffic on the highway. She checked in, and for three months, no one bothered her, except the ghosts of her past. She wondered whether they would haunt her forever.

She replayed it in her head, over and over, knowing where she had screwed up, knowing exactly what she had done that had cost Beau his life. She had let emotion control her. For once in her life, she'd let herself think she could be happy, that a decent man could love her.

Leaving the door open and settling onto a chair, she drew her legs up and shivered in the frosty air. Closing the door or at least getting a blanket to wrap around herself required energy she didn't have. Besides, maybe she deserved to die of a raging fever. It would be a welcome reprieve from the staggering guilt.

Hugging herself, she closed her eyes and let the memories come, seeing them as punishment for the tragedy she had been too weak, and too foolish, to prevent.

When she met Beau Kama nine months ago, she had expected him to be like the other men Slater Nielsen assigned her to: filthy rich, rude, sexist, overconfident, cold. They were so easy to con, ridiculously susceptible to the attentions of a beautiful woman because they thought they were irresistible.

Beau Kama was different. Rich, yes, but not pretentious. He liked money because he enjoyed the luxuries it provided rather than the power that it gave him. Yes, he reveled in the attentions of beautiful women, but he was a handsome man: tall with broad shoulders and thick, dark hair that looked as if someone had just ruffled it. His eyes were blue and kind. She had liked his hands best: big and smooth and gentle.

Over their first dinner together, Beau had told her about his company, KamaTech, which helped companies protect themselves from high-tech crime. His eyes shone with excitement when he described the firewalls his top security adviser constructed to secure corporate computer networks. He laughed when he told her that the same man had hacked into a major corporation's system in less than an hour just to show the firm's chairman how easy it was and ensuring KamaTech a lifetime client.

Margot thought that Slater must have been playing a little joke by sending her to fleece the CEO of a security company. At the same time, she realized that it was the perfect opportunity to get the inside track on the kinds of devices she might be dismantling in the future. Perhaps that was what Slater intended.

The more she got to know Beau, however, the more she didn't care what Slater had intended. Beau's enthusiasm for his career charmed her. His energy, his love of life swept her off her feet. The way he treated her—as if what she had to say mattered to him—was new to her. He didn't immediately try to get her into bed either. Instead, he invited her to dinner several times, even preparing the meals himself. They went sailing on his yacht. They walked on the beach and held hands. Everything they did was only for the two of them.

There were no pesky dinner parties, no annoying social events. Beau, who told her how much he hated the spotlight, said that he wanted her all to himself.

During one of their walks on the beach, he told her about his younger brother. They had been close as children, he said, but drifted apart over the years because they were so different. Beau wanted his brother to take an interest in KamaTech because their father, who had died young from a heart attack, had built it. But his brother, Beau said, had other career plans. First, he had become a photojournalist, traveling to exotic places to take wrenching pictures of war and famine, refugees and soldiers. After seeing too much bloodshed and dodging too many snipers' bullets, his brother had turned to a more creative endeavor. Now, he took incredible pictures that sold for hundreds, sometimes thousands, of dollars.

Beau told her that it amazed him that he and his brother were even related. His brother was far more introspective and could spend weeks at a time on his yacht in the middle of the Gulf, all alone. If Beau took one day off, he'd lay awake all night thinking about all the projects that he needed to take care of once he returned to the office. Margot sensed that, despite their differences and estrangement, Beau admired his brother's courage and ability to live his life the way he wanted. She also sensed that Beau had not shared these feelings with anyone before her.

Shortly thereafter, Beau seduced her. With flowers and music and candlelight. It was the most romantic night of her life.

Margot remembered Slater's anger when she told him it was going to take more time to get the job done, that Beau Kama was not like the other men Slater had sent her after. Beau was decent.

She tried to talk Slater out of carrying through with the plan, but he had refused to change his mind. "The Kama emeralds are worth millions," he'd said. "The extra effort will be worth it."

But it wasn't the extra effort that worried her. Beau had the ability to touch her in ways that no one ever had. She looked forward to being with him, reveled in his attention, relished his company. He made her laugh, which was something she rarely did.

And then she started lying to Slater. "He's not responding," she told him after spending a full day of lovemaking with Beau on his yacht. "But I'm close to cracking him." Even as she said it, she anticipated her next night with Beau with a flutter in her stomach.

"Just do it," Slater said, his ice blue gaze intent on hers. "You're taking too long."

"I'm working as fast as I can," she said.

"Maybe you're losing your touch."

"I don't think that's the problem," she said.

He offered her a snifter of brandy. "Join me for a nightcap?"

She looked at his large, tan hands, remembered how skilled they were, and realized that she wouldn't miss them. In fact, she wouldn't miss anything about him. True, he was an attractive man, with thick dark hair and a well-toned body. The tiny mole on his right cheek had turned her on not that long ago. But Beau was so much more.

"I'm exhausted," she said. "Another time?" She edged toward the door.

"You've been doing that a lot lately."

"What?" she asked.

"Putting me off."

She feigned surprise. "Have I?"

"Is there a problem?" he asked.

"Of course not. Why would there be?"

"I only want what's best for you, Margot. If things have changed, you should tell me."

She paused at the door. "I do have a question for you."

"What is it?"

"Why Beau Kama? He hardly fits the profile," she said.

"Of course he does," he said. "He has twelve of the most perfect emeralds in the world, worth millions."

"But he isn't the type we usually go after. I don't imagine his business dealings are as dirty as what we're used to."

"He's told you about his business dealings?"

"Not specifically," she said.

"Am I paying you to imagine, Margot?"

There was a note in his voice that she couldn't identify. Suspicion? Jealousy? Impatience?

Three months after that conversation, Beau Kama proposed marriage. He said that working ninety hours a week was no longer satisfying. He said he realized that there was more to life than his career. He wanted to cut back on work, settle down, start a family. And he wanted to do that with her.

The next day, Margot went to Slater and said she wanted out.

"You're quitting?" he had asked, and she'd nodded. None of the rage she expected showed in his face or eyes, but she knew him too well to be relieved. "What about your responsibilities?" he asked.

"What do you mean?"

"You have a job to do, Margot."

"Slater, you don't understand. I'm going to marry him."

"I heard." His voice was as smooth as steel. "But you have a job to do."

"You're not going to let me quit, is that what you're saying?"

"I don't allow an employee to quit in the middle of a job."

An employee. That had stung, but she brushed away the hurt, focused only on being with Beau. "What if I finish the job?"

"Fine." His face gave away nothing.

"Fine? That's it?"

"What more do you want, Margot? I'll ask you to stay if you want me to."

"I love him, Slater."

"Maybe you do." The ghost of a smile curved his lips. "Is that all?"

She nodded, her heart thundering in her chest.

"Congratulations, Margot. I hope you and Mr. Kama are happy together."

He had left the room without looking back, and she had watched him go, fear and excitement see-sawing through her. He was letting her go. She couldn't believe it. Perhaps deep down, considering the years she had watched Slater operate, she had known it was too good to be true.

Tumbling back into the present, Margot shuddered and hugged herself harder. Faint nausea churned, and she closed the door, no longer interested in freezing to death. She wasn't ready to face hell just yet.

Rummaging through the cupboards turned up some coffee and bread for toast. The dirty dishes had piled up, and she was down to the last clean coffee cup. In it was the small suede pouch that held eleven marquise-cut emeralds, each about the size of a dime. They were the reason Beau was dead, the prize Slater had sent her to steal nine months ago. Except there were eleven, not twelve, as Slater had told her.

Margot didn't know what to do with the stones. She

thought about them every day, feeling their presence in the tiny cabin, eleven shimmering reminders that she'd betrayed the only man she had ever loved. They were unfinished business.

Yet she didn't know how to finish it. She couldn't return them. No doubt, Slater's henchmen were gunning for her, along with the police. Even her altered appearance wasn't enough protection. She needed an ally, someone who could return the emeralds for her.

Someone she could trust.

And only one person came to mind.

Chapter 4

Meg tried to blink the room into focus. She sensed she was alone but couldn't be sure. The floor rolled under her, and she braced herself on sand-caked hands. As wood creaked and water sloshed, she realized she was on a boat. A very close, warm boat, she thought, pushing hair damp with perspiration back from her forehead.

Cursing herself for losing consciousness, she got to her feet. Pain flashed through one shoulder and knee, and she took a moment to rest and look around. Her eyes had adjusted to the dark, revealing the outline of a lamp on the other side of the room. She limped over and switched it on.

She'd thought she might be on a fishing boat, but this was far more impressive. She didn't know much about boats but was certain this classified as a yacht.

The room was small, maybe ten feet square, with a low ceiling and doors with rounded corners at each end. Drawing a calming breath, she fought down the claustrophobia that threatened to grab her by the throat.

Storage cabinets ran low along one wall, a narrow bed against another. A fire extinguisher hung by one of the doors. A lamp, a digital clock, and a cell phone sat on a storage cabinet that met the right side of the bed.

It was nine. Had it been less than two hours since she and Dayle had stepped out to pick up their pizza? Or was it morning? Could a day, or more, have passed?

Dayle.

Her heart pounded with fear for her friend as she remembered hearing Dayle's scream. She hoped that if Dayle wasn't talking to the cops at this moment, she was at least nearby, perhaps on the other side of one of these doors.

Footsteps overhead brought her head up, and she looked around for a weapon. As the steps stopped outside the door to her right, she yanked the fire extinguisher out of its bracket and pressed against the wall behind the door.

Hinges squeaked and a broad back appeared. Meg swung the extinguisher with all of her strength and struck his shoulder hard. He grunted, dropping what he was carrying, and whirled toward her.

Meg gaped at him. "You."

Mr. Armani winced and rolled his shoulder to test it. "Ah, shit. That hurt."

He looked different in jeans and a white T-shirt. No longer corporate, but not a hood. He lacked the greasiness of a thug—and the manners. At the moment, he seemed more concerned about his shoulder than punishing her for hitting him.

Meg gauged the distance to the door he had just opened. He stood between it and her. She hefted the extinguisher, prepared to clock him again, and calculated the odds of making a break for it.

He eyed her as she brandished the tank like a fat, red baseball bat. Long curls of hair had escaped from her ponytail, and sweat plastered them to the sides of her neck. Her arms were tan and taut, her muscles flexing in anticipation of his next move. Even pale with fear, she was a striking woman.

44

"Put it down," he said, trying to sound unimpressed even though he was acutely aware of the damage that metal canister could do to his head.

"Like hell." She raised her chin a notch, daring him to make a move toward her.

He kicked the door shut behind him and smiled.

A rock of apprehension lodged in her throat, and she resisted the sudden desperate need to retreat. There was only a wall behind her anyway. If he planned to kill or rape her, backing away wouldn't help.

"It'd be in your best interest to drop it," he said, taking a step toward her.

Meg stood firm, but her knees began to tremble. "It'd be in *your* best interest not to come any closer."

He took another step, tensed to fall back if she swung. His shoe bumped something on the floor and they both looked down at the small blue plastic bucket on its side. Several ice cubes were scattered across the floor.

She stared at them in confusion. He'd been carrying a bucket of ice?

He lunged.

She swung the extinguisher up, aiming for his chin.

He jerked back, and the tank whooshed past his face. Catching it on the back swing, he wrenched it away from her.

She dropped against the wall and ducked her head, hands up and eyes closed. *I'm dead.*

The makeshift weapon dangling from one hand, Ryan stared at the woman crouched at his feet, her body tensed for a blow. That surprised him. It also made him angry. He had never struck a woman and couldn't imagine a situation in which he would. But this woman didn't know that, didn't know him. And God, when he'd first seen her, laughing with her friend at the airport as if nothing had happened three months ago, hadn't he wanted to hurt her? Hadn't he wanted to make her pay for Beau's death? Because she hadn't. Obviously, it hadn't devastated her the way it had him.

Clenching his jaw, he turned away.

When she heard him move, Meg opened her eyes to see him putting the extinguisher back in its bracket. She broke for the door. Her injured knee slowed her down, but she reached it and fumbled with the handle, swearing when her fingers slipped across the smooth metal.

He was on her in a heartbeat. Whirling her around, he shoved her against the door, curled his fingers into the front of her tank top, and leaned into her. "If you want to play rough, we'll play rough," he growled. "It's up to you."

A good portion of his body was flush against hers, and she felt what could have been the butt of a gun jammed into the waistband of his jeans. *Oh, Jesus, a gun.*

"What do you want?" she asked.

"I want you to behave. Don't make me force you."

She tried to stare him down, but his gaze bore into hers without wavering. He leaned on her windpipe, pressing her head back. The bump she had sustained earlier sent a sharp ache through her temples. "I'll behave," she said, as if she had a choice.

He backed off, hoping she didn't notice the tremor in his hands. He was beginning to think he had overestimated his ability to intimidate this woman. The expected tears and pleas, the promises to give him whatever he wanted hadn't materialized.

He held out a hand. "Give me your keys."

She gave him a blank look. "Why?"

He snapped his fingers. "Just give them to me." He'd felt them in her pocket when they were thigh to thigh, and he wasn't going to risk losing an eye if she tried to use them as a weapon.

Pulling out her key ring, she dropped it in his palm. He shoved it into his pocket without breaking their locked gazes. "Sit."

Meg, who didn't think her jelly legs could have supported her much longer anyway, slid down the wall until she sat on the floor. A half-dozen aches protested, but they were nothing compared with the anxiety she felt about Dayle. "What happened to my friend?"

"They took her."

Shit. "Who are 'they'?"

He smirked as he bent to pick up the spilled ice cubes. "As if you don't know."

"I *don't* know. What do they want? What do *you* want?"

"Please," he said.

"Look, I don't know what the hell's going on here, but you and your buddies have made a huge mistake." As she spoke, she got to her feet. "Where did they take her?"

He straightened, holding the ice bucket in one hand. "Sit down."

"Just answer me. What do you want from me?"

"Sit," he said.

"No, damn it. Answer me."

"You're getting on my nerves." He took a menacing step toward her.

Meg cringed inwardly but refused to back down. "What are you going to do? Hit me again?"

"I didn't hit you the first time, but I'll knock you flat if you push me."

Her gaze dropped down the length of his body, taking in the sinewy muscles beneath his shirt and jeans. He wasn't a muscleman, but he was strong and agile, steely. She didn't doubt for an instant that he could do major damage with one punch, but she also sensed that he had no intention of harming her. He'd had plenty of opportunity to rape her when she was unconscious. And he could have beat her senseless with the fire extinguisher after she slammed him with it—he'd looked angry enough. Yet he had done none of these things—he hadn't even restrained her in any way.

But she sat as he'd ordered, her back against the wall. If she didn't relent, he might decide he could handle her better bound and gagged. And that would diminish her chances of escaping.

His lips were set in a straight line as he plunked the bucket on the bed. Taking a towel from a cabinet along the wall, he made an ice pack and handed it down to her. "For your head."

She hesitated. Now he wanted to treat her injuries? She accepted the towel and weighed its prospects as a weapon. It wouldn't serve as well as the fire extinguisher, but then, that hadn't proved all that effective. She glanced around for something better as he started another ice pack. The cell phone sat on the table next to the bed, a few feet away.

His movements were swift and jerky as his annoyance grew. "I saved your ass, lady," he said. "For that, I think I deserve better than a fire extinguisher bashed into my back. The only thing that saved me from getting my butt kicked was that the bigger one went after your friend. By the time I got there, the other one was all over you."

He gave the ends of the towel a twist and shoved it at her. His diamond-hard gaze dropped to her lips and then to the left, softening. She was going to have one hell of a bruise along her jaw where Goon Number One had punched her. For a moment, he wished he'd had the presence of mind at the time to beat the guy bloody. But then he wondered why he should give a damn what happened to her. She didn't seem to give a damn what had happened to Beau.

"Put that on your jaw." He turned his back.

Meg scrambled to her knees, seized the phone, fumbled for the power button, and jabbed a finger at nine-one-one.

He faced her. "What are you doing?"

"Calling for help." *What an idiot.*

"You don't even know where you are," he said.

"They can trace the call."

"The battery's dead."

She threw it at him. It bounced off his temple and clattered to the floor in pieces. Meg didn't wait to see whether it stunned him—she dove for the door.

This time, she managed to turn the knob and get it open before he plowed into her from behind. She sprawled headlong into a larger, more elaborate compartment with a door at the other end.

He flipped her onto her back, and she thrashed, kicking and screaming for help, more startled by his strength than the fear of what he might do to her. He had already shown that he had no intention of using the gun—he'd just had the perfect opportunity to shoot her in the back and hadn't.

Still, she was afraid she had pushed him too far as he leaned over her, his face red with rage, blood trickling down his temple. Grappling for the hands that pummeled his face, he captured her wrists and flattened them to the floor on either side of her head. "Be still, damn it."

Meg writhed, fighting his restraint even though she already knew she had lost. "Get off."

"Not until you calm down."

She bucked under him, arching her back off the floor. "Get off!"

"I'm not going to hurt you."

Her breath was coming in quick gasps. Fearing she would hyperventilate, he leaned his face close to hers. "Listen to me. I'm not going to hurt you."

She twisted her wrists in his grasp. "Then let go."

"You don't have a choice here. Calm down."

He sounded so reasonable she wanted to scream. "Up yours."

"You're the one making this difficult."

"Guess I just don't understand the protocol of kidnapping."

"If you can be rational, I'll let you up," he said. "Otherwise, we can conduct this conversation just like this."

"Fine."

"Fine what?"

"I'll behave," she said.

"You said that before."

"Do you want it in blood this time? You're stronger than I am. There's not much I can do to defend myself."

The color had flooded back into her cheeks, and the corners of his mouth twitched. "Yeah, you're helpless."

His amusement irked her. "Are you going to let me up or what?"

"*I'm* going to get up," he said. "*You're* going to stay on the floor. I want you sitting on your hands."

"Good thinking. There's no telling what kind of damage they could do."

Another almost-smile. "You're quite the smart ass, aren't you?"

"Only in life-threatening situations," she said.

"That mouth gets you into a lot of those, I would guess."

"Are you going to get off me sometime tonight?"

He rolled away and got to his feet in one fluid motion. He had to be the most graceful man she had ever seen. Then, cursing herself for finding him the least bit attractive, she sat up.

"Sit on your hands," he said.

"Give me a chance."

"Just do it."

She slipped her hands under the backs of her thighs and glared up at him. "How long have I been here?"

"Couple of hours," he said.

"Who the hell are you? You don't kidnap women for a living."

"I didn't intend to kidnap you. I was just watching you when those goons went after you. Like an idiot, I rushed to your rescue."

He rubbed the back of his neck, asking himself what he had been thinking. But the truth was, he hadn't been thinking. He'd simply reacted. Even when he'd started following her, he hadn't been thinking. He should have called the FBI right away to tip them off. But he'd wanted to see for himself who she was, how she lived. What he'd seen hadn't made sense—the modest beach house, the practical Honda. Is that how an accomplished jewel thief lived? He'd begun to think that maybe he really did have the wrong woman.

But then the two men had jumped her and her friend, and they hadn't seemed the least bit confused about her identity. One of them had even called her by name. Margot.

Ryan knew now that it had been stupid to bargain with them, dangerous. But at the rate the FBI was going, he might never know who masterminded his brother's murder, let alone look the bastard in the eye. And that was something he wanted very much to do. He wanted revenge, pure and simple.

Meg saw the murderous thoughts slide through his eyes, and it unnerved the hell out of her. He looked like he would happily throttle anyone who crossed him. "Who are you?" she asked.

He fastened his damning gaze on her. "Ryan Kama."

Her eyes widened. She knew his last name well. When she had arrived in Fort Myers, the unsolved, two-month-old murder of the CEO of KamaTech had still been huge news. Her fellow reporters had expressed deep frustration at the lack of information that law enforcement had made available to the press. No pictures of suspects. No theories. No motives. No nothing.

Ryan saw the recognition in her eyes and felt a moment of satisfaction. "So you do know who I am."

"I know who Beau Kama was."

"He was my brother." There was accusation in his tone.

"I didn't *know* him. I only know *of* him."

How could she sit there and lie so blatantly without even blinking? But then he reminded himself that she had tricked his brother into thinking she loved him. "I know how you work, lady, so you can drop the act. The police told me all about your methods when they were pumping me for what I knew about you and Beau."

"I don't have methods."

His eyes narrowed in disgust. "You get cozy with rich men. You do whatever you have to do to get them to trust you. When they're sated and sleeping soundly, you steal them blind. Except something went wrong with Beau. None of your other marks have ended up dead. As far as the cops know, anyway."

"I don't remember a woman ever being mentioned in the coverage of Beau Kama's murder."

"The cops—and the FBI when they took over—are keeping the info out of the press. They seem to think that if you're stupid enough to think you got away with it, you'll move on to another mark. Then, once they nail you, you can tell them all about your boss, Slater Nielsen, and how one of your marks ended up the victim of a professional hit man."

"But I'm not her. I must look like her—"

"Right. That's so easy, isn't it?"

"I'm not lying," she said.

"Of course not. You would never lie to get what you want."

Meg put shaking fingers to her temple and rubbed in a small circle. "How do you know all this?"

He gave her a malevolent look. "Hands."

"What?"

"Sit on your hands, damn it."

She obeyed, somewhat satisfied, and a bit relieved, that she made him nervous. She didn't imagine that a ruthless killer would have been so anxious.

He relaxed slightly. "I have a friend who has connections within the FBI. They've shut me out of the investigation, but not entirely."

"I don't understand what you want from me."

"You're going to help me get to the man you work for," he said. "In return, I won't turn you over to the feds."

"I'm a reporter for a newspaper—that's who I work for. I haven't even lived here long."

"Yeah, right. Are we going to make a deal or not?"

"But I don't know what—"

"Fine," he cut in. "Play it your way."

"I'm not playing it any way. You've made a mistake."

He came at her, and Meg shrank against the wall. He jerked her toward him by her shirt. "Listen to me very carefully," he said. "You're in a delicate position right now. If you don't cooperate, I'll turn you over to those friends of yours who seemed to enjoy beating up on women. And you know where they'll take you. Follow me so far?"

Meg didn't have a clue where they'd take her, but she was certain they wouldn't give her an ice pack once they got there. She thought of Dayle, and her stomach tensed. *Please, please, be all right.* She gave a curt nod.

He didn't release her right away, his mouth dry. The subtle, musky scent of perfume clung to her, enhanced by the perspiration that dampened her skin.

She saw the tip of his tongue wet his lips and swallowed back a surge of something that could only be fear. "I understand," she said.

He remembered how she'd tasted when he had kissed her at the airport. Too good for a traitor. But that's what she was. She had betrayed his brother, and now he was dead. Ryan released her and turned away, running both hands through his hair. Linking his fingers at the base of his neck, he tilted his head back. Rage was a loosely chained beast inside him.

Meg still felt the hard nudge of his knuckles against her throat. He hadn't seemed so harmless just now, but even so, he had not hurt her. "Why did you call them my friends?"

"The one who hit you called you by name."

Wisps of fog cleared from her memory. *"Slater's gonna be happy to see you, Margot."* "My name isn't Margot. It's Meg."

"He looked you right in the face and called you by name. He told me he was there to retrieve the one that got away from his boss. That's Slater Nielsen. And you're the one who got away, so drop the act. You're not going to win this fight."

She fought to control her rising panic. There was no reasoning with him. And why the hell had those thugs mistaken her for this Margot? Had none of them ever met her? "What happens now?" she asked.

"Your friends and I arranged a morning meeting with Nielsen."

"Will Dayle be there?"

"Who's Dayle?"

"My friend. You said they got her. Will she be with them?"

"Hell if I know."

Fear returned, along with anger. "You shouldn't have let them take her. She has even less to do with this than I do."

"They wanted insurance. I let them have it."

"What does that mean?"

"I tried to get them to leave her with me, but they wouldn't do it. They wanted to make sure you cooperated with the plan to meet in the morning, and seeing as how she's a friend of yours . . ."

"You bastard. You let them take her so I wouldn't give you any trouble."

"That was the idea, yeah."

She wanted to shake him, to scream at him that he'd made a massive mistake that could get innocent people killed. But she knew he wouldn't believe her. So she tried another tack. "What happens when you meet with this Slater Nielsen?"

He scowled, irritated at her questions, even more irritated that she was so adamant about denying her identity. Couldn't she see that he had her dead to rights? But then it registered what she'd asked. What would happen when he was face to face with the man who'd had Beau killed? What would he do, say? He imagined how satisfying it would be to point a gun at the man's head and squeeze the trigger. Sweet payback.

On some psychological level, he knew it was wrong to want to kill so desperately, to avenge. But he was beyond caring. Someone needed to pay for Beau's death. There had to be justice, damn it. Somehow.

He glared at his captive, telling himself that her wide-eyed fear was an act. A damned good one. He'd wondered how Beau had been so taken in by her, and now he knew. She was a first-class actress. "I'm finished talking," he said. "Get some sleep."

"But—"

"Don't make me repeat myself. My patience is gone."

She was tempted to keep arguing, but he was becoming angrier and more agitated. So she decided to wait. It was several hours before morning. Eventually, he would let down his guard. And she would make another break for it.

Chapter 5

Margot stood at the customer service desk of a Sears store in Green Bay, Wisconsin, while an employee with frosted hair paged the woman she'd asked for. She considered walking out of the store and not looking back, but she didn't have anyone else to ask for help. Besides, she had already dumped the Cavalier, worried that she had kept it too long.

"Can I help you?" a familiar voice asked from behind her.

Pasting a smile on her face that felt more like a grimace, Margot turned. Before her stood a thin woman about her height dressed in khakis and a white blouse wrinkled at the waist. She wore little makeup, and her light brown hair needed combing. "Hello, Holly. Long time no see."

Holly stared at her from behind black-framed glasses with small, round lenses. "Twelve years."

The fake smile faded. Margot didn't know what she had hoped for. A smile and a warm hug? That was probably too much to expect from a friend she had more or less abandoned when they were teens. She'd assumed that Holly knew that running away had been an act of self-preservation. Inwardly, she acknowledged that she should have called long ago to let Holly know she was okay.

Margot shifted. "Look—"

"You've changed. Your hair—"

"I need a place to stay," Margot cut in.

"I see."

Margot tried not to let Holly's knowing gaze rattle her. "You're probably thinking I wouldn't be here if I didn't need something. You're right."

"At least you're honest."

Margot clenched her jaw. "You're my last resort."

Holly gazed at her a long time. "I'm sorry to hear that. Maybe I could have been there for you twelve years ago if you had given me a chance." She walked away.

Stunned, Margot watched her go.

Then Holly looked over her shoulder. "I get off in about an hour if you want to meet me in front of the store."

Margot nodded, feeling very small and shallow.

"Nice shirt," Holly said as she reached for another piece of garlic bread and sopped it through the spaghetti sauce on her plate.

"Thanks."

"I like the way the buttons are its only color. Where'd you get it? I'm always on the lookout for different clothing to suggest to our corporate buyers."

Margot fingered the cloth-covered buttons. It had been twelve years since they'd seen each other, and they were discussing buttons on a blouse. "The shirt is from a store in Door County, and I made the buttons."

Holly looked surprised. "I didn't know you liked to sew."

"I don't. I just . . . needed to keep busy."

"And you chose sewing. Interesting."

There was an awkward silence before Holly cleared her throat. "I figured you were dead," she said. "After the one

58

letter I got from you. Postmark said somewhere in Florida. I can't remember where."

Margot stared at the pasta heaped on her plate. She should have been ravenous, but the thought of food made her feel sick.

"Margot?"

She looked up. "What?"

"I said I thought you were dead, but then, I was only sixteen and feeling very dramatic." Holly sipped from a glass of wine and searched Margot's face over the rim. "How'd you find me?"

"I called your mom."

"Ah. How was she? Cranky as usual?"

"We didn't chat," Margot said.

"So, what happened to you?"

Scooting her chair back, Margot stood and picked up her plate and glass. "Do you have a dishwasher?"

"Just put them in the sink."

With her back to Holly, Margot stared into the drain as the garbage disposal chewed up her food.

"I went to college," Holly said, apparently tired of waiting for Margot to ask her what she'd been doing all these years. "In Madison. Retail management. Took the first job offer I got and ended up here. I bought the Mustang last month brand new, got this great little apartment and a stable enough job. I don't have much to worry about, and I don't have to see my parents more than once every few months and on special occasions. There's a guy I work with—Tom. He's honest, and he likes me. The job's a bitch most of the time, and I'm not the company's best employee, but it's a living. I figure I'll marry a nice guy—maybe even Tom—in the next few years and have some kids. Maybe my parents will take more of an interest in my kids than they did in me. I've got it all planned,

Margot, and you know what?"

Margot closed her eyes, gripping the edge of the sink. "What?"

"I did it in spite of you. After you left without saying good-bye, without even letting me know you were still alive after that first letter, I was real down on human nature. I mean, if you can't trust your best friend, who can you trust? But I'm getting over that now, with Tom. I had friends in college, but I was never as close to them as I was to you. We had a deal, Margot."

"We were sixteen."

"So it didn't count? I hated my parents and school. I hated living in that small town. I wanted out just as much as you did. Maybe it was typical teen stuff, but we said we'd get out together, run away to New York or wherever and make it on our own. And you went without me."

"I'm sorry." It came out a whisper. Margot wasn't sure Holly heard her, but she didn't say it again.

"They looked for you," Holly said.

Margot bowed her head. "I don't want to talk about it."

"You *never* wanted to talk about it. Maybe if you had, you wouldn't have felt like you had to run away."

"It's a little late now, isn't it?"

"Some wounds don't heal without help, Margot."

"Well, I have new ones now, all right?" Turning, she leaned against the counter and pushed hair back from her damp forehead. "I don't want to argue."

Holly drummed her fingers on the table through an awkward pause. "It wasn't your fault, you know."

Margot blew out a ragged breath. She felt the need to sit down but didn't trust her knees to carry her to a chair. She supposed the visit to the past was inevitable.

Holly sat forward. "Margot, your uncle killed himself because he was fucked up."

"He killed himself because I told on him."

"He was raping you. What else were you supposed to do?"

The pressure in her chest grew. "Afterward, Dad was so angry he wouldn't even look at me. He said it was my fault."

"Jesus," Holly said. "I didn't know."

"There was no way I could stay there. I know running away wasn't the only option, but I didn't realize it then. I was scared."

"What about now?"

"What *about* now?" Margot asked.

"You're on the run again. You have that same hunted look in your eyes."

Margot swiped at tears that hadn't fallen. "Someone's looking for me."

"How can I help?"

Margot hesitated, realizing that she couldn't ask Holly to get involved in a dangerous situation she knew nothing about. All she really needed to do was wrap up the emeralds in a package and address it to Beau's brother. She could hire a stranger to walk into KamaTech, plop it on the receptionist's desk, and walk out. She silently acknowledged that coming here hadn't been about that anyway. "You can't help me," she said.

The compassion in Holly's eyes went flat. "Then why did you come here?"

"I don't know."

"You need a friend."

Margot released a soft laugh and rubbed her hands over her face. Holly was right. But she also needed to hang on, and unburdening herself now would undoubtedly knock her into the void she had managed to skirt for three long months. She couldn't afford that until she had returned the emeralds.

After that, there would be no reason to keep fighting. "I just need some sleep."

Holly studied her for a moment. "Who's looking for you?"

"The guy I used to work for," Margot said.

"What'd you do to him that he's out to get you?"

Margot laughed bitterly. "I quit."

Chapter 6

Ryan stared at his captive, trying to keep his exhausted mind blank. It was difficult, though, not to feel like a jerk. At some point during the night, she had curled into a protective ball, the wall at her back. Hair fell in curling tangles across her face, not quite obscuring the bruise along her jaw where the goon had slugged her. Her hands were fisted, held close to her chest as if for added protection. Faint purple marks circled each wrist. Caused by his hands.

Shoving aside the guilt, Ryan told himself that she deserved what she got. He prodded her calf with the toe of his shoe. "Get up."

Meg's eyes snapped open, and she saw him towering above her. She braced herself, her heart banging in her head. He hadn't slept—his eyes were rimmed with red. Day-old stubble darkened his features, and he was even more attractive with that shadow tempering the angles of his face.

"What time is it?" she asked.

Her voice was rough with sleep, dark circles underscoring her green eyes. Ryan hardened his jaw. *No mercy.* "Time to go. Get up."

She gritted her teeth to keep from grimacing as sore muscles protested.

He turned away, annoyed at the way his stomach clenched when her top stretched taut across her breasts. "Bathroom's through here if you need it," he said with a curt gesture.

Meg followed him through the door with rounded corners, the demands of her body more important than anything at this point.

The "bathroom" had just enough room for a toilet and a sink. It was enough for her, and she started to close the door. Ryan cleared his throat.

"Give me a break," she said. "Where am I going to go?"

"Two minutes."

She slammed the door with relief.

She was washing her face when the door swung open behind her. She took her time rinsing away soap, determined to gain some kind of control of the situation. Drying her face on a towel, she turned from the sink.

Ryan leaned against the doorjamb, watching her casually.

The walls of the room closed in, and her breath started to lodge in her chest. "I'm done now," she said.

He tried to enjoy the panic flitting through her eyes. Any discomfort he caused her would be only a tiny payback for what she had cost Beau. "My brother always had great taste in women."

The rim of the sink pressed into the small of her back. "I told you I didn't know your brother."

"Before you, his women were all the same. Classy, articulate blondes with killer red nails."

He was so close, it was difficult to draw a breath. "Then any idiot can see that I'm not his type."

"That's what makes you different. They didn't mean anything to him. He didn't love them."

"He didn't love me, either, because I never met the man."

"He was head over heels for you."

"Then he had a rich fantasy life. Do you mind? I'm done in here." She tried to edge past him. He didn't budge, and she came dangerously close to making frontal contact with his chest before stepping back, careful not to touch him. "You need a shower."

That made him smile, just a little. "Perhaps you think that if you convince me I stink, I'll take a shower, and while I'm occupied, you'll find a way out of here."

Damn it. "I just thought you should know since we're going to be around other people who might be offended."

"Somehow I don't think your pals are that particular about who they hang out with."

"They're not my pals."

"You're so convincing."

"We'll see how convincing I can be when your ass lands in jail for kidnapping and aggravated assault."

He turned away. "Come on."

Meg, grateful to be able to breathe again, followed him. "Where are we going?"

He just steered her by the arm into a larger, more elaborate sleeping area. She had a glimpse of a queen-size bed and windows that looked out over blue-green water. They passed through another door into a compact kitchen and small dining area. Camera equipment—a case, two thirty-five millimeter cameras and several lenses—was piled on a dining table for two.

Snagging a White Sox baseball cap from a chair, Ryan shoved it into her hands. "Stuff your hair under this. No telling how many slime balls out there are after that pretty head of yours."

She did as he said, remembering the thug who had looked her in the face and called her by someone else's name.

Ryan nudged her up a ladder, his hand lingering a second

longer than necessary, the heat of his fingers seeping through the denim of her jeans.

On the top rung, she paused to raise a hand against the glare reflecting off water. The boat was anchored in a marina. "Where are we?" she asked.

His impatient hand at her lower back urged her out onto the deck. The air was still and warm as he directed her into a motorized, inflatable vessel that bobbed in the water next to the yacht.

As he steered the craft toward a dock several hundred yards away, Meg calculated her chances of diving into the water and out-swimming him. One glance at the muscles challenging the seams of his T-shirt told her to wait. She was better off staying put until she knew where she was.

The morning breeze swept stray hair across her face, and she pushed it under the cap. "Will you at least tell me where we're going?" she asked.

"You'll see."

"An abandoned warehouse? An old factory?"

"Sorry to disappoint you."

On land, he led her to the driver's side of a black Jaguar in the marina's parking lot. "You're driving," he said.

Within minutes, they were moving with the flow of traffic, and Meg was relieved to recognize her surroundings at last. They were in Naples, a community about thirty miles south of Fort Myers, where a number of celebrities and other wealthy people had winter homes. She didn't recognize the name of the road when she saw it on a street sign, and she cursed her ignorance of the area. She had only been here once, for a meeting at the newspaper's Naples bureau.

"I need to know where we're going," she said.

"Just drive until I tell you to stop."

"You're not going to get away with this, you know." Even

as she said it, she realized how stupid it sounded. After all, he *was* getting away with it.

"I don't suppose you could just shut up."

"Look, I'm a reporter. My name is Meg Grant. Call the newspaper in Fort Myers and ask them."

"You have the number handy, I presume."

"Call Directory Assistance if you don't trust me."

He cast her a sidelong glance, eyebrow arched. "*If* I don't trust you?"

"You know what I mean."

"Take a right at the stop sign," he said.

Downshifting for the turn, she cursed under her breath when the gears ground. "I haven't driven a stick in a while."

"Seems to me you're driving this car with some familiarity."

He'd tested her, and apparently she'd failed. "This was your brother's car?"

"He often let his women use it."

"My father had a Jag. He taught me how to drive it." It had been one of the few times that father and daughter had connected. She had enjoyed driving the expensive car, and he had adored that she appreciated, for once, something his money had bought.

Ryan was impressed with how easily she lied. "What color?"

"Taupe. Well, that's what Mother called it. It looked light brown to me."

"Nice touch."

"What?"

"The mother thing. That's a very nice touch," Ryan repeated.

"I'm not lying."

"Sure." He glared straight ahead, wondering how far she

could take the lie before giving herself away. "What year?"

" '79."

"Where is it now?"

Meg coasted to a stop. "Which way?"

Ryan glanced at her, saw her swallow. For the first time, he noticed the stress lines etched on either side of her nose. "Straight. What happened to the car?"

"You're testing me," Meg said.

"So what if I am?"

"So maybe I don't like it."

"So maybe you don't have a choice," he said. "You're the one insisting that I've got the wrong woman. I happen to think that I don't. Prove it."

She drew in a slow breath and prayed that her voice wouldn't shake. "It was totaled."

He interpreted the tremor in her voice as fear of being caught in the tall tale. "Daddy's little girl wrecked the precious Jag?"

Her knuckles turned white as she gripped the steering wheel. "No, a drunk driver wrecked the car," she said. "Am I still going straight?"

"I'll tell you when to turn." She looked genuinely distressed, and Ryan marveled at her acting ability. "When?"

"When what?"

"When did the drunk driver wreck the Jag? Make it good, now."

"You son of a bitch."

He leaned closer to her. "Excuse me?"

Meg swerved onto the shoulder and jammed on the brakes. She had her seat belt unbuckled and the car door open before he grabbed her arm.

"Where do you think you're going?"

She yanked away and would have taken a swing at him if

68

there'd been room in the car, or if that had been her goal at the moment. As it was, she just had to get out. Now.

She stumbled, catching herself against the rear end as her knees almost buckled, and threw up in the weeds. She heard the passenger door open and close, then felt his presence at her side. She kept her eyes closed. To her humiliation, her stomach convulsed again.

Exhausted, she pulled off the baseball cap and shoved the hair back from her face as she gulped in air. The sun felt hot on the top of her head, and the humidity made it difficult to take a deep, cleansing breath.

Ryan offered her a white handkerchief with the initials RK embroidered in one corner.

"You're kidding, right?" she said. Afraid she was going to be sick again, she hung her head, grateful for the protective curtain of hair.

Feeling like an idiot, Ryan shoved the handkerchief back into his jeans. She was so white and shaken that he thought she might faint. But he kept his distance, certain she would deck him if he tried to touch her. Besides, he didn't want to. This was just another attempt to win his sympathy, to get her claws into him so she could fool him the way she had Beau. "Okay now?"

She raised her head and might have laughed at his concern, no matter how feigned, if she hadn't felt so sick. "I'm peachy. Thanks for asking."

There was not a breath of color in her face, but he was determined not to give an inch. "Get in the car."

Meg considered running, but only dense, swampy land stretched for miles in most directions. Not one car had whizzed by while she had embarrassed herself in the weeds.

He grasped her arm. "In the car. Now."

She tried to jerk away from him, but getting sick had left

her weak and trembling. She didn't have the strength to do anything but jam the White Sox cap back on her head and return to her place behind the wheel.

As she steered the car onto the road, Ryan cranked up the air-conditioning. "The air will help you feel better," he said.

He was right. Her pulse calmed, and though perspiration still beaded her upper lip, her stomach settled.

They rode in silence, Ryan tapping the tips of his fingers on one knee. She was convincing. Could even the most consummate actress pretend to be violently ill? Yes, he decided, a very talented one could fake just about anything. Even love.

And those goons had called her by name, he reminded himself. They had looked right into her face and recognized her as Margot. He had the right woman, damn it.

Leaning forward, he reached between his feet and pulled the gun from under the seat. At her sharp intake of breath, he glanced over to see her gaze fixed on the weapon as if she had never seen one before. "Pull over," he said.

She obeyed, then watched him load the gun as if he'd never handled one before. "You don't know what the hell you're doing with that thing, do you?"

Reaching over, he yanked the car keys out of the ignition. "Shut up and get out of the car."

She didn't move as she considered their surroundings. They had not passed another vehicle since she had pulled over to be sick. The secluded area was the perfect place to commit a crime. No witnesses but a couple of large banyan trees, several dozen royal palms and pine trees, and plenty of marshy-looking, weedy land.

"I'm not going to tell you again." He opened his door and stepped out.

Meg thought about defying him. She wasn't stupid, after all, and had no intention of walking right into whatever he had planned. Then he came around to her side of the Jag and gave an impatient wave with the gun. Something dark and dangerous in his face compelled her to get out. The damp air closed around her like a loose, wet cloak.

He gestured for her to precede him onto a trail leading into the dense foliage. She could smell the salt of the Gulf.

"Does this place have an address? I'll need it for the police report," she said over her shoulder.

Ryan remained silent and tried to keep from admiring her body. Her jeans hugged the firm length of her thighs, the tight, rounded shape of her butt. He would have bet money that she was a runner. Then he chastised himself for letting the sight of her backside distract him. He had never been drawn to any of Beau's women, except on a superficial level. He would've had to be dead not to appreciate the blond-haired, blue-eyed goddesses Beau had escorted to the few social events he had grudgingly attended.

Maybe that was what was so disturbing about the woman shoving aside low-hanging branches just ahead of him. She was different. Beautiful, yes. But not in the supermodel, too-thin, that's-not-her-real-hair-color fashion. Her attractiveness was natural, unplanned.

And she was smart. He could see it in how she was studying the situation from every angle at every moment, working it in her head, trying to chart an escape. She hadn't given up, hadn't resigned herself to what was happening. She still believed that she would walk away from this unscathed. She was either a fighter or unwilling to accept that her game was over.

Meg paused where the trail forked. "Which way?"

"Left."

They stepped out of the trees onto a beach littered with the pieces of millions of shells that had been pounded into de-

71

bris by Gulf waves. Only yards from where they stood, those same, gentle waves caressed the shore.

They both stopped the moment their feet touched sand, and Meg's heart began to pound in her ears. "Dayle," she said under her breath.

Ryan curved his fingers around her elbow, not willing to take the chance that she would bolt.

Meg swallowed back the new sickness that bubbled into the back of her throat at the sight of her friend, the Gulf at her back, a gun aimed at her temple. Someone had hit her more than once—both eyes were surrounded by purple, swollen flesh. Blood had caked at one corner of her mouth and under her nose.

Meg flicked her gaze to the man who held the gun to Dayle's head and vowed revenge. She registered the dark ponytail, square jaw and skin that was leathery brown. Two paces behind him stood another man, also with a gun. He had a military haircut, a scar stretching from one temple to the corner of his mouth, a wide, sunburned forehead, and thick, blond eyebrows. He had mean eyes that squinted against the sun.

"Drop it," Scar said, gesturing at the gun in Ryan's hand.

Ryan cocked the weapon instead.

Meg heard the hammer click as if it were right next to her ear, then realized that it was. He had leveled it at her head in much the same way the thug threatened Dayle. Meg didn't dare breathe, conscious of the dampness of Ryan's hand on her shoulder.

"Who's your new friend, Margot?" Leather asked.

How could he look right at her and not realize she was not Margot? But with a gun aimed at her best friend's head, she wasn't going to deny him what he wanted to know. "Says his name is Ryan Kama."

"Shut up," Ryan hissed near her ear, incredulous that she

had given him up so easily. Anonymity had been his best weapon. They'd had no idea what he wanted with their boss. "Where's Nielsen?" he snapped.

Leather smiled. "I'm afraid he had other plans for the morning. If he'd known you were a Kama, he may have been willing to rearrange his calendar."

Too late, damn it. Ryan's fingers tightened on Meg's shoulder, digging in. "Then I suggest you get him the hell out here *now.*"

Meg sought Dayle's eyes. *Are you okay?*

Dayle nodded, then winced as Leather jammed the gun against her temple. Meg's chest tightened with rage and with fear for her friend. Dayle might not survive another night with these two. She had already been beaten or worse. Meg knew she had to do something. Anything. "Are you boys interested in a trade?"

Ryan stared at her in disbelief. What the hell was she doing? "No trades." He yanked her closer to him as if to show that she was his.

Meg kept her gaze on Leather. "Give her to him, and you can have me."

Nodding, Leather smiled, his tongue snaking over his lower lip, as if "you can have me" meant something really good to him. "Sure, Mags. Excellent."

Ryan felt a moment of panic as control was almost snatched from him. Clamping an arm around Meg's neck, he dragged her back against him. "No deal. Tell Nielsen he blew his chance to get his hands on her. She's mine, and I'm guessing she'll sing to the feds for all she's worth." He pointed the gun at her head. "No fast moves or the con artist here buys it."

Scar and Leather raised their hands in a gesture of submission.

Ryan backed toward the line of trees at the edge of the beach, bracing as Meg's struggles became frantic. "Don't leave her with them!" she cried. "You can't leave her with them! Dayle!"

He kept her in check as he edged backward, his main concern to get the hell away before someone shot him and swiped his only key to finding Beau's killers.

As he half-dragged, half-carried her from the trail into the dense woods, Meg kicked and bucked and tried to throw him off balance, her voice hoarse from calling Dayle's name.

"Shut up," he hissed. "You're going to get us both killed."

But her desperation only increased. Cramming the gun into the waistband of his jeans, he clamped his hand over her mouth, vaguely noticing that she had lost the baseball cap in her struggles.

At the car, he levered her against the passenger side, pinning her even as she continued to fight. "We can't leave her with them," she said. "Did you see what they already did to her? They'll kill her."

"You're nuts if you think I'm going back—"

A gunshot cut him off, and he let her go to whirl toward the sound. He hadn't noticed how noisy the wildlife had been. Now, he listened to the silence, straining his ears for the sounds of men crashing through the woods toward them.

There was nothing. Only dead quiet.

Meg slid to the ground, her back against the car, her face in her hands. "Oh, God. Dayle."

Ryan didn't waste a second. He hauled her up by the arm. "Get in the car."

She was limp, defeated. He grasped her by the arms, shook her. "Listen to me, damn you. You're going to get into the car, and we're going to get the fuck out of here."

Opening the door, he shoved her inside and slammed it

shut. He ran to the other side as fast as he could, but it wasn't fast enough. Meg fumbled her door open, tumbled out of the car and dashed back into the woods, her only thought to get to Dayle.

Ryan crashed into her from behind, taking her down in a full-body tackle.

The crushing weight of his body drove the air from her lungs, and she lay beneath him, stunned and breathless. The edges of her vision wavered in and out. The damp, spongy ground beneath her cheek smelled musty. All around her it was too warm—the air, the ground, the man on top of her—but the heat couldn't ward off the chill that crept through her.

Ryan scrambled off her, afraid he may have hurt her but more frightened by what would happen to them both if the brutes from the beach found them. He caught her arm, pulled her up. "Get up."

"You bastard!" She twisted, took a swing at him, and narrowly missed landing a solid punch.

He seized her wrists, clamped them together and secured them with the white cotton handkerchief he'd offered her less than an hour before when she'd been sick. He felt like a jerk, but he didn't have time to fight with her. "You've got a choice. Either stay here and let those assholes get their hands on you or come with me."

He didn't wait for her response. He just started off at a fast clip toward the car, his fingers gripping the handkerchief that bound her hands. She kept pace with him, and he took that as her answer.

Back in the Jag, she sat in silence, staring straight ahead while he did a U-turn and gunned the engine. When he'd put several miles between them and the beach, he glanced sideways at his captive. Tears were streaming unchecked down her cheeks. "You don't know what that gunshot was about," he said. "It could have been a warning shot."

"Did they look like the kind of people who are going to just let her go now?"

He didn't know what to say. She was right. Dayle would have to serve some kind of purpose for them to keep her alive. Now that he had broken off contact with them and had no way of reaching them to negotiate further . . . He stopped himself. Damn it, he refused to feel guilty for something he had no control over. "She wouldn't be in this mess if it hadn't been for you," he said in a low voice.

Closing her eyes tight, Meg bit into her bottom lip.

At the marina, she gave him no trouble getting back on the yacht, though he sensed she was waiting for the right moment.

That moment came when he turned from securing the dinghy. One second his gun had been tucked in his waistband, and the next it was in her tied hands, cocked and pointed at his chest. Not allowing her the opportunity to feel triumph, he kicked the weapon out of her hands. He saw the pain register in her eyes a moment after he had her on the deck, her bound wrists pinned above her head. "That was stupid," he said, his lips inches from hers.

She glared at him with hatred, scalding tears rolling back into her hair. "She was my best friend." A dry sob escaped before she could choke it back, and she fought the wave behind it.

Taken aback by the raw emotion, he loosened his grip on her.

She jerked her hands free and shoved at him. "Get off!"

As he sat back on his heels, she rolled onto her side, drawing her knees up to her chest.

Rubbing his hands over his face, he tried to block out the sobs she muted with clenched fists. He'd thought he could handle it. He'd thought his rage at Beau's senseless death would carry him through, make him ruthless enough to get the revenge he wanted. But he hadn't counted on this woman whose claims of innocence were becoming ever more convincing. He hadn't counted on more people getting killed . . . innocent people. He had taken on an entire organization, and he was just one man.

But damn it, he hadn't known what the hell else to do.

Chapter 7

After only one day at Holly's, Margot decided that she had to go. Staying put for too long was foolish. In fact, she may have already endangered her only friend.

Rising from the sofa she'd slept on, she saw on the VCR clock that it was nine in the morning. A glance outside told her it was snowing. Margot didn't relish the thought of hitchhiking in frigid, snowy weather and considered asking Holly for a ride. But that would mean saying good-bye, something she liked even less than hitchhiking in the winter. Of course, there was Holly's brand-new red Mustang parked out front.

She paused while folding a blanket and sat on the sofa's arm.

A new car would get her somewhere fast, and it was safer than hitching. She could swipe Holly's keys from her purse and be on her way. The chances of Holly immediately reporting the car stolen were slim because Holly didn't have to get ready for work for another two hours. Those two hours would provide enough time for Margot to get to Milwaukee and trade the car for another one.

Or she could just ask.

Walking to Holly's bedroom door, she opened it a crack and peered in at her sleeping friend. No, she couldn't afford to ask. When it came to self-preservation, being polite wasn't part of the equation.

Margot took a shower and tried to figure out the easiest way to get the emeralds back to Beau's brother. Hiring a courier seemed the obvious choice. By the time anyone figured out who had sent them or from where, she'd be long gone.

To where?

She couldn't picture what came next, and she remembered another time when she hadn't been able to imagine what her future held. Then, no one had been chasing her but her own demons. She'd been sixteen, hitchhiking alone from Wisconsin to Florida, searching for someone she didn't really expect to find and too broke to even buy herself a cheeseburger. Slater Nielsen had been so nice when he had picked her up in his limousine along the Florida highway.

He smelled like heaven and wore expensive tailored clothing. Sipping a cognac, he offered her a soft drink and seemed genuinely interested in her story, edited as it was. After only three hours, he made her a proposition. All she had to do, he said, was learn a trade that he would teach her himself.

Her initial explosive denial prompted a belly laugh that turned his face bright red. He explained that he wasn't a pimp, that he would never ask her to earn a living by using her fabulous body. No, he said, he was interested in her brain.

Intrigued, Margot listened to what he had in mind.

Think of it as an education, he said. He would teach her about art and literature, music and theater. He would introduce her to wine and gourmet cooking, tutor her in politics, history, and economics. And he would teach her how to outmaneuver any security system ever designed.

She'd planned it all at that moment. She would work for him six months, long enough to save some money, then she would move on. It seemed simple, uncomplicated by emotional ties and unpaid debts. Slater made it easy.

The first year flew by, and surprisingly, she enjoyed Slater's game. She liked outsmarting people and security systems, delighted in the discovery that she was good at something besides being a bad girl. She had talent. She was smart. Slater had often said so.

As another year passed, she grew reluctant to leave the safe haven he provided. At the estate on his private island, he gave her a room of her own and let her decorate it as she pleased. When she turned eighteen, he bought her a car—a convertible with a stereo that would have made even the most jaded teen drool. At twenty-one, he presented her with diamonds and promises for the future.

They became lovers shortly after that, and she discovered that her fantasies about him had fallen far short of the reality. He had pleased her in ways she hadn't thought possible.

Never did she question what he asked of her professionally. She knew it was wrong, even though she liked it. Sometimes, she was ashamed that she was a professional thief. Yet it all somehow seemed justified. Slater's targets were carefully chosen. Not one of them, until Beau Kama, seemed undeserving of the crimes she committed against them. They were the kind of men who would have treated her like trash if they had happened upon her hitchhiking rather than Slater.

For twelve years, she enjoyed the thrill, the danger, the perks. Then Slater had sent her after Beau, and everything had changed.

Realizing she'd lingered in the shower too long, Margot shut off the water and swept aside the shower curtain. At the same moment, the door burst open and one of Slater Nielsen's most vicious hit men grabbed her by the throat and slammed her back against a wet tile wall.

Jake "The Bloodhound" Calhoun's lips parted in a wide grin, showing crooked, tobacco-stained teeth, his breath reeking of cigarettes. "Hey, Mags. Long time no see."

Ryan sat in his car and stared at the Illinois license plate on the practical, silver Honda Civic. It was parked in front of a small house on stilts, on Fort Myers Beach. It seemed like days since he had followed her and her friend here from the airport.

In his hand, he clutched the keys he had demanded she give him the night before to keep her from using them as a weapon. The first key he tried admitted him into a sparsely decorated living room that looked as if it had been left in a hurry. Luggage and a purse lay just inside the door, mail and another purse cluttering a desk nearby.

He circled the room, taking it in. The sofa was new and looked comfortable. Several newspapers and magazines were stacked next to the desk, as if saved for later reading.

A Victorian dollhouse sat on an antique table in one corner. On the floor under the table was a wooden crate, MOMS KRAFT BOCKS stenciled in black letters on its side. It contained small cans of paint, miniature furniture, and tiny rolls of carpeting and wallpaper. The dollhouse was evidently a work in progress.

A bookcase packed with books and pictures demanded a closer look, and in some of the pictures he recognized the woman who had his stomach in knots. In one, she wore scuba gear and stood next to the woman she had called Dayle. In another, she was younger and grinning, an arm propped on the shoulder of the same friend.

Ryan picked up the frame and stared hard at the image. In the background was an older-model Jaguar. Taupe, she had called it.

81

"Damn," he said under his breath.

Putting the picture back, he turned to survey the room. His gaze landed on the purse by the baggage. Feeling like a thief, he opened it and withdrew the wallet. The driver's license inside identified Dayle Richmond of Arlington Heights, Illinois. Further inspection turned up a lawyer's ID.

The other purse yielded another driver's license and a Fort Myers newspaper ID, both showing pictures of a woman identified as Meg Grant.

Pulling out his cell phone, Ryan punched in some numbers. When he got an answer, he said, "Special Agent Sam Loomis, please."

Jake Calhoun gentled his grip, and Margot gulped air into her starved lungs as his gaze dropped down her naked body. She was wet from her shower and shivering, and he nodded in appreciation. "Nice, Mags. Real nice."

She tried to jerk away from him, but his fingers tightened on her throat like a vice. She bit back the urge to scream, thinking of Holly sleeping in the next room. *Please, still be sleeping.* But she'd known Jake for years, knew how he worked. He would have scoured the apartment before cornering her, would have eliminated any potential witnesses.

But maybe there was a chance. Maybe Jake had gone straight for her, bypassing her friend.

Still grinning, Jake said, "Got something to show you."

He dragged her forward out of the tub, and she winced as her shins knocked hard against the porcelain lip. He pushed her out into the hall, one arm locked around her neck, the other around her waist.

The first thing that struck her was the bright red handprint on the wall. A trail of blood, as if someone who was bleeding had been dragged down the hall, led into the bedroom. *Fuck.*

Jake walked her forward into Holly's bedroom, and Margot was helpless to stop him as despair welled inside her. She knew that smell. Coppery and sweet.

Her friend was lying in a pool of blood on the floor next to the bed, and Margot gagged. Holly hadn't screamed. Margot was sure she would have heard her if she had. *I'm sorry, Holly. Jesus, I'm sorry.*

"See that?" Jake whispered near Margot's ear. "That's what happens when you underestimate our boss. You'd think you would have learned that lesson the first time."

Hot tears blurred her vision as he levered her against a wall. Jake's grinning face blocked her view of Holly's body. "Aw, Mags, you're not going to cry, are you?"

She concentrated on breathing, on getting the rage, and grief, under control. She wasn't in any position now to try to overpower him.

Jake didn't seem to notice her struggle as he trailed his hand over her bare breast. "Much as I hate to pass up this golden opportunity, we don't have much time. You're going to get dressed and meet me in the kitchen. I've already been all over this place, and there's no easy way out. So don't even bother to try a back window. Got it?"

When she failed to indicate that she did, he gripped wet hair and yanked her head back. "Got it?" he repeated.

She glared at him through narrowed eyes, making a silent promise to make him pay for what he'd done to Holly. Somehow. Some way. "Yes."

He let go. "Good. Get moving."

Chapter 8

Meg raised her head, and her stiffened neck muscles protested. Pushing damp hair back from her face with her tied hands, she listened carefully. She had heard a thump from above. Had Ryan returned?

As if in answer, the cabin door slammed open. The man who had held a gun to Dayle's temple several hours before stepped inside. The leathery skin around his eyes wrinkled as he grinned. "Mags," he said. "Good to see you again."

Heart slamming against her ribs, Meg shifted to her knees and rose to her feet, conscious of how his gaze fixed on her bound hands.

"Were you a bad girl, Mags?"

She swallowed hard, cleared her throat, and was able to take a breath only when he lifted his gaze back to hers. "What did you do with Dayle?"

He gave a shrug. "What do you think? Your buddy didn't want to make a deal. It's not like we have time to be lugging her around while we track you down."

She forced herself not to lunge at him, her muscles twitching with the effort. "Is she dead?"

"You know the rules, Mags."

"I'm not Mags. And that's not an answer."

His grin broadened. "Way to go, dropping Kama's name like that. I was able to track down his home address in no time." He looked around, whistling. "And I must say, nice digs."

"I said I'm not Mags."

He stood between her and the door, nodding as if enjoying the game. "Okay. Who are you?"

"Meg Grant. I'm a reporter with the Fort Myers newspaper."

He kept nodding. "Okay."

"I don't know anyone named Margot."

"You must think I'm stupid, Mags. I mean, *really* stupid."

"I'm telling the truth."

"Sure you are." The tip of his tongue toyed with his upper lip.

What she saw in his eyes frightened her into action. Feinting right, Meg dove left when he reacted. She got past him and charged for the door, but he caught her heel with the toe of his boot and swept her feet out from under her.

She went down hard on one hip, unable to break the fall with her tied hands, and rolled onto her back. Her feet slipped on the polished floor, and before she could find traction, he was on her, all grasping hands and sharp elbows. He smelled of sweat and alcohol.

Meg fought blindly, pounding at his head with her clasped hands. She thought for an instant that she might be gaining some leverage, then his fingers clamped around her throat and shut off her air.

She gagged as black spots snatched away the edges of her vision. *Oh, Jesus, this is it.* She was going to die, and no one would ever know what had happened to her or why.

Then he was lifted away.

She rolled onto her side and gasped for the air that slashed at her throat. She saw Ryan punch her assailant and ram him against the wall. His body started to buckle, but Ryan grabbed him by the collar with one hand and slammed a fist into his face before letting him drop.

A man wearing a dark suit charged into the compartment as Ryan braced a knee on the fallen man's throat and prepared to deliver another blow. The man in the suit drew a gun and ordered Ryan to back off twice before Ryan let the guy go and stood.

Ryan glanced over his shoulder at Meg, and his stomach rolled when he saw her curled in a ball, hugging bound wrists to her breasts. Something inside him had snapped when he had seen the son of a bitch choking her. "Are you all right?" he asked in a hoarse voice.

Meg didn't acknowledge him, her jittery gaze fixed on the guy in the suit as he flashed a badge at her. FBI. *Thank God.*

The agent flipped out handcuffs, snapped them on her attacker, and hauled him to his feet.

Ryan moved toward Meg, holding out a hand to help her up. "Are you okay?"

She shrank back. "No!" She pressed shaking fingers to her throat. She couldn't think straight, couldn't stop trembling. Every move he made seemed like a threat.

Ryan shoved both hands through his hair. Jesus, she'd almost been killed. He'd left her helpless and tied up, an easy victim.

Another man, this one older and beefy, entered the cabin, flashing an FBI badge. "Special Agent Sam Loomis," he said, helping Meg up.

She swayed, but Loomis steadied her, and she thrust her hands toward him. "Please, untie me."

Ryan watched the agent work out the knot he'd put in the handkerchief. She was shaking, and he noticed she kept her gaze on her wrists, as if Loomis couldn't free her fast enough. Stress had drawn her features taut.

When the handkerchief fell away, Meg rubbed one wrist and then the other. Over, it was over. For her. "My friend is in trouble," she said to the agent, coughing as the words tore at her throat.

Loomis said, "Turn and brace yourself, miss."

Meg didn't move. "What?"

"Brace yourself against the wall, miss. I need to frisk you."

"*Frisk* me?" Surely she had misunderstood him.

"Brace, please, miss."

"You don't understand. My friend Dayle may be hurt or—"

"Don't make me force you."

Head spinning, she did as he said, hands flat on the wall. "Please. I can show you where she—"

"You have the right to remain silent."

She broke off, alarmed. "I'm being arrested?"

He finished reading her her rights, then grasped her arms and angled them behind her. Cold steel encircled her wrists, followed by the zip of metal against metal.

Bound again, she was caught between disbelief and rage. "What's the charge?"

"For starters, grand theft and fleeing the scene of a crime."

Chapter 9

In the bathroom, Margot pulled on her jeans and the blouse with the homemade buttons. Her hands were shaking so hard, she had to stop and brace herself on the vanity. Taking deep breaths, she told herself she couldn't afford to fall apart. But Holly was dead, and it was her fault. She had led Jake right to her.

Margot squeezed her eyes shut and clenched her jaw against the emotion. The shaking spread to her legs, and she sat on the edge of the tub. Lowering her head to her knees, she willed the tears back. If she let them come, they would never stop, and she couldn't let grief cloud her thinking, not if she was going to survive whatever Jake had in mind. Surviving was imperative if she was going to get the emeralds back to Beau's brother. And make Jake pay for killing her only friend.

Forcing herself not to think, Margot finished dressing and left the bathroom. Guilt and rage almost overwhelmed her again when she saw that while she'd dressed, Jake had torn Holly's apartment apart. She found him in the kitchen, guarding the only way out of the apartment.

His thinness always surprised her. His face was shaped like a triangle, his wide forehead narrowing down to hollow cheeks and a pointy chin. Thick black hair made his skin appear even paler than it was. He may have looked anorexic as he leaned against the sink, a cigarette dangling from his mouth, but he was strong and ruthless.

Water tinged with pink spotted the floor at his feet, and Margot realized that he had washed Holly's blood from his hands here. Swallowing against a surge of nausea, she gave him a cold look. Striking out at him now would do her no good. The only way to play this man was to be cool.

Jake looked her up and down and focused on her hair. "Nice 'do, Mags."

"Fuck you, Jake."

"Is that any way to talk to an old friend?" He dropped his cigarette on the tile floor and ground it under his heel. "See what I'm doing, Mags?"

She refused to look down. "Yeah, message received loud and clear. Cut the shit, Jake. I know you're not going to kill me or you already would have. I'm guessing that means Slater wanted you to pick me up. So take me to him, collect your cash, and be on your slimy way."

"I have something else in mind."

She met his black eyes, and goose bumps raised on her arms. "If you defy him, he'll kill you," she said.

"And how would he find out he's been defied? I'm thinking you're not the most trusted source these days."

She resisted the urge to rip his face off. "What do you want, Jake?"

"The Kama emeralds."

Her breath stopped. That's what he'd been looking for when he'd ransacked the apartment.

"I know you took them, and I know they belong to Slater," Jake said.

"Like hell they do. They belong to . . . who they belong

to." She thought of Beau and the bullet hole in his forehead. As if emeralds would do him any good now.

"Don't want to make a deal?"

"Why would I? So you can go back to Slater and ask for a better one than I gave you? Maybe I didn't take them."

"I know you took 'em. I checked the safe after I offed your boyfriend."

The blood drained from her head. "You?"

"Nice shot, huh?"

Margot charged him, fingers hooked for optimum damage. He caught her wrists and pivoted, shoving her back against the refrigerator. She fought hard, not caring what he might do to her, wanting to hurt him. But he was stronger, and she was weak, drained by desolation. When she stopped struggling, he didn't release her.

"Let me go," she ground out.

"Not until we cut a deal, baby."

"I'm not cutting a deal with you, asshole."

He twisted a wrist in one hand until her eyes teared with pain. "Your options are limited, Margot," he said, as if discussing what to order on a pizza.

She spat in his face.

He released one wrist and backhanded her. She fell against the counter, stunned. His fingers bit cruelly into her cheeks as he forced her face up to his.

"Listen to me real good, Mags. I'm the one in charge here, and you're going to do what I say or I'll kill you. I don't give a shit what you decide because I'm going to get my money whether I give you to Slater dead or alive. You follow me? He'd be just as tickled to have your corpse dropped on his doorstep as he would to have you still breathing."

He let her go, and she slid to the floor. Pulling a crumpled pack of cigarettes out of his jacket, he lit two cigarettes and held one down near her head.

She accepted it with a shaky hand and took a deep drag. It was as if she had sucked a tranquilizer into her lungs. As the calm settled over her, she thought about what he'd said. She didn't believe that Slater had put out a dead-or-alive contract on her. She had betrayed him twice—first by falling in love with another man and again by taking off with the emeralds. He would want to exact his revenge in person, while she was very much alive and able to experience every torture he inflicted. Jake was trying to intimidate her.

"Are we making a deal or aren't we?" he asked.

"What's the deal?"

"Give me the emeralds, and I let you go."

"How do I know you'll let me go?" she asked.

"Guess you'll just have to trust me on that one, Mags." Hooking a hand under her arm, he hauled her up. "We got a deal?"

She tasted blood where he'd split her lip. Making any kind of deal with him was dangerous, but what choice did she have?

"I'm feeling a bit impatient, Mags."

"Fine," she said.

"Fine what?"

"I'll take you to the emeralds."

He arched an eyebrow, then pushed her against the counter.

"What are you doing?" she demanded.

He frisked her with rough hands, shoving his fingers into the pockets of her jeans, feeling carefully up and down her legs and arms. Snarling, he got in her face. "You don't have them on you?"

"Hell, no. What am I, an idiot? I'm going to carry millions of dollars' worth of jewels in my pocket? Jesus."

"I don't believe you." He went for the buttons on her blouse.

Margot batted his hands away. "What the hell are you doing?"

"Open the blouse."

"What?"

"Do it or I'll do it for you."

She began undoing buttons, her cheeks flaming with rage. She made it through four before he seized a wrist and dragged her to him so he could check the front of her bra.

"What the hell is this?" He held up the object in question.

"You've never seen a paper clip?"

"Not on a bra. What's it for?"

"It's for picking locks, you jerk."

Releasing her with a grunt, he flicked the clip at her. "Where are the stones?"

"I said I'll take you to them."

"Don't fuck with me, Mags."

There were tremors in her fingers as she affixed the paper clip to the fabric of her bra and buttoned her blouse. "Captiva."

"If you're lying to me, I'll—"

"They're on Beau's yacht, anchored in a marina off the island. I swear to God."

He smiled. "You don't have a God."

"You want to make a deal or what?"

"You're telling me you dumped the emeralds on Kama's yacht before you left the state," he said.

"Yes."

"What were you trying to do? Unsteal 'em?"

She raised her chin a defiant notch. "Maybe."

"That's precious."

"Bite me."

He grinned. "Sure thing, and then we're going to Florida." Cocking his head to one side, he pretended to be glum. "You know, it's a shame that Slater's not going to get his hands on you. He's got a scheme in the works that'd knock your socks off."

"What are you talking about?"

"Our buds Turner and Dillon are tracking down a sweet thing in Florida that looks a lot like you but ain't you."

Margot's heart began to thud in her ears. "What?"

" 'Course, the boss didn't bother to fill them in on the details. They think they're hauling your ass back to him just like I'm supposed to. Shit, I'd love to see how this plays out, but we just made us a deal."

Shivering, she hugged her arms across her chest. "I need to use the bathroom before we go."

"You were just in the bathroom."

"What do you care? There's no way to get out, remember?"

His grin widened. "Take your time."

In the bathroom, Margot washed her face with shaking hands. Her ears were ringing, her mouth swollen where he had struck her. The water stung the split in her lip.

Bracing her hands on the sink, she stared into her own eyes in the mirror. *"Turner and Dillon are tracking down a sweet thing in Florida that looks a lot like you but ain't you."*

Last year, Slater had asked her if there was anything, anything at all, she wanted that she didn't already have. She'd told him years before that she was adopted, but she'd never asked him to try to find the sister she'd never known. She'd always planned to do that on her own once she broke away from him, once she lived a life that wasn't criminal. At the time, that life no longer appeared to be imminent, so she'd asked him to do it. *"Find my sister for me, Slater. You would make me the happiest woman in the world."*

A few months later, Beau Kama happened.

Margot forced back the despair so she could concentrate on what she needed to do now. Jake thought he was smart, but Slater had taught her to be smarter than the average thug.

When she left the bathroom, Jake was standing by the door, the keys to Holly's Mustang dangling from his hand. "Looky what I found," he said. "New wheels."

Chapter 10

"I want a lawyer."

The man who'd arrested her, Special Agent Stan or Sam Loomis—Meg couldn't remember which—took his time removing his jacket, revealing a white, coffee-stained shirt. As he loosened the navy tie at his throat, he called out to no one in particular, "Somebody get the lady a lawyer."

Meg glanced at the large mirror on one wall of the room, which was about the size of a small walk-in closet. Apparently, they had an audience, and she wondered whether Ryan Kama was watching from behind that one-way glass.

The FBI agent sniffed hard as he flipped open a legal pad. "You don't mind if I ask you a few questions while we wait for your lawyer, do you, Miss . . . ," he made a big show of checking his notes, "Grant?"

She sat back in the creaky, gray metal folding chair, slouching in spite of herself. "Fine." She had nothing to hide, and she just wanted this to be over. The sooner she answered his questions, the sooner they would all find out who she was and she could get the hell out of here. And the sooner she would be able to find out something more about Dayle. All she had been able to get out of him was that federal agents were scouring the beach area where she and Ryan had last seen her.

"Let's start with you telling me what you were doing October fifteenth," Loomis said.

The date—her birthday—startled her, but she had no trouble remembering what she did that day. "I spent most of the day at work, as a reporter in Arlington Heights, Illinois."

Loomis lit a cigarette, blowing a cloud of smoke into the already stuffy room. "You're awfully quick with that answer. Are you sure you don't want to think about it some more?"

"No. On October fifteenth, I worked. All day."

"We'll have to verify that, of course."

"Go ahead."

He narrowed bloodshot eyes. "Don't waste my time."

She didn't know how to respond, so she just stared at him, her gaze level.

Leaning forward, he tapped the end of his pen on the table in front of her. "I've been looking for you for a very long time. However long this takes is fine with me."

"I'm not her."

Sitting back, he cocked his head to one side. "Do you know what happens to pretty women in prison?"

"Don't tell me you're going to go down that street. It's such a cliché."

"You'll be popular, trust me," he said with a small smile.

"Except I'm not going to prison because I didn't do anything wrong. If you want to nail a criminal that bad, I'd suggest taking a look at Ryan Kama. He's committed all kinds of crimes. Kidnapping. Aggravated assault—"

"Harboring a fugitive," he said, blowing a stream of smoke through his nose.

She didn't look away because she knew that's what he wanted. He wanted her cowed. But she knew better than to show any sign of weakness that he could somehow exploit. "I don't suppose there's a lawyer waiting to see me."

He stubbed out his cigarette with controlled taps. "You know what will happen to you if you manage to convince me that you're not Margot Rhinehart, don't you?"

"I imagine you'll let me go."

"And where would you go?" he asked.

"Home sounds pretty good."

"There are some nasty people looking for you, Margot."

"I'm not Margot."

"One of those people put those bruises on your throat."

She swallowed against the soreness. "Lucky for me, he's in your custody."

"Maybe not for long."

"What does that mean?"

"It might work better for me to cut him loose, maybe see where he leads me," he said. "If I cut you loose, too, what do you think might happen?"

She didn't answer as she remembered the man's brutal hands on her throat, cutting off her air. *"You must think I'm stupid, Mags."*

"The thing is," Loomis said, lowering his voice as if they were conspiring, "I can protect you from thugs like him. All you have to do is be straight with me. Tell me about Slater Nielsen."

"I don't know anyone by that name."

"He had your lover killed. Don't you want to fuck him over for that? This is your chance. Right here, right now."

"I don't have a lover," she said, chagrined to hear the tremor in her voice.

"Not now you don't. And if I were you, I'd be pretty damned pissed off."

Meg pushed herself out of the chair, clenching one hand

into a tight fist. *Keep it together.* In the mirror's reflection, she saw the detective reach for a fresh cigarette. Helpless anger made drawing a breath difficult, and she told herself to ride it out. He'd realize his mistake. He had to.

Loomis sat back as he lit the cigarette, as relaxed as a man at a bar with a drink in his hand. Narrowing his eyes through the smoke that swirled around his head, he said, "How about this, Margot? I've got Turner Scott sitting in the next room. Before I came in here, he was eager to chat me up about you."

She faced him. "I don't know who he is."

"Turner Scott's the man who tried to strangle you, Margot."

"Because he tried to kill me, that means I'm supposed to know him?" Hysteria crept forward, and she struggled to hold it back.

Loomis rapped a thick knuckle on his legal pad. "Thanks to Mr. Scott, I've got fourteen pages here about you. I've got stuff on you that would put you away so long that the only way you'd leave the slammer is in a pine box." He flipped through the pages. "Jewel heists, cons, home burglaries, museum thefts, insurance fraud. Shall I continue?"

"That's not about *me*. It's about a woman who apparently looks a lot like me."

"That's an old line, Margot. Why don't you try something new?"

"Why don't you try doing your job? You've got the wrong woman."

He rose, unperturbed. "I'm going to show you something that might persuade you to reconsider your level of cooperation."

He opened the door, and as a young man in a suit wheeled in a TV and VCR, Loomis gestured for her to sit. She did because exhaustion and fear had made her legs weak.

He pressed play on the VCR, and Meg watched the black-and-white tape with mounting alarm. The woman on the TV worked fast, her expression determined, unaware that a security camera placed above her head was recording her crime.

Anyone unfamiliar with every angle and nuance of Meg's face could easily have mistaken her for this woman. The hair had the same curls, the same wisps that aggravated Meg every day. The eyes were the same shape. She imagined that if the tape were in color, those eyes would be the same deep-sea emerald green, the hair the same dark auburn-brown.

When the tape was over, Loomis ejected it and popped in another one. Now, the same woman stumbled out of what appeared to be the front door of a house, her face contorted with terror, her hands dark and wet, her hair wild. She half-fell, half-leapt off the porch and was gone. All that she left behind was a smeared hand print on the front wall.

Loomis hit the pause button and looked down at Meg, an unlit cigarette dangling from his lips. "Both tapes were made at Beau Kama's home on October fifteenth, the first in the early hours of the afternoon, using a fancy, new-fangled camera designed by KamaTech's security chief. Perhaps your lover, Mr. Beau Kama, told you about him. Nick Costello?"

Meg shook her head, numb.

"Right," Loomis said, his tone laden with sarcasm. "The second tape was made later that night, just after a woman called nine-one-one." Sitting across from her, he slipped back into his conspiratorial manner. "You called for help. That works in your favor."

"That isn't me," she said, her voice almost a whisper. "I don't know who that is." The possibilities tumbled through her exhausted brain. "I was adopted. Maybe she's . . ." She trailed off, staring at the frozen image on the TV screen. "Maybe we're related."

He gave her a smile that didn't reach his eyes. "This is the deal, Margot. I'm only going to offer it once. Give me Slater Nielsen, and there's a chance you could score immunity."

Meg shot to her feet, slamming a fist on the table. "Damn it, I'm not jerking you around here. Call the newspaper in Fort Myers, talk to my editor. Check my fingerprints against hers. Go to my house. I have yearbooks from high school with pictures of me, with my name—Meg Grant—all over them."

Bored now, Loomis fished in his pocket for a lighter. "I suppose I could let the newspapers know the FBI has secured the testimony of a woman with intimate knowledge of Nielsen's crime syndicate. Perhaps I could give them a nice little mug shot of you to run with the story. Then let's just say I let you go. Hell, I'm not going to need your testimony for a few months at least. I'll give you a minute to picture it, Margot."

Meg began to pace, raking her hands back through her hair. Perspiration had plastered ringlets of it to the sides of her neck. *Shit shit shit.*

The agent blew more smoke into the smoke-choked room, content to let her pace.

Meg, her heart pounding in fury, in fear, took a deep breath and faced him. "I'm done talking," she said, her voice low with tension. "I want a lawyer. Now."

"You're making a mistake, Margot," he said.

"You're making the mistake if you don't get me a fucking lawyer now."

The chair legs screeched against the floor as he stood. Glaring at her for a moment, he seemed to be considering another tack. Then, shaking his head in disgust, he went to the door.

Alone and shaking, Meg tried to talk herself back into control. Her head ached, and her brain felt as if it were short-circuiting.

The room was too close and warm.

Dayle was probably dead.

Close to caving in on herself, Meg lowered herself to a chair and cradled her head in her hands.

As Special Agent Loomis walked into his tiny, dusty office, Ryan rose from the chair he had occupied for the past two hours.

"How is she?" he asked.

"She's not talking," Loomis said, tossing his cigarettes onto his cluttered desk. "Other than to insist that she's not Margot Rhinehart."

"Maybe she's telling the truth. What I saw at her house was pretty convincing."

"Don't let her fool you, Mr. Kama. People like her are experts." He sat in the worn leather chair behind the desk. "We'll know soon enough anyway. I've got people checking her story in Fort Myers and Illinois, and we'll have a read on the fingerprints any minute."

"I want to see her."

"Sorry, Mr. Kama. Only person who's going to see the lady is a lawyer."

Ryan nodded. "I called someone in Tampa. She should be here soon."

Loomis leaned way back, seeming to test the strength of the chair, and propped his feet on the desk. "Now why would you go to the trouble of doing that when we've already summoned a lawyer?"

Ryan had no clue. Other than he worried he'd made a horrible mistake getting the FBI involved. Not only had he given up control of the situation, but he feared for Meg's safety. Slater Nielsen was a powerful man. Arranging a hit at a small FBI field office like this one might be even easier than Ryan could imagine.

He told himself that he was being paranoid. But, damn it, he had a right to be. He'd underestimated Nielsen and his people. One woman might already be dead because of it. And the thug who'd attacked Meg had had no problem finding her on the yacht.

"Mr. Kama?" Loomis asked.

Ryan looked up, realizing he had not responded to the agent's question. "I need to talk to her."

"Not going to happen. Besides, she hasn't asked to see you." Loomis stroked his chin as if checking for razor stubble. "What would you two have to talk about anyway?"

That was a good question, Ryan thought.

Dropping his feet to the floor, Loomis peered at Ryan. "Maybe you've gotten too attached to the fugitive, Mr. Kama."

Ryan rejected that suggestion. All he was attached to was getting the people responsible for killing Beau. "It's because of me that you've got her in custody," he said, still trying to reason. "Surely that counts for something."

"The FBI appreciates your help, sir, but the truth of the matter is, you're done here. It's out of your hands. You might as well go home, take a swim, get a massage or whatever it is you rich folks do when you've had a rough day. I've got it under control."

Ryan crossed his arms. "I'm not going anywhere."

"Then you'll have to wait in the break room. I have work to do in here." Loomis waved him toward the hall. "The next door on the right. Have some coffee. Relax."

Outside Loomis' office, Ryan stared down the corridor at the room where he'd seen them take Meg. Relax? How could he relax when he was the one who'd put her in such a vulnerable position?

Chapter 11

Meg sat on the cold concrete, her back against the wall, her forehead resting on her knees. Her eyelids were gritty with fatigue, yet her brain kept going over the videotapes. *Margot's my sister. She has to be.* The resemblance was too striking. Perhaps they were even twins. The graininess of the black-and-white tape had made it difficult to tell for sure.

The door to the interrogation room opened, and a tall woman in a navy, tailored suit stepped into the room. She had short, blond hair and sky-blue eyes. The hand she extended was well-manicured. "Kelsey Sumner, Ms. Grant."

Meg didn't trust her. It wasn't the way she looked, but Meg thought she probably wouldn't trust anyone ever again. At least the woman hadn't called her Margot. "Who are you?" Meg asked.

"You asked for a lawyer." Kelsey, who looked about thirty, walked to the table and set down her briefcase. "I'll be up-front with you," she said. "I'm a friend of Ryan's."

Meg's shoulders sagged. She imagined a hell where everywhere she turned, Ryan Kama would be there, always in control, always taunting her. "I don't have anything to say."

"Why don't you take a seat? Let's talk."

"I'm not talking to *you*," Meg said. "I want a court-appointed attorney. Unbiased representation."

"I'm among the best, Ms. Grant," Kelsey said.

"Make that modest, unbiased representation."

"Meg . . . may I call you Meg?"

"No."

"Okay." Kelsey seemed to think a moment, her gaze lingering on Meg's neck. Something shifted in her eyes before she cleared her throat. "Do you need anything? I understand you've been here awhile."

"I need to know what happened to my friend."

"Your friend?"

"She was kidnapped by the same two men who tried to kidnap me," Meg said. "No one will tell me what happened to her."

"I'll be right back."

Meg lowered herself to a chair, tangling her hands on the table and clinging to the prospect of good news. She rose again when Kelsey returned, but she could tell by the look on the other woman's face that the news was not good.

"The FBI is doing what they can to find her," Kelsey said, her tone gentle. "I'm sorry." She paused, obviously feeling awkward. "Is there anything else you need?"

"I need out of here," Meg said.

"I can probably help you with that."

"Sure, you can."

Kelsey helped herself to a seat, unruffled by Meg's surliness. "Ryan told me you'd be stubborn."

"I'm sure he told you I helped get his brother killed, too."

"They have some pretty damning evidence, Ms. Grant."

Meg let her eyes slide closed for a moment, then opened them. She had nowhere to turn, no one to turn to. If only Dayle were here . . . "If the evidence is so damning, why would you take my side?"

"Because Ryan asked me to."

Surprise arched Meg's eyebrows, but it lasted only a moment before she realized what was happening. "That makes it *so* much easier for him, doesn't it? He can virtually guarantee I go to prison."

"He wants to help you."

Meg's legs gave out, and she sank onto a metal chair. The planet was spinning off its axis, and she was just trying to hang on. "I don't understand."

Reaching out, Kelsey covered Meg's hand on the table. "He's trying to figure it out as much as you are."

The kind gesture caught Meg off guard, and for a moment, looking at this woman's hand covering hers, she felt a connection, the forming of a bond. She supposed it was ridiculous. Kelsey had admitted that she was with the enemy. But something about her reminded Meg of Dayle, and more than anything right now, she needed someone to be on her side.

"Well, Ms. Grant?"

"He held a gun to my head," Meg said. "I'm sure you can understand my hesitation."

Kelsey gave a short nod, her face showing nothing, but Meg saw the fury, controlled but ugly, slip through her eyes. "I'd like to hear from you what happened."

"I'd rather talk to a court-appointed attorney."

"Your chances are better with me, Ms. Grant. I have a very good record."

"He accused me of setting up his brother to be killed, and now he wants to help me? Where is the sense in that?"

"I know it's confusing," Kelsey said.

"He almost got me killed." Pulling her hand away, Meg told herself it was foolish to trust this woman. Even a little. "You know what? I don't need his help. As soon as the feds figure out I'm not her, I'm out of here. And then Ryan Kama can go screw himself."

"And while Ryan is screwing himself, what happens to you?"

"Agent Loomis already worked that angle. You people can't scare me into doing what you want."

"I'm not trying to scare you," Kelsey said. "I'm trying to get you to think about where you'll be when the feds release you."

"I'll be free."

"You'll be free all right—*free game.* The feds might verify that you're not Margot Rhinehart, but the people who are after her won't know that. And they're still out there."

Ryan sat in the break room of the FBI field office and rubbed at the ache in the back of his neck. Kelsey had been in with Meg for an hour, and the waiting was driving him insane. Loomis wouldn't talk to him anymore, so he was right back where he'd been before he'd spotted Meg at the airport. Shut out of the FBI investigation into his brother's murder. Stripped of control.

Dropping his head forward into his hands, he couldn't stop seeing the image of the thug on top of Meg, choking off her air, her hands tied together with his white handkerchief. If he and the federal agents had arrived a minute later . . .

Kelsey stormed through the door, and Ryan scrambled up in surprise. Her eyes snapped blue fire as she cornered him. "You held a *gun* to her head?"

He raised his hands, palms out. "Kelsey, Jesus, the safety was on."

"Like that matters, you idiot. What else did you do to her, Ryan? She looks like she's been knocked around. The bruises on her throat—"

"I barely touched her. You know me better than that."

Whirling away as Loomis ambled in, she leveled a threatening finger at the agent. "No one talks to my client without me being present," she snapped. "Especially you. Got it?" Turning back to Ryan, she asked, "When was the last time she ate?"

"I don't know. Not since I picked her up last night."

"That was almost twenty-four hours ago. No wonder she looks like she's about to collapse. Those bruises on her throat are nasty. There could be permanent damage."

Ryan felt his face flush with shame. It hadn't occurred to him that Meg could be injured.

Before Ryan could respond, Loomis cleared his throat. "We're letting Turner Scott go."

Ryan rounded on him. "What? Why?"

Loomis patted his front shirt pocket, looking for cigarettes but coming up empty. He settled for coffee and poured some into a Styrofoam cup. "Besides Ms. Rhinehart, he's our only link to Slater Nielsen. We let him go, a couple of agents tail him, maybe he leads us to Nielsen."

"Maybe?" Ryan shouted.

Kelsey's hand on his arm reined him in. "Let him explain, Ryan."

"The FBI has been tracking Slater Nielsen for a year," Loomis said, sipping coffee. "We know his name. We know what he does and how he does it. We don't know where he's based, and we don't know how to get to him. And seeing as how Ms. Rhinehart is reluctant to turn on Nielsen, Turner Scott is our best bet."

"Don't you think Nielsen will be smart enough to know what you're up to once he gets word that one of his henchmen has been arrested and released?" Ryan asked.

"Perhaps. But maybe Nielsen will come after him."

Ryan saw again Turner Scott's hands wrapped around Meg's throat. "Jesus," he said. The bastard had almost killed her, and he was going to walk. "What about the woman he may have killed on the beach? Doesn't she matter to the FBI?"

Loomis pocketed one hand, jingled change. "Nielsen is the big fish here, Mr. Kama. Turner Scott, he's just a little guppy in a great big pond. We've got the opportunity to dangle him as bait and see if the big fish will bite. Even if Nielsen himself doesn't come after Scott, maybe he'll send someone else after him who's easier to squeeze. Catch my drift?"

Kelsey, a hand on Ryan's arm to keep him from lunging, asked, "What do I tell my client about the man who attacked her going free?"

Loomis gave her a humorless smile. "Tell her whatever you want. The fact of the matter is, he's out of here."

"What about her friend? Can you make an educated guess at the chances she's alive?" Kelsey asked.

"The people we're dealing with are professionals, counselor. Professionals don't leave loose ends. That's my educated guess."

A woman, who appeared to be an assistant or secretary, entered carrying a file folder. "Your fingerprint analysis is in, Agent Loomis."

Ryan held his breath as Loomis flipped open the file and scanned the paperwork inside. When the agent pursed his lips in thought, Ryan prodded, "Well?"

Loomis snapped the file closed. "She's not Margot Rhinehart."

Ryan didn't know whether to be relieved or disappointed. Or even believe him. "What now?"

Loomis shrugged. "We let her go."

"That's it?" Ryan asked.

"What else would you like me to do?" Loomis asked. "She hasn't done anything wrong. You, on the other hand, could be in a world of hurt if she decides to press kidnapping and assault charges."

Ryan refused to be intimidated. "There has to be something you can do, some way to protect her. Nielsen's people are still gunning for her."

"I'll offer her a safe house," Loomis said. "If she doesn't want it, it's her choice."

As Loomis left, Ryan pulled away from Kelsey's grasp. "I can't believe this crap," he said. "He's going to let her go, then sit back and wait for Nielsen to come after her. He's going to dangle *her* like bait, too."

"You don't know that, Ryan."

"Are you willing to take that chance?"

Kelsey's forehead creased with worry. "What are you going to do?"

Ryan yanked his cell phone out. "I have an idea."

"You're free to go, Ms. Grant." Special Agent Loomis looked downright contrite as he stood before Meg in the interrogation room, his hands in his pockets.

Relief turned Meg's knees to water, but she locked them straight. She didn't know what to say. Thanks for the hospitality? Bite me?

His brow furrowed as he scratched his chin, as if he were giving what he was about to say some serious thought. "You have the option of pressing kidnapping and assault charges against Mr. Kama."

Meg was tempted. Sweet revenge. But she longed to go home. Her control was already starting to splinter, and she wanted out of there before it disintegrated altogether.

"Do I have to decide now?"

Loomis handed her a business card. "Just give me a call." Then he gave her arm an awkward pat. "Please accept my apologies."

She didn't bother to try to muster a smile of forgiveness. Maybe she would have if his regret had seemed genuine.

"I can arrange for you to stay at a safe house until we find Margot Rhinehart," he said. "You'd be safer."

Meg rolled shoulders tight with tension. "How long would it be?"

"I don't know. It could be months."

"I can't sit in a safe house that long. I have a job."

"What about a long vacation out of the country with friends or relatives?"

Meg felt the despair well up. How could she turn to friends when Dayle, her dearest friend, might be dead because of this? Feeling the agent's expectant gaze, she said, "I'll figure something out." For now, she just wanted out.

Loomis gestured toward the door. "I'll have an agent drive you home."

She didn't have to be invited twice to leave that claustrophobic room. In the hallway, she spotted Ryan at the other end and froze. He was talking on a cell phone, one hand pressed over his ear to block out noise. Beside him, Kelsey tapped her foot and looked stressed.

"Is there another exit?" Meg asked.

"Afraid not," Loomis said. "It's a small office. One way in, one way out."

Squaring her shoulders, Meg reminded herself that Ryan had no power over her anymore. In fact, if anyone held the power now, she did. All she had to do was tell Loomis she wanted to press charges.

She walked by Ryan without a glance, though she felt his

intent gaze on her. She was surprised he didn't make one last effort to persuade her to help him continue his search for Margot. But perhaps now that he knew she wasn't Margot, it didn't matter to him what happened to her. That worked just fine for her.

As Loomis paused to speak with Ryan and Kelsey, Meg walked out of the FBI office into bright afternoon sunlight. Breathing deep, she tried to ease the tension that made her muscles ache, feeling the exhaustion in her bones.

The sound of a racing engine brought her head up, and she stumbled back as a police car roared to a stop in front of her. Two officers piled out, guns drawn. "Police! Get your hands up!"

Meg was too stunned to move as one of the officers seized her arm and shoved her forward against the car. In an instant, he'd snapped handcuffs on her wrists. "You have the right to remain silent . . ."

Chapter 12

Meg couldn't believe she was in yet another claustrophobic interrogation room, this time at a Naples police station. The cops seemed to be taking their time verifying with the FBI that she was indeed Meg Grant and not their missing jewel thief. Meg suspected the delay had much to do with Ryan's influence.

As if her thoughts had summoned him, he stepped into the room and closed the door behind him. Meg rose, shaking with rage. She pictured herself landing a punch on that square jaw. Her hand clenched with anticipation. "You have a lot of nerve," she said.

Ryan kept his face neutral, but his stomach lurched at the sight of her. Purple shadows marred the skin under her green eyes, her complexion ashen. The pallor made the bruises encircling her throat all the more prominent. Shoving back the guilt, he said, "Someday you'll thank me for saving your life."

"You arrogant son of a bitch. You called the cops."

"You're safe here," he said. "You wouldn't have been safe going home."

"So you had me arrested a second time? I was questioned all over again. The same damned questions. I suppose you

112

couldn't be bothered to let the police know that the feds have cleared me?"

"I'm afraid the feds and the police aren't cooperating on this case," he said.

"How convenient for you." Her voice broke, and she moved as far away from him as the tiny room allowed. *Jesus, don't lose it. Not in front of him.*

She heard him pull out a chair, heard the metal squeak as it took his weight. "The thing is, just because Agent Loomis said you're not Margot Rhinehart doesn't mean you're not."

She faced him. He was sitting on the edge of the chair, his elbows braced on his knees. "This is unbelievable," she said. "*You* are unbelievable."

"The feds cut Turner Scott loose. Did you know that?"

"No." She rubbed at her eyes, so tired she didn't even care.

"They let him go because they're hoping he'll lead them to Slater Nielsen," Ryan said. "I think they're doing the same thing with you. And I think Agent Loomis told me you're not Margot to get me off his back."

"I've got news for you," she said. "The cops are going to tell you the same damn thing. I'm not her."

"Frankly, it doesn't matter who you are. You look enough like her to help me get to the people who killed my brother."

"And what makes you think I'd be stupid enough to do that?"

"I don't think you're stupid at all," he said. "But you might be desperate."

Meg glared at him so hard her eyes burned. "I'm not desperate."

He smiled, as if to say, not yet. Straightening in the chair, he crossed his legs. "The district attorney is a good friend of mine. I can pull strings to get you out of here. Probably within the hour."

"I see. But you wouldn't let me just walk away."

"No," he said, "I'd protect you from Nielsen's henchmen."

"In exchange for what?"

He picked at a piece of imaginary lint on his knee. "You're going to help me avenge my brother's murder."

She leaned against the wall at her back, needing its support. "Vengeance is against the law, Mr. Kama."

"Justice isn't."

"What if I refuse?"

Ryan shrugged, forcing as much boredom into the gesture as possible. "Arranging a hit on a woman in a jail cell probably wouldn't be that difficult for a man as powerful as Slater Nielsen. With me, at least you've got a shot at surviving." Pausing, he gave her a grim smile. "Feeling desperate yet?"

Yes, she thought, and trapped, and there was nowhere to run. She fought down the rising panic. "You know I'm not her."

"I *don't* know that. Not for sure. And the fact of the matter is, I don't care."

"This is blackmail."

"Not really. If it works right, we both get what we want."

"You get vengeance," she said. "What do I get?"

"Your life." He stood, pushing the chair back under the table. "I'll give you some time to think about it."

Alone, Meg dragged a hand through her hair, feeling the filth and longing for a shower. She didn't know what to do. Ryan was right. She wasn't safe here. She wasn't safe anywhere. But how was she supposed to help him get to Slater Nielsen when she didn't know anything about the man?

The door opened, interrupting her thoughts, and a police officer said, "Your lawyer's here."

Meg straightened from the wall, expecting Kelsey Sumner. Instead, a man she had never seen before sauntered in.

He grinned when he saw her. "Hey, Mags."

In the precinct break room, Ryan dropped onto the ratty sofa next to Kelsey. Defeat was a lead weight on his shoulders.

"Any luck?" she asked.

Shaking his head, he zeroed in on the Styrofoam cup in her hand. "Is that coffee?"

Kelsey handed it to him. "It's weak, but it'll do the trick."

He swallowed a gulp of the bitter brew. "She's not budging," he said. "I guess I can't blame her. She's been through hell."

"You've put her through hell," Kelsey said.

He glanced at her. "I'm not the only one. I didn't sic Nielsen's goons on her."

"And if she's innocent?" Kelsey asked.

"It doesn't matter. She's involved."

"It does matter, Ryan. You know it does."

He dropped his head back against the sofa and scowled at the water-stained ceiling. "Damn it, Kelsey. Don't you think I know that?"

A woman in uniform stuck her head in the door. "Isn't one of you supposed to be Margot Rhinehart's attorney?"

Kelsey rose. "I am."

"She's got another lawyer in there talking to her now," the officer said.

Ryan sprang to his feet. "Who is he?"

"Don't know. He just said he's her attorney."

The woman left, and Kelsey said, "Nielsen must have sent him."

"But how did he know?"

"Turner Scott's been gone a couple hours," she said. "Or maybe Nielsen has an informant in the precinct."

Ryan crumpled the cup in his hand. "She's not safe in there with that guy."

Meg warily faced her visitor.

He wore a not-that-cheap suit, clean white shirt open at the throat and an expensive gold watch. His hair was greased back and in need of a trim. Wire-rimmed glasses slid to the tip of his nose, and as he looked her up and down, he pushed them up with the middle finger of one hand. Meg couldn't tell whether he made the gesture deliberately or if it was just how he repositioned his glasses.

"How's it going, Mags?" he asked, grinning. She'd expected to see the flash of a gold tooth, but his teeth were straight and white.

"Who are you?"

The grin widened. "Told them my name's Jimmy Buffett. Stupid cops didn't even blink."

"I'm not Margot." She wondered how many more times she'd have to say that.

"You can drop the game. It's just us."

"I've never seen you before," she said.

"No one's watching."

She leaned her hands on the table. "Look at me. I'm not her."

"You knew it would come to this, Mags."

"Look at me, damn it."

"I'm looking. Jesus." He gave an uneasy laugh.

She held his gaze. "Look at my face. Her face is thinner than mine. Look at my hair."

"Yeah, whatever. Look, he sent me to get you out of here,

so maybe there's a chance."

"A chance what?"

"You know. Maybe you'll be okay."

She pounded a fist on the table. "I don't know who you are. I don't know who *he* is. Are you talking about Slater Nielsen? Is that who *he* is?"

His eyes shifted from side to side as if she'd said something she never should have dared to say. "Jesus, what's wrong with you?"

"What happens?" she demanded.

"What?"

"If I go with you, what happens?"

"Is this a trick? Are trying to trick me, Mags? Are you wired?" He shifted around the table fast, and his hands were on her, moving over the knit of the tank top that covered her ribs and down to her waist in a quick, rough frisking.

She shoved him back. "Get away from me."

Glancing at the door, she expected a police officer to bound through it to protect her. But it remained closed, and apprehension clamped down. What was she supposed to do if the guy got violent? Would anyone hear a scream for help? Ryan had said Slater Nielsen was powerful enough to have her killed, even in police custody.

Her pulse, already charging, became a deafening thud in her ears. She was on her own. Ryan was not here to protect her, and despite every punishment she had wished on him, she missed him.

Jimmy Buffett was straightening his jacket. "No one else will help you out, Mags. He took care of that."

"Who took care of it? Slater Nielsen?"

He winced as if she'd said something very bad again, then stepped closer to her, lowered his voice. "If you turn me away, you're sending a message. You know that."

117

She narrowed her eyes. "What message?"

"Mags, come on." He adjusted his jacket again.

Could he be wearing a shoulder holster? Surely the police would have checked him for weapons. "Tell me what you mean," she said.

"It's time to choose a side. You know the rules, Mags."

"I'm not Mags! Look at me!" She wanted to grab him by the collar and shake him, but she kept her distance, gauging how many paces she was from the door. Was it locked?

He didn't react, as if he were used to a woman who resembled her having a similar temperament. "He's not going to like your attitude."

"Get out."

He stepped back. "Excuse me?"

"Get out of here or I'll tell them so many lies they'll detain you into the next century."

"Mags—"

"I'm not kidding, asshole. Get the hell out." She pointed at the door, praying he couldn't see her shaking, praying he couldn't see her certainty that he would take out a gun and shoot her dead in one motion.

Jimmy Buffett squared his shoulders, at a loss for what to do next. "He won't like this."

"Tell Slater Nielsen he's after the wrong woman."

"Christ, Mags, why do you have to be so difficult?" He reached into his jacket, and she charged him, screaming for help and thinking only that he couldn't shoot her if she were on top of him. They had hit the floor and rolled up against the wall by the time the door slammed inward and two officers barreled in.

The first one lifted her off of him, and Jimmy Buffett scrambled to his feet, his hands raised above his head. "Whoa whoa whoa. I was just getting a mint. Jesus."

"We're done here," Meg said.

The officers were leading her visitor out the door when Ryan and Kelsey came running. "What's going on? What happened?" Ryan demanded.

"She jumped him," one of the cops said.

Ryan glanced at Meg, saw she was pale and shaken but otherwise fine, then focused on the man secured between two cops. "Who is she?"

Jimmy Buffett laughed, his white teeth flashing. "What the hell is this, Mags? You've actually got these people thinking you're not you?"

Meg grasped the back of a chair for support. "Tell them I'm not her."

Ryan stepped between Meg and the man she'd attacked. "Do you know this woman?" he asked her visitor.

One of the officers said, "Mr. Kama—"

"Let me talk to him a second," Ryan said. "Answer me. Do you know this woman?"

The thug's lip curled. "Me and Mags go way back." He sneered at Meg over Ryan's shoulder. "Don't we, baby?"

"He's lying," Meg said, her voice wavering.

"Sure, baby, whatever gets you through," he said. "You haven't changed a bit." He tried to jerk away from the cops but failed. "I assume I'm free to go. She's the one that attacked me."

As the cops hauled him out, Meg tightened her grip on the chair, her knees weak. Ryan was right. Until Margot was found, Meg would never be safe. Anywhere.

She looked at Ryan, waited for him to meet her eyes. "Let's deal."

Chapter 13

Margot woke but didn't move from where she had snuggled up to the passenger door of the Mustang. Cool wind rushed in as Jake Calhoun tossed a cigarette out the window.

Margot shook her head to clear it. It was almost dark, and she guessed it was around six in the evening. "Where are we?"

"Just went through Paducah. What do you say we check in to a cheap motel for some cheap food, cheap wine and cheap sex?"

"Up yours, Jake." Stretching her legs, she turned her head left, then right.

When Margot first met Jake, she'd asked him how he got his nickname, the Bloodhound. He said he had a talent for finding people who were trying to hide. His secret? "I smell their fear," he had said. "Like a bloodhound."

Now, Margot shifted in her seat, coughing as he blew thick smoke in her direction. "Comfortable?" he asked, grinning.

She scowled, helping herself to the pack of cigarettes stuffed in his shirt pocket. "Doesn't seem fair that you smoke twice the crap that normal people do, and you're still breathing," she mumbled.

He grinned wider as she tapped out a cigarette and pushed

in the dashboard lighter. "Thought you kicked that habit," he said.

"Kicked the Slater habit, and that didn't last," she replied. "So how'd you know where to find me?"

"Finding you was the easiest job I've had in a long time. See, the thing about people like you is they always think they need someone's help or they're not going to make it. They usually end up looking up people who knew them before they were fucked up. Good ol' Slater told me you're from some podunk town in Wisconsin, so I hung out there a few days, asked around about you. It's amazing how many people yapped my ear off after I gave 'em a sob story about how you broke my heart and took off with our kid and I didn't know the first place to look for you so I could try to win back your heart. Small town folks don't have a fucking clue. Anyway, finding my way to your best bud in Green Bay was a cinch after that. I only had to hang out there a couple of weeks before you showed up. You played it exactly right, Mags."

The lighter popped out, and she held it to the tip of the cigarette. Nothing happened. She checked the end that should have been glowing red.

"It's broken," Jake said. "What a bitch, huh? A new car like this."

"Thanks for the tip. Matches?"

"Try the glove box."

"Hit the light, would you?" Margot said as she flipped open the glove box.

A pair of old and scratched sunglasses tumbled out. Wayfarers. The kind she and Holly had bought after trekking to the only Kmart in their small town. Five bucks they had paid for the cheap imitation Ray-Bans. And Holly still had hers.

Despair welled anew, and she pushed it and the sunglasses aside, only to see the other thing in the glove box that she instinctively knew didn't belong to her friend. A gun.

"Jesus, Jake," she said. "Isn't there somewhere else you can keep this? What if kids got into the car and—" She broke off as it occurred to her that this may have been the gun he had used to kill Beau.

Her hatred for Jake and Slater Nielsen overwhelmed her, like a giant wave that she saw coming faster than she could ever run. All she could do was brace herself. When her fingers closed around the butt of the gun, Jake's foot lifted off the gas pedal.

The gun was heavy in her hand, the metal cold. She weighed it in her hand, considering.

It would be easy to kill Jake and avenge the murders of Beau and Holly. She imagined making Jake beg for his life, then blowing his head off anyway. Simple. Cold. Oh so satisfying.

"You haven't got the guts, Mags," Jake said.

The Mustang picked up speed.

She hated him even more for his confidence. She pulled the hammer back, and it made a hollow, clicking sound.

Jake smiled. "Don't be a fool. You'd kill us both."

"That really isn't all that important to me right now." She placed the barrel of the gun against the pulse that beat at the base of his neck, amazed that her hand was so steady.

He raised his chin, looking down his nose at the road. "Mags—"

"How's it feel, Jake?"

"It isn't loaded."

"Liar. A hit man always keeps his guns loaded."

"Then pull the trigger." He wasn't even sweating. The cocky son of a bitch.

She squeezed the trigger, and the hammer clicked on an empty chamber. Trembling with relief and disappointment, she sagged back against the seat.

"I'm not a fool, Mags. I'm not going to keep a loaded gun around where you can get to it."

She threw the gun back into the glove compartment, finished the search for matches, and came up empty-handed. Slamming the glove box shut, she sat back to stare into the dark, crumbling the unlit cigarette in one hand.

Chapter 14

"Where are we going?" Meg asked.

"Back to the scene of the crime," Ryan replied, steering the Jaguar into Naples' early evening traffic. He checked the rearview mirror to ensure that a car carrying two of his most trusted security people followed close behind.

He didn't glance at Meg, worried by the clutch in his gut every time he saw her bruises. He was amazed that she hadn't passed out from fatigue. At least she'd eaten something while he had worked out the details of her release with the district attorney.

"Are you all right?" he asked.

"Couldn't be better."

He allowed himself a small smile. "You bounce back fast."

She turned her head to look at him. "Is this the part where we make awkward conversation and pretend you didn't just blackmail me?"

"I got you out, didn't I?"

"I wouldn't have been there if you hadn't called the cops," she said.

"I did it to save your ass."

"You did it so you could blackmail me."

"Forget it," he said, and concentrated on driving.

Meg suspected that maybe he really had saved her life. But he hadn't done it for her, so she'd be damned if she'd express gratitude, even if she did feel safer with him.

Closing her eyes, she told herself she would turn the deal to her advantage when she was able to think more clearly. After all, Ryan could help her find out everything she could about Margot and why they looked so much alike.

For now, Meg focused on the scenery beyond the passenger's side window. Darkness had fallen, but the lights of the city revealed towering palm trees, pink stucco motels, ritzy strip malls, fancy restaurants and office buildings that seemed constructed entirely of glass.

As the road curved, the scenery gradually changed—from ranch-style homes with carports and short driveways to houses with tall windows, four-car garages and rambling drives. Ryan turned the Jag down one of those drives banked on both sides by flowering trees, spotlights shining up into them to showcase leaves that spurted bright orange and magenta. A house with tall, white columns came into view.

As they got out of the car, Ryan said, "The killer entered the house through a sliding door at the back of the house. The security cameras back there were shot out."

On the porch, he ducked under yellow crime scene tape to unlock the front door, then gestured for Meg to precede him inside. The air in the house was stale and damp, the tile floors covered with a thin layer of dust. Plushly carpeted steps led upstairs.

Ryan hung back, watching her for a hint of familiarity, waiting for her to make the next move.

"Where did it happen?" she asked.

"Bedroom." He waited a beat, but she didn't budge. "Upstairs."

She mounted the steps, and he followed close behind, so

close that she caught his scent—wind and soap. Goose bumps dimpled her skin, and she hoped he didn't notice.

About halfway up, she paused to look at a smattering of dark brown marks that marred the white wall, as if someone with a blood-covered hand had braced against it. Feeling Ryan behind her, watching intently, she continued until she was outside a door criss-crossed with more yellow tape.

He pulled the tape down and opened the door. As she walked in, she saw a large, dark brown stain, stark against the white carpet. Her stomach flipped, and she backed away, covering her mouth with one hand.

Ryan stood close behind her, blocking her from backing up more than a step. "Beau was shot at point-blank range as he stood at the foot of the bed," he said near her ear. "That means the killer stood as close as I am to you right now."

She braced a hand on the doorjamb as an image flashed in her head of Dayle, dead, or worse, dying slowly, her blood soaking into the hot Florida sand, no one to help her, no one to hold her.

Meg stepped sideways this time, away from Ryan.

"Blood was smeared across the mirror," he said. "As if whoever killed him had left a message and whoever found it didn't want anyone else to see it." Taking a creased photo from his back pocket, he handed it to her. "A copy of this was pressed into the edge of the mirror."

The woman in the photograph could have been Meg, arm in arm with a man who had a cleft in his chin and dark, wind-blown hair similar to Ryan's. It was the first color picture she had seen of Margot Rhinehart. She had the same green eyes, the same auburn highlights in dark brown hair. *Who are you?*

Ryan shifted near her elbow, and Meg flinched back from him.

He gave her an impatient look, but then his gaze dropped

to the collar of bruises on her neck, two stark thumbprints at the base of her throat. Swallowing the sudden ache in his own throat, he said, "I guess you have a right to be jumpy."

"Tell me about Margot." She kept her face blank, her voice even.

"About three and a half months ago, Beau told me he was going to marry the woman he loved. He sounded happy, relaxed, like I'd never heard him sound. He e-mailed me this," he said, indicating the picture. "Less than two weeks later, he was dead and the police were showing me the security tapes starring the woman in the picture. I thought I'd found her when I spotted you at the airport."

She could understand how he would think she was the woman in the photo. There were differences, but perhaps they were too subtle for anyone who hadn't looked at a similar face in the mirror her entire life. But there had to be differences that were evident to other people: the timbre of their voices, the way they spoke and gestured, the way they laughed.

It struck her then how odd it was that apparently Ryan had never met Margot. "I had the impression that you and your brother were close. Why didn't you know his fiancée?"

"Beau and I were close when we were kids, but we hadn't spoken much in the past ten years."

"That's a long time."

"We had a difference of opinion."

"It must have been huge."

"Beau was devoted to our father's business, and I wasn't. He couldn't accept that my interests were creative rather than business-oriented. It wasn't his fault, really. That was how our father was, and my brother was just like him." He paused, remembering how Beau had gushed about his fiancée. "I didn't think Beau would ever get married. He was too focused on his work, too driven. Margot changed him."

"Love can do that, I guess," Meg said. "Change you."

"Spoken by someone who has serious doubts."

"Spoken by someone who's never been changed."

"Maybe you have to want to change. Or maybe you wanted to, but you weren't allowed. That would be understandable, if someone had power over you that you couldn't control."

She handed him the picture. "I'm not her."

Before she could turn away, he grabbed her arm, saw the temper flare in her eyes. "I want to believe you," he said.

She tugged away, telling herself that anger, not his touch, caused the frantic flutter of her heart. "No, you don't. If you wanted to, you would. You're not a stupid man."

Looking into her green-blue eyes, he realized that she was right. He couldn't afford to let himself believe that she was innocent. Not if he was going to use her to get at Slater Nielsen.

"We're done here," he said. "Let's go."

Half an hour later, Ryan was letting them into a house that wasn't as large or as elegant as Beau's but was still the home of a wealthy person.

This house, unlike Beau's, was airy and clean and felt lived in. Sand trailed across the black tile where sliding glass doors opened onto the beach, the waves of the Gulf caressing the beach several yards away beneath a bright moon. An elaborate computer station that included two laptops, a printer, a fax machine and a multiple-line phone was set up in what would normally be a formal dining room. Hundreds of papers were strewn across the surface of a massive desk.

"Who lives here?" Meg asked.

"You'll meet him soon enough. Guest room is upstairs."

It was simple but contained all the necessities, from a

double bed and dresser to a bedside table with a phone. Ryan gestured at a bag that sat on the bed. "Kelsey picked up some clothes for you. Shower's through there."

Once he left her alone, Meg didn't waste an instant getting into the shower. With the spigot blasting needles of hot water at her body, she started to feel human again for the first time in days. Afterward, she didn't dry herself off but wrapped the towel around her body to let time do the job. Then, sitting on the edge of the bed, she thought about sleep. She needed it. Her body demanded it. But there was something else she had to do.

She picked up the phone and dialed.

Ryan chugged down several fingers of whiskey. He didn't feel it burn its way down. He didn't enjoy it. He wanted its anesthetizing effect. After another liberal gulp, he clunked the highball glass on the black, glossy surface of the bar and braced his hands on its edge.

Tension had settled in his shoulders, and he rolled them, stretching stiff muscles. He tried not to think about the woman upstairs, tried not to think about how he was using her, how his mistakes in judgment had almost gotten her killed. Her friend was probably dead because of those same mistakes. He tried to think of a way to cut her loose, racked his brain for a way to walk away and forget she existed.

But Beau's image was there every time he squeezed his eyes shut. Not the smirking twenty-something Beau who'd chided him about his lousy luck with women. Not the happy Beau telling him about his beautiful Margot, the catch of the century. Not the shrewd, business-minded Beau who had kept KamaTech afloat after their father died.

No, the image that assailed him was a dead Beau with a gaping red hole in the center of his forehead.

Margot Rhinehart was responsible, at least in some way, for that gaping red hole. And Ryan wanted her to pay for it. And he wanted the man she worked for to pay. He wanted them all to pay. He didn't care how.

Meg Grant, whoever the hell she was, could help with that. If he walked away from her now, he was nowhere. He had accomplished nothing. Beau's killers were that much closer to getting away with the murder of a good man.

He sloshed more whiskey into the glass and tossed it back before reaching for the phone. That's when he saw the tiny red light that indicated someone else in the house was using a line.

He charged up the stairs.

Meg was hanging up the phone when Ryan slammed open the door and glowered at her as if he could have snapped her in two. She self-consciously checked the security of the towel's end tucked between her breasts and rose from the bed.

Standing in the doorway, he attributed the rapid banging of his heart to his race up the stairs. It had nothing to do with the way the skin across her chest glistened with moisture. Or the way a few remaining drops of water dribbled unchecked down her toned arms.

Meg shifted her weight from one bare foot to the other. She'd had her share of hungry looks before, had returned plenty. But this man was so ravenous that it took her breath away. Even as her head didn't trust him, her body responded. How could it not? He was a rugged, gorgeous guy with that cleft in his chin, angular jaw, thick, messy hair, and dark, sensual eyes. She could see that he was having an explicitly sexual idea. It was exciting, and frightening.

"Did you want something?" she asked, her voice husky.

Ryan forced himself to look down at the floor. He had to clear his throat of the tightness there before he could look at her without mentally ripping that towel away. What the hell had he come up here for? he asked himself, then remembered. She'd been using the phone. Suspicion replaced all thoughts of her naked. "Who did you just call?"

The disappointment she felt as his mood changed surprised her. Or perhaps she had just imagined the lust that had darkened his eyes.

When she didn't respond, he stepped into the bedroom. "The light was on on the phone downstairs. Tell me who you called."

She moistened her lips. "I made two calls. One to my boss to explain that it could be several weeks before I can return to work. And the other to Dayle's family to tell them—" She broke off, unable to finish as emotion swelled into her throat. Damn it, she was going to cry. Right in front of him.

As the first tears trickled down her cheeks, his suspicion abated. He thought of Dayle, and the guilt was crushing. "I'm sorry," he said, taking a step toward her. "I'm so sorry about Dayle. I was stupid." His voice cracked. "I wish I could take back what happened."

His words nearly shattered what was left of her control. He moved toward her again, and Meg edged back in alarm. Her hip bumped the bedside table before he caught her elbow and drew her to him gently. Putting his arms around her, he cupped the back of her neck and urged her to put her head on his shoulder.

Holding her breath, she closed her eyes, the heaviness in her chest close to bursting. No man had ever touched her like this. She couldn't recall ever *allowing* a man to touch her like this. She had had lovers, though not many, but she had always held her emotional self back from them, preferring a relationship that was physically, rather than personally, intimate. She had learned that no real personal investment equaled very little pain after the breakup. And the breakup had seemed inevitable somehow—perhaps because she had realized that no investment also meant no chance of a future.

"It's okay to cry," Ryan murmured.

She relaxed against him in slow degrees, telling herself her resources were so depleted that she had no strength to step back. Because she was so tired, she let him hold her, let the clean scent of him soak in. It was tempting to let the emotion go, but she didn't trust herself to keep it under control.

As the tension in her chest eased, she became aware of his fingers sliding under the damp curls resting against her neck. She felt the brush of his lips at her nape, felt the graze of his tongue as he sampled the flavor of her skin. His teeth followed, just a slight, teasing nibble that sent a shudder through her knees.

Ryan moved slowly, prepared to stop if she pushed him away. But even if she did, he'd felt the leap of her pulse when his lips had closed on her skin. "You're shaking," he whispered.

"I'm not."

He let his hands move over her back, up under her hair where the towel ended and damp skin warmed beneath his fingers.

Lifting her head from his shoulder, she met his dark gaze. "What are we doing?"

"I don't want to talk about it." He lowered his head and kissed her, his mouth tentative at first, then growing more demanding.

The kiss tasted like whiskey and carried a hint of desperation. When he trailed damp kisses from her mouth to the hollow of her throat, she dropped her head back and let herself enjoy it.

He hooked his fingers in the top edge of the towel so that even a slight tug would loosen it. She grew still, held hostage by his fingers and his mouth and not caring. His lips burned a path to just below her ear lobe. God, he knew the right spots, the right amount of pressure. By the time his tongue found her ear, she was ready to strip the towel away herself.

Frustrated with his leisurely pace, and a little amazed at her own need to hurry, she dragged his T-shirt free of his jeans, ran her hands up the ridges of his—

The phone rang.

They sprang apart, and Meg grasped the towel to keep it from falling.

Ryan seized the phone next to the bed and spoke only two words—"Yeah" and "Fine"—before hanging up.

"Nick's on his way," he said, shoving a hand back through his hair. He watched her tuck the end of the towel back in place and wished he had time for a cold shower—or something hotter and steamier—to quell his desire. One time would be all it would take, he thought. Just to get her out of his system.

Meg put some distance between them. Her cheeks felt too warm, her pulse erratic. "Who's Nick?" she asked.

"Get dressed. You'll meet him soon enough."

Chapter 15

Meg sat on the bed long after he walked out of the room. What had just happened? What had she been thinking? But she hadn't been thinking. That was the problem.

She was feeling alone and cornered. Perhaps it was a given that she would respond to a human touch. She didn't know for sure because she had never been in such a situation. But then, she had never been drawn to a man the way she was drawn to Ryan Kama. She would have been lying to herself if she didn't admit that she was attracted to him. What red-blooded woman wouldn't be? He was a beautiful man.

But it was more than that. She had known beautiful men, had dated a few. But even as well as she had known some of them, she had never experienced such an overwhelming urge to rip their clothes off. Not like what she had felt moments before.

That was it, she thought. Lust. It made sense. Ryan had saved her from God knew what when he'd intervened in her kidnapping. He'd shown concern for her well-being. He'd comforted her when she'd been at her most vulnerable, her most needy. He hadn't bolted at the first sign of emotion. He had come right to her, had taken her into his arms. Because that was what *she* had needed.

She closed her eyes. So was her response to him lust or something else, something she'd never felt before? And did it matter? She was exhausted and scared and confused. Whatever she was feeling was no doubt a product of everything that had happened leading up to that moment.

Getting up from the bed, she shoved the questions aside. There were more important things to worry about right now.

After dressing in jeans and a white T-shirt from the bag of clothing that Kelsey had provided, Meg left the bedroom. In the hallway, she heard voices in the living room below and paused at the head of the steps.

"I don't know what the hell to think, Nick," she heard Ryan saying. "Maybe I'm just too damned close to it all. I've lost my objectivity. But, damn it, that slimy lawyer at the jail looked her right in the eye. So did those thugs on the beach that first night. All of them looked her right in the *face* and couldn't tell the difference. Even if the two women look that much alike, don't you think one of those guys would have noticed *something* different?"

"Maybe none of them know Margot that well," said a man Meg couldn't see. Nick, Ryan had called him. Nick went on, "You asked me to turn up what I could on Meg, and so far she's clean. I've got the details on the computer—"

"*Meg Grant* comes up clean, but *Margot Rhinehart* works for a very sophisticated, well-resourced operation that no doubt churns out new identities for people like Margot all the time."

"The feds cleared Meg," Nick said. "Her prints and Margot's don't match. I verified it during my last scouting trip through the FBI's computer network."

"How difficult would it be to go in there and change a set of fingerprints on record?"

135

"You're reaching, Ryan. Even I wouldn't be able to do that."

Ice clinked in a glass. "What about your FBI source?" Ryan asked. "Anything new there?"

"Afraid not," Nick said.

"She wouldn't lie to you, would she?"

"Jesus, don't you trust anyone?"

"I don't trust the FBI," Ryan said. "They shut me out of the investigation, and it pisses me off. Another drink?"

"Maybe you should slow down with the drinks," Nick said.

Meg decided now was a good time to interrupt. As she entered the living room, she noted the black leather sofa, large armchairs, matching ottomans, and glass-topped, wrought iron tables. Framed, black-and-white photos adorned the walls. One in particular caught her eye—two toddlers playing on a beach. "Ryan Kama" was scrawled in the bottom corner. Before she had a chance to wonder at that, both men turned toward her.

Meg focused on the man Ryan had called Nick because it saved her from having to see Ryan's scowl. Nick wasn't as tall as Ryan, but he was as darkly handsome. His silver-streaked black hair stuck out around the ears where a teal Florida Marlins baseball cap had flattened it to his head. He had warm brown eyes and ruddy cheeks covered with a light growth of beard. The laugh lines in his face were numerous. As he took her in, his eyebrows arched.

"Nick Costello, Meg Grant," Ryan said. "Nick is the chief of security at KamaTech. He designed the camera that caught Margot helping herself to the emeralds in Beau's safe."

Nick crossed to her and looked her in the face, neither friendly nor combative. "Beau Kama was a good friend of mine," he said.

Recognizing his dare to look away, she held his gaze. "I'm sorry for your loss."

"He was a good man."

"So I've heard."

"Have a seat," he said, gesturing at an armchair.

She started to sit, but tensed at a movement outside the sliding glass doors beyond the office area she had seen earlier. A man in dark clothing, a gun strapped to his hip, stood on the other side of the glass.

"Relax. He works for me," Ryan said.

Not knowing whether to feel safer or more afraid, she settled into the leather chair as Nick leaned against the arm of the sofa facing her and withdrew a crumpled pack of Marlboros from his shirt pocket. Placing a cigarette between his lips, he offered her the pack. "Want one?"

"No, thank you."

"What about a drink?"

She shook her head, impatient. "What do you know about Margot Rhinehart?"

"We'll get to that." He put the pack back in his pocket. "You're a reporter?"

She didn't look at Ryan, though she felt him watching her. The memory of his lips on her skin was distracting, and she was certain her face was still flushed from the experience. What had Nick asked her? Oh, yes, he was establishing control of the conversation. "Yes, I'm a reporter," she said, not having the energy to wrestle him for the upper hand.

"What's your beat?" he asked.

"I'm sure you already know that."

"Nothing wrong with playing along, is there?" Nick asked.

"Is it really necessary? I overheard the part about you researching me," she said. "Certainly, you've turned up more than you'd ever need to know."

"Humor me."

She pressed her lips together. Showing her frustration would achieve nothing. "I cover courts."

"That must be interesting."

"Most of the time it's intensely dull."

"How long on the courts beat?"

"Including the time I was at the paper in Arlington Heights, a year and a half," she said.

"What'd you do before courts?"

"Cops."

"Cops," he repeated, nodding and smiling around the unlit cigarette flopping between his lips, which made him look ridiculous. "Bet you saw a lot of action on that beat."

"Not really."

He faked surprise. "No?"

"Reporters usually arrive on the scene *after* the crime has been committed." She wanted to tell him that he shouldn't act. He wasn't good at it. And she suspected he had no intention of smoking that cigarette.

"Lots of crime up there in Arlington Heights?" he asked.

"It's about average for a town its size."

"There was a case up there not too long ago. Didn't get national attention. Some guy was laid off from his job the same day he found out his wife was fooling around. Went home with an Uzi and shot up his entire family, including the dog. Remember that? Guy was a postal worker, I think."

Meg sensed that the two men watching her were holding their breath. "What is this? A test?" She glanced at Ryan, who gazed back at her without expression. She saw his fingers tighten around the half-full glass in his hand, saw him zero in, for just an instant, on her lips.

She turned her attention to Nick. "I wouldn't put too

much stock in your source of information, Mr. Costello. The man was an engineer, and he used a hunting rifle."

"You covered the case when it got to court?"

"It never went to court," she said.

"Why not?"

"The man—his name was Jack Curtis—turned the rifle on himself before the police arrived."

"I see."

"Anything else, Mr. Costello?"

"One more thing," he said. "Is that your natural hair color?"

"What?"

"Is it?" Ryan asked.

She kept her gaze steady on Nick. "Yes."

"What about the curls?"

"Yes, they're natural," she said through clenched teeth. "The eyes also are mine, and so is the rest of the body."

Nick flashed a grin at Ryan before circling her. "We might have to lighten it."

Meg twisted in the chair to watch Nick. "Excuse me?"

Ryan drained the rest of the drink. "It seems like a perfect match to me."

"It's darker," Nick said. "Probably not as much sun exposure. It might not even be noticeable, but we won't want to take any chances."

"Hello? I'm right here. What are we talking about?"

"You're going to become Margot Rhinehart," Ryan said, as if he had just told her that the day would be mostly sunny with winds out of the southwest.

Nick thrust the pack of cigarettes at her. "Time to take up smoking."

Meg didn't know what to say. At first, she thought it was another test, perhaps a ploy to get her to say, "Please don't send me back there, they'll kill me." But then she thought of Jimmy Buffett and the two men who had abducted and most likely killed Dayle. They were all associates of Margot Rhinehart. Ruthless, brutal murderers. And she wore the perfect disguise to walk into their midst and nail every one of them. For Dayle. For herself.

She accepted a cigarette from Nick's pack.

Ryan watched her as his friend held a lighter to the tip of her cigarette. He had seen the suspicion that first darkened her eyes, followed by panic, then fury, and finally, a surprising resolve. She didn't argue. She didn't fight it or whine about the danger. He didn't know whether he should be impressed by her courage or frightened for her life.

Meg was aware of Ryan's tension as he poured himself another drink, but she ignored him. Concentrating on drawing smoke into her lungs, she remembered Dayle standing in her living room with the ashtray in her hand. She'd thought Meg sitting on her balcony alone trying out a bad habit had been worrisome. What would she have thought of this?

Pushing away the memory, she asked Nick, "How do you know Margot smokes? Do you know her?"

His forehead creased as if with regret. "We never met. We found cigarette butts with lipstick on them in an ashtray on Beau's deck."

Meg squinted at him through the smoke. "Did you have a falling out with Beau, too?"

"No. I was working overseas for KamaTech when Beau was killed. I'd been there about a year. I moved back to do what I could to assist in the investigation."

She picked a tiny piece of tobacco off the tip of her tongue. "If Beau and Margot were a couple, how come there were never any pictures of them together in the media? I mean, Beau was a mover and a shaker, wasn't he?"

"Beau hated the spotlight," Nick said. "He had a talent for avoiding it, and my guess is that that suited Margot's plans just fine." He pulled an object out of his pocket. "This is hers, too. We found it at Beau's."

Accepting the watch, Meg examined it. The face was encrusted with tiny diamonds, its band slim and silver, elegant. "It's beautiful. How do you know it's hers?"

"Leap of faith. You might want to get used to wearing it."

After removing her own watch, she slipped on Margot's. "How am I going to hook up with Slater Nielsen when you and the feds have no idea where he's based?"

"His henchmen know where he's based," Ryan said. "And they're eager to get their hands on you."

Her pulse stuttered, and she thought she saw him smile. But then Nick blocked her view, saying, "We're going to have to adjust your makeup."

"That shouldn't be a problem," Ryan said. "She's not wearing any." Stalking to the glass door that led outside, he slid it open, stepped into the darkness beyond and slammed it shut so hard it was a wonder it didn't shatter.

Arching a questioning brow at Nick, she hoped her relief at Ryan's exit didn't show.

"Don't worry about him," Nick said. "He's a bit conflicted, which is something he's never handled well." Then he startled her by running his fingers through her hair, inspecting it as if for flaws. "We're going to have to cut your hair some. Do you mind?"

"Whatever gets the job done." Taking a drag on the cigarette, she thought about what she had just agreed to do—impersonate a woman she had never met. Had she lost her mind? But she reminded herself that she was doing it at least partially for Dayle.

"Damn." Nick's ruddy cheeks paled as he eyed her throat.

"That psycho on the yacht really did a number on you."

"Yeah, he did." She shoved hair behind her ear and stubbed out the cigarette in an ashtray on a nearby wrought iron table. "Are you a detective, Mr. Costello?"

"Please, it's Nick. And no, I'm not a detective. I'm a security expert."

"It apparently pays well," she said. "You have a beautiful home."

"I've managed to invent some handy security devices over the years."

"Such as the camera that caught Margot stealing the emeralds."

"Actually, that was one of my more simple devices," he said. "It's part of the hook you'd hang a painting on. When the painting is removed, the camera starts recording. Most thieves would expect a camera to be inside the safe or mounted on it in some way." He stopped, as if realizing that he'd gotten carried away. "Anyway, KamaTech's business is state-of-the-art security, and I happen to have some handy, uh, computer skills."

She remembered the comment he'd made to Ryan about his many trips through the FBI's computer network. "You're a hacker."

"Not in the illegal sense."

"The FBI doesn't mind letting you peruse their files?"

He flushed. "Not in the illegal sense professionally," he clarified.

"So you're one of those people who hack into a company's network to show them where they're vulnerable."

"That's part of what I do, yes."

"You're also researching me for Ryan, aren't you? Going other places with that computer that you're not supposed to go."

"He's my friend. Friends help each other out," he said.

"Suppose I tell you something about me that your computer probably hasn't turned up? Something that might explain what's going on here."

"I'm listening."

She took a breath, held it. "I was adopted. I don't know anything about my biological family. Their name, where they live, who they are. I think Margot and I might be related, maybe even sisters." She paused, wishing she'd accepted his earlier offer of a drink. "Or twins."

He opened his mouth to speak but seemed to think better of it and shut it.

"Would you be able to look into that for me?" she asked.

He sat across from her, his cheeks pink again. "Have you told Ryan about this?"

"I'm afraid he would think I'm trying to trick him. But if you turned up the paperwork, the proof . . . he'd believe you."

Leaning back against leather, Nick pressed the palm of his hand to his forehead, nearly dislodging his Marlins cap. "Jesus."

She didn't give him a chance to dwell on it. "There's something else," she said. "A concern I have."

He lowered his hand and sat forward. "I'm still listening."

"What if Slater Nielsen just wants Margot dead? When I refused to deal with the lawyer who came to see me at the jail, he said to me, and I quote, 'It's time to choose a side.' I then accepted help from the brother of the man Nielsen's hit man allegedly killed. That's going to look to Nielsen like I made my choice, isn't it? I mean, what will he think if I let his men take me to him and pretend to be his little lost sheep after all the protesting I did with his henchmen and all the time I've been spending with his enemies?"

Rising, Nick crossed to the door through which Ryan had

escaped and stared outside.

Meg cleared her throat to get his attention, and he turned his troubled brown gaze back to her. "I'm not stupid, Nick. This is a win-win situation for Ryan. I imagine you're going to hook me up with some kind of wire and a locator device. If I *am* Margot, then I know what I need to say to get Nielsen to incriminate himself, and your locator device leads you and Ryan right to him. If Nielsen just kills me, whether I'm Margot or not, it'll be on tape. Either way, you've got him on murder. Mine."

Nick went back to peering outside, as if he could will Ryan to return. "Ah, here he is," he said, sliding the door open. He stumbled back when Ryan rushed in on a stream of salty air, blood wetting the front of his white shirt.

Meg shot to her feet. "Are you all right?"

Ryan swooshed the door shut behind him and hit a nearby light switch. Darkness claimed the room. "We've got trouble."

"What is it?" Nick asked.

"Two of my security people outside are dead."

Meg stood frozen, waiting for her eyes to adjust to the dark. The moonlight outside was bright enough to outline the shapes of the two men by the door, and she told herself that Ryan didn't sound or act hurt. But she was certain she had seen blood, fresh and dark red.

She didn't have a chance to analyze her fear for his safety before he was coming toward her. Grasping her by the arms, he gave her a firm shake. "Who did you call earlier?" His voice was low and urgent.

Confusion paralyzed her. "What?"

"You called someone to come get you, didn't you? I was such an idiot. I completely bought the tears. And now he's out there, or in here, and my employees are dead." He was hissing the words, so close to her face that she felt the warm moisture of his breath on her cheeks, smelled the whiskey he had consumed. "Was that the plan?" he demanded. "Get away from the cops, so it would be easier to stage an ambush to free you?"

She shook her head. "No, I—"

Nick was beside them. "Ryan, if someone's in the house—"

Ryan released her on a vicious oath. "Goddamn it, I knew it. *Goddamn it.*"

Nick tried again. "Ryan—"

"Close the blinds. I'll call the police." Ryan seized the cordless phone off the table by the sofa, but then a creaking sound near the stairs jerked his head in that direction.

Meg saw the gunman pause on the steps, saw his white teeth reflect what little light there was, saw the gun in his hand. He raised it and started shooting.

She felt a sharp tug, followed by quick, burning pain.

Ryan, lunging for Nick, heard several more shots before he and Nick hit the floor behind the sofa. He had a glimpse of Meg dropping and rolling behind a chair and wondered what the hell she was doing—shouldn't she be racing for the door while the gunman had him and Nick covered?

Fumbling with the phone still grasped in his hand, Ryan called nine-one-one, the silence a roar as he strained to listen for footsteps coming toward them or approaching from another direction. Maybe there was more than one gunman.

The ringing seemed to go on forever. Why the hell did it take so long to get an answer? Then footfalls thudded against ceramic tile, followed by the slamming of the front door. Silence again.

Ryan fixed his gaze on the chair so he would see her when

she ran. He'd take her down so fast her head would spin. His hands shook with the anticipation of it.

Finally, an answer. He barked the address into the phone, still watching the chair, waiting for her to make a move. But she made no attempt to escape. What was wrong with her? The gunman had bolted. She should have been right behind him.

Nick scrambled to his knees beside Ryan. "The son of a bitch ran." He released a jittery laugh of relief. "What a lousy fucking shot."

Dropping the phone, Ryan stumbled over Nick to get to the chair a few feet away where, behind it, he discovered what he had feared: the gunman was not a lousy shot.

Propped against the back of the leather chair, Meg had one hand clamped to her left side, blood seeping between her fingers.

Seeing Ryan standing over her, she felt a moment of panic that his head could get blown off at any instant. "Get down," she rasped.

He dropped to his knees beside her, fighting back the terror at the sight of blood on her, yelling at Nick to get help. Seeing consciousness fading from her eyes, he clasped her shoulder. "Don't do that, Meg. Stay with me."

Nudging her bloody hand aside, he searched for the source of the blood. Her soaked T-shirt was in the way, and he shredded it. She gave a weak protest, but he ignored it as he clamped his hand over the wound along her left side, not allowing himself to ease up at her whimper of pain. Her fingers gripped his wrist, tried to pry his hand away, but he kept the pressure on, knowing there was too much blood, way too much.

Looking into her green eyes, he sought assurance that she was not bleeding to death right in front of him. Shock had knocked them out of focus. "Are you with me, Meg?"

She didn't respond.

"Nick! Hurry!"

With each second that ticked by, Ryan felt the life of the woman under his hand trickle further away. As if verifying his fear of how fast it was happening, her head rolled to the side, her fingers slipping away from his wrist.

"Don't give up," he said under his breath, then raised his voice. "Don't you give up, Meg. Are you listening? Don't give up."

"Ambulance is on its way."

Ryan glanced up at Nick. "Jesus, Nick. I thought the bastard was after us."

"So did I."

"I thought—" He choked off and looked down at her, at her face, bloodless and slack, and his heart tilted in his chest. "Where the hell are they?"

A siren in the distance answered.

Chapter 16

Ryan was dead tired. He knew he looked it when he walked into the waiting room and saw the concern in the faces of Nick and Kelsey.

"How's she doing?" Nick asked. He had not recovered his color since the shooting.

"Doctor said the bullet went right through her, didn't hit anything important. They're giving her blood, but she'll be okay."

"Thank God," Kelsey said.

Ryan could tell by the sheet creases on her face that she had been in bed when Nick had called. "Thanks for coming so fast," he said.

Now that the worry was over, Kelsey's anger surfaced. "How the hell did she get shot, Ryan? You said she'd be safer with you."

Ryan started to rub both hands over his face but stopped when he saw them. They were coated with dried blood. Meg's blood. His stomach lurched. "Shit."

Nick put a hand on his friend's shoulder. "You should sit."

While Ryan and Kelsey settled into a corner of the waiting room, Nick went in search of coffee.

"What happened, Ryan?" Kelsey asked, her tone gentle now.

"I don't know. I saw the guy on the stairs. It was the son of a bitch who came to see her at the jail. Someone had to let him know where we were. I thought it was her."

"If it wasn't her, then who?"

"Hell if I know. One of my guards. One of the cops. It could have been anyone. Who knows who this Nielsen guy controls?"

Nick returned with three cups of steaming coffee. They each sipped, then grimaced in turn. Kelsey set hers aside. "So what now?"

Braving another sip, Ryan was rewarded with a burned tongue. The pain startled him, and he realized that he had been numb since Meg had been shot. "She can't stay here," he said. "She's a sitting duck."

"Even with twenty-four-hour security?" Nick asked.

"I had that set up at your place."

"Then what? Who can you trust?" Kelsey asked.

"No one. We just have to get her out of here."

"The woman's been shot," Kelsey said. "She's not going anywhere."

"I can take care of her. We just have to get her away from here before Nielsen's henchmen find out the job's not finished. They could be crawling all over this place already."

"I don't like this," Kelsey said. "What are you going to do?"

"I'm going to make sure she's not dead before dawn."

Chapter 17

Jake parked the Mustang in an unauthorized space and shut it off. He and Margot sat staring out the windshield at the green-blue water, fascinated by its expanse. This was Margot's favorite part of the Gulf off Captiva, where the waves were a little more urgent than the ones that rolled onto the shore of Sanibel, the island they had just crossed to access Captiva.

The water was prettier here. Greener, with white caps. The sand was made up of partially demolished shells. Walking barefoot could be treacherous, but to Margot, it was beautiful. It was on this beach that she had fallen in love with Beau Kama. In the distance, anchored several hundred yards out in one of Captiva's marinas, was his yacht.

"Christ, it's hot," Jake muttered, slipping a finger between his collar and neck. "What is this, a freaking heat wave?"

She glanced at him with disdain in her green eyes. "You'd think you'd be used to Florida by now, Jake."

"Whatever." He began inspecting his fingernails. "Okay, we're going to take a dinghy out there and get the emeralds," he said. "Once I've got all twelve of them in my hand, I let you go. I go back to Slater and tell him you gave me the slip. You ever meet up with him, this never happened. Are we clear?"

"Slater will send someone like you after *you* when he finds out you swiped them out from under him."

"I don't think so, Mags. He's more interested in retrieving you than he is in the jewels. They didn't come up once in our conversation."

Margot did the rowing while Jake hung onto the sides of the boat as if he expected to get tossed into the water at any moment. She ignored him, thinking instead about what she was going to do about the woman Slater was tracking. He was going to use her sister against her for revenge. *How can I stop him? What can I do to protect her?*

Glittery green lettering on the yacht's hull caught her eye, and she squinted, wishing she'd grabbed Holly's sunglasses. As she realized what it was, she stopped rowing, her heart in her throat. Emblazoned on the hull was the new name of Beau Kama's yacht: *The Emerald Eyes*. He'd promised her a surprise the morning he was killed. This evidently had been it.

"Why the hell are you stopping?" Jake demanded.

She bent forward, afraid she was going to be sick.

Jake grabbed for the side of the boat as it rocked. "What the fuck are you doing? Get up."

She straightened, fighting the weakness back by slow degrees, and fumbled with the oars.

Jake glared at her. "We need to get there sometime today. Move it."

Sweat trickled down one side of her face, and she swiped at it with a shoulder. "Don't worry, Jake. I'm fine. Thanks for asking."

"Shut up and row."

At the yacht, she hauled herself up the ladder that hung suspended over the side and staggered onto the deck. While Jake climbed up behind her, she dropped onto a cushioned bench to catch her breath. Her heart drummed in her temples, and she still felt ill.

"Where are they?" Jake asked.

Pushing herself up, she tried the door that led to the inner cabin and found it locked, as she'd expected. She quickly tripped the locking mechanism with the paper clip from her bra. Inside, the unmoving air was sweltering. She bypassed the living room area while Jake oohed and aahed over the expensive leather furniture and plush carpet. In the stateroom, she ignored the memories that surged to life at the sight of the queen-size bed and windows that framed the shimmery water of the Gulf. Her focus was on a cubbyhole near the side of the bed.

She had Beau's gun in her hand and was aiming it at Jake's head when he ambled through the portal. He froze. "What the—"

Surprisingly, her vision blurred with tears that she blinked back, but her hand was steady. "You know I'll pull the trigger."

He raised his hands, his face ashen. "Let's talk about this."

"There's nothing to talk about. You're going that way." She used the gun to gesture toward the door at the other end of the room. "Move."

His gaze was fastened on the gun as he edged backward through the portal into a small room lined with storage compartments. "On your knees," she ordered.

Instead, he attacked. She jerked the trigger, but nothing happened. They hit the floor hard, Margot on the bottom, Jake grappling for her hands. He was laughing. "Who's the moron, Mags? The safety's on."

She drove her elbow into his face and felt a satisfying crunch. Grunting, he grabbed for the gun, jerked it out of her hand, then backhanded her across the mouth.

Stunned, Margot lay still while he lurched to his feet, blood streaming down his face. "You bitch! You broke my nose!"

Enraged, he yanked her to her feet and thrust the barrel of the gun into the flesh under her chin. His thumb flicked the tiny lever that was the safety as he got in her face. "I could make your pretty little head disappear in a cloud of blood and bones and gray matter right this minute. How'd you like that?"

"Fuck you, Jake."

He shoved her away, and her body crashed against a door. It popped open as she fell to her hands and knees, various supplies spilling onto the floor. Trying to get her breath, she focused on the fire ax that landed just inches from her hand.

From behind her, Jake seized a handful of her hair, pulled her head up, and pressed Beau's gun to the back of her skull. "Any last words, Mags?"

If she was dead, she thought, it'd all be over. There would be no need for Slater to try to use her sister against her. Granted, the emeralds might not make it back to their rightful owner, but she'd rather die now than let Jake get them. "Do it," she rasped, and braced for the bullet.

Laughing, Jake released her hair and uncocked the gun. "Yeah, you'd like that. But then I wouldn't get what I want, would I? I can retire on those stones. Get your ass up."

When he bent down to grab her arm, she swung the ax up like a croquet mallet. The flat side of the blade struck him under the chin with a sharp crack, and he crumpled to the floor, unconscious, the gun falling harmlessly to his side.

Margot dropped the ax and staggered into the main stateroom, where she slammed the portal to the storage compartment and threw the latch used to secure the door during rough weather. That would hold him for a while, but she had to work fast.

As she unbuttoned her blouse, she sought a clean T-shirt among the clothing she'd kept on the yacht, then went into the galley in search of a knife. It took her only a minute to re-move all the buttons of her blouse and slice through the fabric covering each one. When she was done, eleven dime-sized gems glittered dark green on the black marble countertop.

Rummaging through kitchen cupboards and drawers for a hiding place, she found a mini flashlight. She unscrewed the bottom and dumped out the batteries. Gathering up the em-eralds, she spilled them like ice cubes into the slim barrel, then replaced the bottom and dropped the flashlight back into the drawer. Mission accomplished.

Breathing normally now, her head and back aching from her tussle with Jake, she looked around and regretted. She and Beau would have had a good life together, she thought. With laughter and love, warmth and understanding. Children.

Her stomach clenched, and she pressed a hand to it. The cabin was suffocating. After grabbing a cell phone out of the same cubbyhole where Beau had kept his gun, she shakily climbed up the ladder onto the deck. The sun shot diamond shards of light into her eyes, and she narrowed them, shocked when her head started to spin. Damn, she was going to faint. Sitting down, she dropped her head between her knees. It couldn't be the heat, she thought. The heat had never af-fected her this way.

The dizziness passed, and she raised her head, ready to sink it again if the weakness returned. She felt clammy and tired, and sat for a moment, thinking about what to do next. She would have liked nothing more than to return to the bed below and curl up for the next twenty-four hours. But who knew how long she had before Jake woke up, pissed off and ready to kill?

Rowing back to shore drained her remaining energy. On solid ground, the first thing she did was call nine-one-one to let the police know where they could find an unconscious professional hit man. Then she checked the Mustang for keys and found that Jake must have taken them with him out to the yacht. Hot-wiring a car was not among her talents, so she started walking along the side of the road, her legs like lead.

She was no longer sweating. Her skin was dry and hot, her head pounding. Nausea came in waves, and she had to stop several times to catch her breath. As the sun beat at her, and her head grew heavier, she knew she was in trouble. The thought was frightening. She was not the kind of woman who got sick suddenly. And she had never fainted.

The scuff of footsteps brought her head up, and she saw a man approaching. He was older, with skin subjected to the Florida sun for so many years it had turned to leather. His shaggy hair was bone-white, and he had blazing blue eyes that were slits against the brightness of the sun. "You okay, miss?" he asked.

Margot tried to give an I'm-okay-go-away wave, but the ground beneath her feet rolled. "Oh, shit," she said.

Stopping before her, the old man cocked his head. "You don't look so good."

She opened her mouth to say that she didn't feel so good, but instead, she passed out at his feet.

When Margot came to, she was on a narrow bed, surrounded by curtains and covered with a light sheet. A device attached to the end of her index finger kept track of her pulse, and an IV line snaked from a pouch filled with clear fluid to a needle taped to the back of her hand.

A woman dressed in white pants and a pink top pushed aside a curtain. "Ah, you're awake. How are you feeling?"

The headache was only a vague throb in her temples. She still felt tired, but her stomach had settled. "Fine," Margot croaked, and cleared her throat. "Thirsty."

As if she had anticipated her, the woman offered a plastic cup with a straw. "Sip slowly."

Margot obeyed, relieved when the cool liquid soothed her parched throat.

"Do you know where you are?" the woman asked as she jiggled the pouch of fluid that hung from a metal hook.

"Hospital?"

"Captiva Urgent Care. You fainted on poor Bailey."

"Bailey?"

"Old guy who fishes from the bridge that connects the islands. Said you dropped like a twenty-pound grouper jerked out of the water and smacked onto the pavement. Want to tell me your name? You didn't have any identification on you."

Margot swallowed. "Mary."

The nurse made a note on a clipboard. "Mary . . . ?"

"Louis."

"Know anything about heat exhaustion, Mary?"

"I'm not a tourist."

The woman smiled. "Had you pegged for one the instant you were brought in. They're usually the ones ignorant of such things. You were dehydrated." She gestured at the IV line. "We're taking care of that. You're lucky you fainted in a public place, Mary. You could have gone into shock and died."

Margot closed her eyes. Dying from shock rather than mind-bending torture or a bullet in the head—what a relief that would have been. "Tell Bailey I said thanks."

"We took some blood, ran some tests, just to be sure the heat was your only problem."

Hearing the woman's hesitation, Margot opened her eyes.

The nurse gave her hand a squeeze. "Honey, I hope you think this is good news."

Chapter 18

Meg woke to a rocking motion. Ryan, in white shorts, a blue T-shirt and bare feet, sprawled in a white plastic deck chair next to the bed, his head fallen to one side as he gently snored.

She blinked, bringing the dark-wood ceiling into focus, then, turning her head, the rest of the room. She was surrounded by teakwood that looked familiar. The room swayed, and she remembered. Ryan's yacht.

As if she had poked him, Ryan jerked awake and stared at her for several moments. Realizing that she stared back, he smiled. "Hi."

"Hi."

Leaving the chair, he knelt by the bed so that they were at eye level. He resisted the urge to brush the hair off her forehead, fought the need to tangle his fingers with hers on the sheet. He had to remind himself that he still didn't know for certain that she was innocent. All he knew was that nothing in his life had stopped his heart like seeing her blood on his hands. "How're you doing?" he asked.

The deep concern she saw in his eyes was foreign to her. "Fine. How are you?"

His smile grew. He couldn't help it. He was so relieved to see her gazing up at him with clear eyes. "I'm fine, thanks."

She had a vague memory of being wheeled down a sterile-looking hallway in a wheelchair, then being carried out an emergency exit and bundled into the back seat of a car, blankets and all. She remembered someone holding her hand, stroking her hair, telling her everything would be okay, that very soon she would be safe. She'd felt no pain, no fear, only disorientation.

She wasn't able to recall anything after that. Sitting up would help, she decided, would get the blood flowing to her sluggish brain. She shifted, tensed her stomach muscles, and gasped. Suddenly, she was wide awake, slapped into full awareness by pain.

Wincing with her, Ryan reached for her hand. Her fingers clamped around his. "Relax and breathe evenly," he said. "Tensing up will make it worse."

"Easy for you to say," she said, clenching her teeth against another wave.

"If you relax—"

"I'm trying."

"Breathe with me," he said.

She thought he was kidding, but then he was staring into her eyes and breathing in an exaggerated way, as if they were having a baby. Squeezing her eyes shut, she tried to ignore him.

"Look at me, Meg."

The pain was not easing up, so she obeyed, thinking only of relief.

"Good. Now, breathe with me."

Eventually, as she relaxed, the agony in her left side receded to a sharp, gnawing pain. She concentrated on not tensing again.

Blowing out a long breath, Ryan pried her fingers from around his. He was lucky he was the stronger one or the bones in his hand would have been dust.

As he rose, Meg asked, "Where are you going?"

He smiled, liking the note in her voice that suggested she didn't want him to leave. "The doctor gave me some drugs for you. Think you could use them, don't you?"

She managed a weak smile. "Drugs, excellent."

"Be right back."

The room seemed to expand without him in it, and she stared up at the ceiling. She knew she'd been shot. But she didn't know how long ago or how she came to be on Ryan's yacht and not in the hospital. Or how it was that she was wearing a T-shirt that wasn't her own and not a stitch of anything else.

Returning, Ryan sat on the edge of the bed. "Let me do the work," he said. Carefully lifting her shoulders, he slipped under her so that she was propped against him, then reached around to give her a glass and some pills. "Muscle relaxants and pain killers. The doctor said they'd put you to sleep."

She swallowed them, handed him the glass and felt him shift to set it aside. He didn't move out from under her, and it occurred to her that she didn't mind. "Are we at sea?" she asked.

He toyed with a curl of her hair feathering his forearm. It was dark brown with a flash of red sunlight. "Since late last night. What do you remember?"

"Not much. Did you kidnap me from the hospital?"

"Nick and Kelsey helped. Your doctor wasn't too hot about it, but Kelsey assured him he wouldn't be held liable for anything, and he'd already determined that once they'd given you blood and patched you up, your life was no longer in danger. He loaded us up with antibiotics and the other drugs before we took off."

"So Nick's okay?"

He could tell by the tiny catches in her breathing that the pain still clawed at her. "He's fine."

"Are you okay?"

He rested his chin on the top of her head. "I am."

"What time is it?"

"Just after seven," he said.

"In the morning?"

"Yes."

Closing her eyes, she let the rhythm of the waves lull her. "Does your boat have a name?"

"The *Christina.*"

"Named after a woman," she said.

He heard the disappointment in her voice, and his pulse stuttered even as he realized that her system was soaking up the drugs, that she wasn't thinking clearly. "Not a woman," he said. "A dog."

"Oh." Her head lolled against his chest, and he felt the caress of her breath on the inside of his elbow. "What kind of dog?" she asked, her lips barely moving.

"A retired racing greyhound. She and I sailed together for about six years."

"What happened to her?"

"She had arthritis, and the humidity made her miserable. I gave her to a retirement home about a year ago. It's air-conditioned, and she gets more attention from the residents there than she got from me alone."

"Why didn't you name the boat after Kelsey?"

He smiled. "You're full of questions."

"My job."

"Of course," he said.

"You loved each other."

"Sometimes love isn't enough." He listened to her breathing, which had slowed and deepened. "How're you doing? Feeling better?"

"I'm your prisoner again."

He could tell by the way she slurred her words that she was almost gone. "What makes you say that?"

"Why else would we be on your boat?"

"Ah."

She dropped off.

Later, while Meg slept, Ryan checked in with Nick. "You didn't get a chance last night to give me details on what you turned up on Meg."

"Let me pull up her file," Nick said.

Hearing the clack of computer keys, Ryan picked up a pen and prepared to take notes.

"Here we go," Nick said. "Her parents, Richard Alan Grant and Kari Ellen Grant, died about six months ago when their car was struck by a drunk driver. They left her a shitload of money in a trust fund that she can't touch until she's married and has a kid. Richard was the president and CEO of a bank corporation based in Chicago. Kari headed up several local charities and had her eye on a political career—she was running for alderman when the accident happened.

"Meg doesn't have any siblings, aunts or uncles. Both sets of grandparents died naturally several years ago. Employment history is stable. She started working as a reporter at the newspaper in Arlington Heights just out of college before moving to the Fort Myers newspaper last month. I talked to a woman in the personnel office at the Arlington Heights paper, and she confirmed that a woman named Meg Grant worked there for six years. Had the usual jobs while in school—retail and college paper. Medical records don't go back that far, but that's not unusual if she's always been healthy. Only illness I could find was an emergency appendectomy about three years ago.

"Debt includes a two-year-old car loan and a somewhat hefty college loan. The house on Fort Myers Beach is a rental. Apparently, her very rich parents weren't providing any financial support. She's had two moving violations, and they occurred in the same year ten years ago at age eighteen, both in a '79 Jag registered to Richard Grant. No arrests, no outstanding warrants, no FBI file."

"She's too good to be true," Ryan said.

"Or she's one of those people who plays by the rules."

"Why did she move to Florida? She has no family here."

"Nope. The newspapers are affiliated, though," Nick said. "Maybe she wanted a change of scenery. She moved during the winter. Ever been to the Midwest this time of year? It's freaking cold."

"Did her parents have a house?" Ryan asked.

"Uh, hang on. Here it is. A big one in Barrington, a ritzy Chicago 'burb. Summer home in Michigan."

"Did she sell either one after they died?" Ryan asked.

"No."

"Rent them?"

"No."

"Do they exist?" he pressed.

"What are you getting at, Ryan?"

"I want to know more about Richard and Kari Grant. It's easy to create an identity for one person."

Nick didn't speak for a moment, as if weighing the advantages of what he was about to say. "Look, Ryan, there's something I need to tell you. Meg told me that she was adopted."

"What does that have to do with anything?"

"She seemed to think that Margot might be related to her because they look so much alike."

Ryan didn't know what to say. It would make sense. But was it too easy? "You believe her?"

"I don't know. I don't know her like you do."

"I don't know her either," Ryan said.

"I think you do."

"It could be a lie, Nick. She's an expert, remember?"

"*Margot*'s the expert. Meg's the woman who almost died in your arms last night."

Ryan couldn't speak for a moment as the panic and helplessness he'd felt then returned. When he had it under control, he said, "Can you get proof?"

"I don't know," Nick said. "Adoption records are sealed pretty tight."

Ryan kneaded the back of his neck. "Meg and Margot don't just look alike, Nick. They look *exactly* alike."

"So if they're twins, then Margot might be adopted, too," Nick said, his voice rising as an idea struck him. "The FBI might have that in their profile of her. I'll check with Delilah."

"Delilah?"

"My FBI source."

"Oh. You've never mentioned her by name."

"We met in college. We still get together every so often for some fun. She's a bit of a tiger," Nick said, wistful.

"When can you talk to her again?"

"I'll give her a call when we're done here. Even if the feds turned up an adoption in Margot's past, it's unlikely they would have pursued the details without an apparent connection to the crimes." He paused, and Ryan heard typing before Nick said, "Before I forget, Delilah told me the feds lost track of Turner Scott."

"Jesus. That guy isn't even the brightest bulb on the chandelier." Ryan wished he had something hefty to throw at a wall. "What about Margot? Are the feds making any progress locating her?"

"Delilah says not yet. I'm thinking that if they could have, they'd have found her by now. In the meantime, I've been working on something myself."

"Fill me in."

"Delilah told me that Margot has several identities that she's used over the years, all set up through Nielsen's network. Passports, credit cards, driver's licenses, bank accounts. The feds are watching them all for recent activity. So far, according to Delilah, no flags have popped up. Which means she's either staying put or she's using an ID that the feds haven't flagged. Which is what I've been working on."

"Haven't the feds been tracking Margot for a while? What makes you think you can turn up an identity that they haven't?"

"Couple of reasons. First, I'm a lot smarter than they are."

Ryan laughed, and some of his earlier frustration eased. "It's good to know your ego is under control."

"Hey, I earned this ego. But, seriously, it makes sense that if Margot is hiding out from Nielsen—and it appears that she is—she wouldn't use an ID that he set up for her."

"True, but I would think the feds have thought of this."

"Right. Well, I have an advantage that they don't. I was Beau's best friend. He told me things about Margot that they can't know."

"Such as?"

"Such as her nickname."

Ryan let his shoulders droop. He'd thought Nick might actually be onto something. "Her nickname is Mags."

"That's not what Beau called her," Nick said.

Ryan perked up. "What did he call her?"

"Mary Lou."

"How do you know this?"

"Beau and I talked, Ryan. He wanted to marry her."

Ryan was reminded of how little he knew his brother. "How does knowing Beau's nickname for Margot help locate her now?"

"I've fed all kinds of details like that about Margot and Beau into a database that sorts through it all and spits out hundreds of name variations. The software then combs databases throughout the country for sudden or unusual activity under those names."

"Wouldn't the feds be doing the same thing?"

"Yes, but you're missing my point. The feds are focused on Margot's details. They don't have the kind of access to Beau's personal details that I do. She didn't break from Nielsen's organization until after Beau was killed, so it seems to me that if and when she creates her new identity, there's going to be some kind of influence from her relationship with him."

"Such as his nickname for her," Ryan said, doodling "Mary Lou" onto the pad of paper under his hand.

"I know it's a stretch," Nick said. "But it's something. Maybe the feds will find her, and I'll have wasted a whole lot of time. Either way, the woman can't hide forever."

"She can if she's made herself into someone else."

Nick was silent a moment.

"Are you still there?" Ryan asked.

"Why are you so reluctant to admit that Meg and Margot are two different women? It seems pretty clear to me. And it was clear to the feds or they wouldn't have let Meg go."

"It'll be clear to me when I can see the two of them side by side."

"You're in denial, my friend."

Ryan released an indignant sound. "Denial of what?"

"I saw what you went through when Meg got shot. You were a wreck."

"You were, too, as I recall," Ryan said.

"For different reasons. I was facing the realization of my mortality. You were facing the realization of hers."

"Yeah, if she ends up dead, I end up back at square one. Are we done with this conversation?"

"Just making an observation," Nick said.

"Let me know what you turn up on the Grants."

Margot was curled on a wooden chaise, facing the waves of Captiva as she dozed. The late afternoon sun was warm on her face. In the distance, she heard a mother calling to her small children and focused on their sounds.

A mother. *She* was going to be a mother.

Her stomach muscles twitched at the thought, and she put a hand on her abdomen. Beau's child was in there. Thinking of it left her dazed. She couldn't grasp the concept, even after a week.

When she had thought Beau was gone, that she would never hold him again, she hadn't wanted to live. She had kept going because she'd had unfinished business—returning the emeralds she had taken from him. Giving them back was a poor substitute for what she wanted most to return—his life. She would gladly have given up her own in exchange for his. If only she could.

Now, she had a new responsibility to Beau. She carried his child. She owed it to him to live, to bring his son or daughter into the world.

But Slater Nielsen wanted her dead. Undoubtedly, the police were looking for her, too. She wouldn't be able to hide forever. Even checked into this Captiva resort under another name, she knew she was not safe for long.

And if the police found her first, Slater could easily have her killed in jail. Not to mention what he might do to her sister in the name of revenge.

No one—not her, not Beau's child, not her sister—would ever know peace of mind as long as Slater breathed.

It was clear what she had to do.

She had to get a gun.

Chapter 19

Piano music brought Meg to semiconsciousness. Easy, subtle, relaxing. She lay with her eyes closed, listening, trying to get her bearings. Fresh-brewed coffee teased her senses.

"Are you awake?"

She opened one eye, saw Ryan peering at her, and reluctantly opened the other. The last time she'd seen him, he'd helped her to the bathroom, then back into bed, where he'd given her two more pills. She didn't know how long ago that had been, but he wore different clothes now: denim shorts and a red T-shirt.

"Is it morning already?" she murmured.

"Afternoon, actually," he said, sitting on the plastic chair by the bed and resting his elbows on his knees. "How're you feeling?"

Meg let her lids drop over her eyes. "Powerful drugs."

"Don't get attached to them."

"Wouldn't dream of it," she said, drifting away.

He called her back. "Meg. Want to wake up and talk to me?"

"Not particularly."

With a soft laugh, he moved to the edge of the bed, where he tapped her cheek with gentle fingers. "Come on, you're hurting my feelings."

Blinking sluggishly, she wondered whether she had the strength to smack him. "Is there a problem?"

He gave her a tolerant smile. "Yeah, you're sleeping too much. The doctor said you should be up and moving around by now."

"Sorry."

"No you're not," he said. "How about some food? You need to eat something."

"Okay."

"Meg?"

"You decide," she said.

"How about a blowfish and peanut butter sandwich?" he asked.

"Sounds great."

"Want to sit up?"

"Sure," she said.

"Maybe a walk is in order," Ryan suggested.

"Whatever."

"A dip in the Gulf?" he asked.

"Splendid."

Leaning over her, he heard the evenness of her breath and realized that she had gone back to sleep already. He pulled back the covers, but she didn't stir. Wrapping a sheet around her, he scooped her up in his arms. She was slow enough to react that he began to wonder whether he should crank up the yacht's engines and steer back to shore and the hospital.

But then she sputtered to life, throwing her arms around his neck. "What the hell?"

Grinning, he was pleased to see color rushing into her pale cheeks and annoyance flashing in her green eyes. "We're going above deck for some cool, fresh air. It'll be good for you."

When she saw the ladder with its eight rungs leading through the hatch to the surface above, she started protesting. "I don't think this is a good idea."

"Why not?" he asked, playing innocent.

"Well, that's a ladder."

"I was a volunteer fireman in my younger days."

"Fire*fighter* is the PC term," she said.

"I figured you for one of those women."

"One of *those* women?"

"Bleeding-heart liberal feminists, all of which is probably redundant, and which I'm sure you'll tell me is completely un-PC," he said.

"If you're trying to bait me—"

His grin cut her off.

Meg bristled in his arms, conscious of the thud of his heart against her upper arm. His body was warm and solid, his scent—wind and soap—familiar. She noticed he had a bit of a sunburn, and his grin seemed to be widening. "What?" she asked.

Enjoying the emotions that shifted through her eyes as she became more aware of him, Ryan was glad that he was not the only one affected by their proximity. "I see you're awake now."

"You can put me down," she said, her voice an octave lower.

He paused at the base of the ladder. "Think you can make it up this thing by yourself?"

"Of course. It's only eight rungs, for God's sake."

"Think you could have taken eight rungs right after you had your appendix out?"

Staring at him, she tried to figure out how he could know something so personal. Then it struck her that he'd seen her scar. Her face grew hot. "You're a pig."

The blush made her eyes all the more green, and God help him, he wanted her. He felt like a jerk. She'd just spent two days drugged in his bed, and assuming she was indeed as innocent as everyone thought, she was a marked woman at least partially because of him. But all he could think about was how she was wearing one of his T-shirts and there was not much in the world that was sexier to him than a woman in one of his shirts.

"Can you handle the ladder?" he asked.

She nodded. Even if she found she couldn't, she would die trying to get up it to avoid having him put his hands on her. She couldn't think with him touching her—at least beyond what it would feel like to have those strong hands skimming across her bare skin. She swallowed against the constriction in her throat, wondering at what point she had stopped thinking of this man as a threat and begun thinking of him as, well, naked.

Ryan let her legs slide down his body, shifting her in his arms to allow her to test the strength of her limbs before he released her. It was sweet torture, and he silently lectured himself for letting so much time pass since his last encounter with a woman. Perhaps then this ache for her would not have been so powerful.

When her feet touched the floor, Meg discovered that her knees had mutated into a substance similar to Silly Putty. "Damn," she said, clinging to his shoulders for balance.

He held her around the waist, careful to steer clear of her injured side. "Carrying you is not a problem."

"You just want to show off what a macho stud you are."

"Naturally. So put your arms around my neck and hang on."

She complied, certain her knees were close to wobbling out from under her anyway, which would be one more embarrassment she did not need.

He smiled down at her. "Can you at least pretend to be an impressed chick?"

She suppressed an answering smile. "I don't do the chick thing."

"My ego may be irreparably damaged."

"Get over it."

"You're so tough," he said.

"As nails."

"Upsy daisy." He lifted her as she was laughing at the absurdity of those words coming out of his mouth. When the laugh dissolved into a small moan, he froze, paralyzed by the helpless sound. "Am I hurting you?"

Clenching her teeth, she shook her head.

"Liar."

"Just don't make me laugh," she said.

"Hang on tight."

They climbed the ladder without incident, and as he set her on a chaise, she was impressed by his strength and agility. While he disappeared below deck, she searched for a comfortable position. He returned with a pillow and a blanket that he tucked securely around her. "Can't have you catching a chill."

"You think of everything." She let her head sink into the pillow, exhausted from the little amount of activity.

"How about some coffee?" he asked, reading the fatigue in her eyes.

"How about some sleep?"

"Maybe later."

She closed her eyes. "Now would be good."

He snapped his fingers in front of her nose. "Stay awake, Meg, come on."

She opened her eyes to narrow slits. "Are you *trying* to aggravate me?"

"I'm not going to leave you alone until you eat something and drink some coffee."

She sighed. "Fine."

"Would you like a bagel?"

"A bagel, great. Am I going to have to leave you a tip?"

"Yeah, and it had better be a good one," he said. "Don't go anywhere."

"Cuba is just a short swim, isn't it?"

His answering chuckle faded away as he scooted below deck.

Meg gazed up at a sky crowded with fluffy, gray clouds that looked heavy with moisture. Water quietly sloshed, the boat shifting on its surface. The air, fresh and salty, held a slight chill that was warded off by the blanket. At any other time, all would seem right with the world.

But nothing was right. Dayle was probably dead, and even if it was not Meg's fault directly, she bore at least some responsibility. If she had not moved to Fort Myers. If she had not invited Dayle to visit. If she had not had the burning need to find her biological family, which was what had brought her to Florida to begin with—

"Still doing okay?" Ryan asked, interrupting her thoughts as he set a tray of bagels and coffee on a white table that matched the chaise and the few other chairs on the deck.

"Fine."

Glancing over his shoulder, he saw the anxiety that had impressed a crease just above the bridge of her nose. Some of the earlier shine in her eyes had dulled, and he suspected she was thinking about her friend. He wished he could tell her that the pain of loss would, if not go away, at least ebb with time. But he knew from experience that it didn't ease. Not when the loss was so senseless and violent. If anything, the pain worsened, the firestorm of it fanned by rage at the injustice. He didn't imagine that anything could vanquish the fury except vengeance.

Handing her a coffee mug, he waited while she ventured a sip.

"You make good coffee," she said.

The compliment pleased him. "Thank you."

"What day is it?"

"You've been in and out for two days."

"I don't remember much."

"Not much to remember."

"You remember the scar."

He put half a bagel on a plate and brought it to her. "Relax. Kelsey is the one who helped you into my T-shirt, and I was a very good boy the entire time you were snoozing."

"But you know I had my appendix out. If you didn't see the scar, how did you know?"

"Nick told me about it."

"Oh. Right."

Returning to the table, he snagged the other half of her bagel and his own coffee and settled onto a chair that faced the chaise. "Comfortable?"

She nodded and tried the bagel, not at all certain she wanted it. Her stomach expressed disinterest at first, then growled for more. She washed down a bite with a sip of coffee. "So what are we doing in the middle of the Gulf? I assume it's the Gulf."

"You assume correctly, but we'll have plenty of time to talk about it when you're feeling better."

"The gunman screwed up," she said.

He set aside his food. "The only thing he screwed up was not inflicting a mortal wound."

"He wasn't shooting at me."

"Let's not talk about it," he said.

"He was aiming at you and Nick. I must have been hit by a ricochet."

Lowering his coffee, he said, "I thought he shot you on purpose."

"No. I saw him on the stairs. He shot at *you*. I was hit by accident."

He held her gaze over the rim of his cup. The food and caffeine were agreeing with her. Normal color had seeped into the hollows of her cheeks, and the soft focus of her eyes had sharpened. "We'll talk about it later," he said. "Right now, we need to concentrate on getting you back on your feet."

"We?"

"Yes," he said. "We."

"Why?"

He smiled, pleased that she was fishing. "Why not?"

"You're wasting time. The longer we're at sea, the colder Margot's trail gets."

"Her trail has been cold for months."

"Unless you still think it leads to me," she said.

He arched a dark brow. "Does it?"

She refused to look away, wondering how many times she would have to return that stare without flinching before he believed that what she said was the truth. "No."

"Then our only concern at this point is healing."

"You could have left me in the hospital under police guard," she said. "I might have been fine."

"Perhaps I was looking for a guarantee."

"Why?"

"You're an intelligent woman," he said.

The implied "you figure it out" was all the more frustrating with a groggy mind. Letting her head drop back to the pillow, she closed her eyes. "You exhaust me, Ryan Kama."

She didn't hear him move until she felt the warmth of his

breath on her face. Firm lips settled on hers.

The surprise kiss was over too soon. One moment, his lips nudged hers apart, his tongue, quick and coffee-flavored, grazed hers, and the next, he was gone. She opened her eyes to see him on his knees next to the chaise, confusion shadowing his expression. The drugs were clinging to her system, she decided. She wanted him to kiss her again, only longer.

It stunned him that a quick kiss could have the same devastating effect as their deeper, more explicit embrace three nights before. He had acted on impulse to prove to himself that the thrill, the heat of that first kiss, had been a fluke, the result of stress and lack of sleep. But the plan had backfired.

Now he wanted more.

Chapter 20

All her life, Meg had healed quickly, and this time was no exception. By day seven, she could take the ladder as if it had never turned her muscles to jelly. Nightmares still tugged her awake at night, but she spent less time in bed each day. While she was not ready to run a race, even a short one, she was ready for the next step. If she only knew what the hell the next step was.

Meanwhile, Ryan was impressed, and a little troubled, at how quickly she bounced back. He had thought he would have more time to plot his next move, but her bruises had already faded, replaced by a darkening tan and a healthy glow. She was anxious, asking questions, pumping him for information.

Her inability to sleep well concerned him, and he noticed that her gaze often turned inward. He knew that those were the times when she was thinking about Dayle, struggling to manage the grief and lingering anger. He felt helpless, unable to lend comfort because he knew what she was feeling and that there wasn't a damned thing anyone could say or do to make it go away. So they didn't speak of it. Instead, they discussed the recent Florida heat wave, current events, politics, pop culture. Sometimes, like now, they just sat and watched the clouds, content in a silence that was surprisingly companionable.

Meg, wearing a white T-shirt tucked into a pair of his khaki shorts loosely secured at the waist, sprawled on her back on the chaise that she had claimed as her own. Sleeves and shorts were rolled up to allow maximum sun exposure. A pair of sunglasses, also his, shaded her eyes.

"How long do you think this heat wave will last?" she asked without looking at him. She didn't have to. The image of him standing over a gas grill, tending to a pound of barbecued shrimp, was firmly in her head. He wore denim shorts and nothing else. The sculpted ridges of his body had been too much for her. And there was something about this man in bare feet that made her breath catch. So she pretended interest in the mounds of fluff in the sky.

"Weather report says a few more days," he said.

"Then what? Back into the low seventies?"

"Probably."

"Even that beats the Midwest in January any day."

He chuckled. "I imagine it would."

Tipping the sunglasses down, she eyed him. A light sheen of moisture glistened on his skin, and she marveled at the ache in her belly that had nothing to do with healing. She'd never bothered much with men. She knew what she liked, and the few times that she had been lucky enough to encounter it, she had enjoyed the good times and bailed at the first sign of bad.

When it came to relationships, she wasn't a fighter, mostly because she had never felt anything that was worth fighting for. All of her relationships had ended with the requisite "let's be friends" and a final kiss good-bye. No raging, no tears, no broken, or even slightly damaged, hearts. She'd always been proud of that. It felt adult, mature. Safe. If the relationships lacked passion, she figured it was because passion existed only in books and movies. She could live with that. Besides, she had a career—*that* was something she was passionate about—and the hours she devoted to it left little time for emotional entanglements. She liked it that way.

Glancing over, Ryan saw her watching him and smiled. There was something satisfying about having her gaze follow him.

Caught, Meg slid the glasses back in place and told herself the mysterious ache was simple restlessness. "I'm starving," she said. *What an understatement.*

Ryan grinned at her, noting the huskiness of her voice. *I know what you're thinking, and I'm right there with you,* he thought, liking the way her hair caught rays of sunlight and translated them into bold red sparks. "Almost done."

"You're a great cook. In case I haven't mentioned that." He was a master with a grill and had served up meals of grilled grouper, crab legs, and a fish called amberjack that had tasted like steak. Meg had not eaten so well since moving away from the professionally prepared meals of her childhood.

"You've shown your appreciation with a hearty appetite," he said.

"Are you saying I eat too much?"

"Nope."

"It's best you don't," she said.

"Hadn't planned on it."

She studied a cloud that had taken on the shape of a duck with a very large bill. "What do you do? For a living, I mean." She was surprised that she had not thought to ask him that sooner.

"Started out as a photojournalist but had my fill of that after dodging bullets covering a war. Now I'm an artist."

She remembered the camera equipment she'd seen strewn

across the table that first night on his yacht. "There was a photo at Nick's that had your signature on it."

"Yes. The kids on the beach."

"I liked it."

"Thank you. It reminded me of when Beau and I played on the beach when we were little."

She twirled a curl of her hair around one finger as she watched the cloud shift, become a blob with frayed edges. "Are your parents alive?"

"My father died several years ago of heart failure. Mom died two years ago. Cancer."

"I'm sorry. I bet they were proud of you."

"I think so." He judged another couple of minutes before the shrimp had to be turned.

"Mine weren't proud of me," she said.

"Why wouldn't they have been?"

The cloud now looked like a poodle with large, fuzzy ears. "I thought for myself too much, and I could never quite live up to their expectations. I was lucky, though. Dayle's family was an excellent surrogate. And convenient, too. Just down the block." Sadness tinged her tone.

"You're going to miss her for a long time."

"She was a good person. I'll never have a better friend."

"I'm sorry," he said, knowing how inadequate that was.

Avoiding his gaze, she rose from the chaise. "Do you need anything from below?"

"I'm good. Shrimp'll be ready in a few."

"I'll just be a minute."

He watched her go, wondering how long it would be before she was able to let him see her grief.

Below deck, Meg washed her face in the bathroom, then took deep breaths to control the emotion that threatened to burst out of control. Each time she felt her composure slip, she tried to tell herself that she didn't know for sure what had happened to Dayle. But she knew. In her heart, she knew.

When Meg hadn't returned after a few minutes, Ryan transferred the shrimp from the grill to a plate and went to check on her. He found her sitting on the edge of his bed, a sheet of paper gripped in her hand, her face set in tense angles. Too many nights of restless tossing had left their mark on her—in the lines of her face, in the hollows under her eyes. But there was something else.

"Are you okay?" he asked.

"I was on my way back up when I heard a noise," she said. "This was coming out of your fax machine."

Accepting the piece of paper, he saw that Nick had sent him photocopies of the driver's licenses of Richard and Kari Grant.

"You're stalling," Meg said in a low voice. "We've been out here for more than a week because you're waiting for something, and it's not for me to regain my strength. This is just a makeshift prison for me until Nick gives the okay on my existence as Meg Grant, isn't it?"

He met her gaze, forced himself to keep his eyes steady on hers. "We're out here to keep you safe."

She pointed at the paper in his hand. "Then why would someone be faxing you my parents' driver's licenses? Why would Nick be telling you about my appendix? He's digging through my life, through my parents' lives. Why? After all this time, what is he looking for?"

"Meg, I had to be sure—"

"It's not right," she cut in, getting up to pace to hold back the emotion that again surged too close to the surface. "I'm a good person. I deserve better than this." She stopped in front of him, thumped her chest with a closed fist. "I *deserve* better than this. You don't have any right to dig through my past. I am *not* Margot Rhinehart, damn you. I shouldn't have to prove it to *anyone*. Especially you."

He grabbed her by the arms before she could whirl away. "Why shouldn't you have to prove it to me?"

She didn't try to get away from him, even as her heart stuttered with the knowledge of how close she was allowing him. "Don't you know me by now, Ryan?"

"All I know is how much I want you."

She blinked up at him, startled by the unexpected confession.

And then he was kissing her.

An intense swirl of desire caught her, and she flowed with it, helpless. God, it had never been like this, had never felt like this. It scared the hell out of her. She pushed him back and turned away.

Ryan released a frustrated groan and shoved both hands through his hair. He wanted to yank her back to him and satisfy the need once and for all. But he was beginning to wonder if once would be enough with her. He pulled in a long breath, let it out. "Look—"

"Don't you dare apologize," she snapped over her shoulder.

"I wasn't—"

"Yes, you were."

"All right. Maybe I was. What's wrong with that?"

"It's decent, and I'm sick to death of seeing how decent you are. It makes me feel like dirt."

"Well, Christ, should I say I'm sorry for that?"

"You don't get it," Meg said.

"Then explain it to me."

She faced him. "You're a decent man, Ryan. I see it in everything that you do. You saved me from those goons on the beach that first night. You got me a good lawyer. You did what you had to do to protect me after I was arrested. You've taken good care of me all week."

"And all of that was the wrong thing to do?"

"It was the decent thing to do," she said. "But you've done it all because of who you are, not who I am. Every time you look at me . . . I see the suspicion in your eyes. You won't let yourself believe that I'm not her."

Stepping to her, he put his hands on her shoulders. "You're not. I know you're not."

And lowering his head, he kissed her.

She felt his hands tighten on her shoulders, as if he was holding himself in check. And she realized that she didn't want him to hold back. She wanted him. She wanted him so much she would have sacrificed breathing to have him.

He felt her surrender and lost himself in it. Tugging her T-shirt free, his hands skimmed bare flesh, welcoming it into hands that teased and caressed as he walked her backward toward the bed and tumbled her onto it. He took command of the moment, stripping away her shorts and tossing them aside.

Meg thrilled to the caresses that carried with them just a hint of roughness, a hint of desperation. His hands were ruthless, carrying her over the first peak within minutes, wringing from her a long, shuddering moan that would have been a scream if she had not managed to swallow it back.

Boneless and shaking, she reached for him, intending to return the favor. He smiled and held himself back. "I'm not done with you yet," he said.

"I couldn't—" She broke off on a gasp.

This time his hands were gentle, just as determined in their quest to have her quivering and helpless at his fingertips. She moved under his caresses, unable to focus on anything but what he was doing to her. Her body strained against the building surge as his mouth plundered hers, then moved down to her breasts, where he nuzzled and nipped each in turn, before moving lower. His tongue grazed the sensitive skin of her belly, dipped into her navel, and sank lower still.

Realizing with a start what he intended, she arched up on the bed. "What are you doing?" she asked, her voice hoarse with desire and a sudden, uncertain fear.

His breath whispered across her quivering tummy. "I'm loving you."

But she wasn't ready for so intimate a kiss, and clutching at his hair, she urged him up. As their lips met, he brought her to another peak. She buried her face in the pillow as the pleasure slammed into her, and while her muscles were still tense with the rolling climax, he dragged her up and lifted her onto his lap. She released a sound of surprise that evolved into a purr as he guided her onto him. Then he was pumping into her, forcing her up again, higher this time, then higher still.

He said something, but she was unable to do little more than cling to his shoulders. He took her over another impossible peak, and she bit back a scream, her nails digging into his back.

He spoke again, through clenched teeth, and she struggled to focus on his face. "Let go," he rasped.

She didn't have the chance to decipher his meaning before another, powerful climax rocked her. Even as she floated down, he was shifting their positions, easing her onto her back where he restrained her wrists on either side of her head and resumed the onslaught at a dragging pace that had her arching her body up to meet his, desperate for the next, shattering release. But he pinned her hips to the bed, used his weight to immobilize her.

"Don't move," he said in a low voice, gulping in a deep breath.

She gave a moan of protest, and he felt her body contract around him, a tight, velvet fist. He couldn't hold back. He let control spin away as the pleasure ripped through him with blinding force.

Sanity was slow to return as they lay tangled together on top of the sheets, slippery with sweat and fighting for breath. When he focused on her face, her eyes were closed, a smug smile curving her lips. He knew how she felt.

"Wow," she said.

"Wow?"

"Um hm."

"That's all you can say?" he asked.

"I can't even move, and you want me to be articulate?"

He grinned, kissed her shoulder. He was proud of himself, he wasn't ashamed to admit. But he knew, as mindless as she had been, she had not let go. A trust issue that he would have to work on, he decided. "Want to join me in the shower?"

"Only if you carry me."

"All right." He scooped her up, and she laughed, throwing her arms around his neck and letting her head drop back.

"The room is spinning," she said.

He carried her into the bathroom, set her in the shower and turned on the water. She yelped when the water struck her, but then Ryan was under it with her, his knowing hands moving up to cup her breasts, his thumbs stroking her nipples into peaks. She melted against him as the water warmed, not an ounce of strength in her legs.

"God, not again. I don't think I can take any more."

"Hold onto me." Backing her into the corner, he drew her arms around his neck, then lifted her legs up around his hips.

Aching with the anticipation of having him inside her

185

again, she shifted to allow him easier access. Fascinated, she watched his face as he slipped into her. The muscles in his jaw bunched, and she saw him swallow. Then all she could do was hang on as he built a new tower of passion inside her, higher and higher until the world exploded into sparks of light.

She thought she might have blacked out as she became aware of the water raining down on them. Ryan started shampooing her hair, and she had to grip his arms to keep from collapsing at his feet.

He couldn't stop grinning. She was pliant against him, not the least bit resistant as he angled her head into the spray to rinse. Her eyes slid closed and stayed closed.

"How're you doing?" he asked, lathering her up with a bar of soap, taking particular care with her most sensitized parts.

She clutched at his wrist. "I'm going to die a slow, agonizing death if you start that again."

He relented, figuring there would be plenty of time for more later. After shutting off the water, he wrapped a large, fluffy towel around her and carried her to the bed.

Meg would have protested, but she didn't have the strength to walk. Every muscle in her body hummed with the aftershocks of their lovemaking.

Drawing a sheet over her, Ryan sat on the edge of the bed. He brushed wet hair back from her forehead and placed a chaste kiss at her temple. Clasping his hand, she kissed his palm.

"Sleep now," he said.

She couldn't keep her eyes open. "What are you going to do?"

"Watch."

She let the heaviness of her lids win. "Watch me sleep?"

"Yep."

186

"Why?" she asked.

"Ssh."

She drifted off without another thought.

Ryan sat with her for several minutes, until her breathing became shallow and even and he was assured her sleep would be calm for the first time since they had met.

Only then did he crawl between the sheets beside her and allow himself to rest.

Later, while Meg still slept, Ryan called Nick. "Stop the research."

"Too late. I'm done. Want to know what I found?"

"I don't need to know," Ryan said.

"What's going on?"

Ryan rubbed at his right temple. "God help me, Nick, I think I'm in love with her."

A loud laugh answered him. "Gee, that's a shock."

"I'm serious."

"So am I. And just for the record, she's squeaky clean," Nick said. "Every little detail checks out."

"It wouldn't matter."

"Yes, it would."

"Maybe it would," Ryan said, then let his breath out in a shuddering huff. "I think I can walk away now."

"From Meg?"

"God, no. From Slater Nielsen and Margot Rhinehart. The FBI is on Nielsen, and they'll get him eventually," Ryan said. "Who the hell knows where Margot is? All I want now is to concentrate on Meg."

"Do you think you can do that? Walk away, I mean. I've never known you to leave something unfinished. Don't get me wrong—I've never thought that going after Beau's killers was the wise thing to do, and I agree that the feds will get them. But it's not like you to walk away."

"The more I pursue this thing, the more I put Meg at risk," Ryan said. "I'm walking away. I've got to try, Nick."

"Uh, look, before you walk away, there's something else I have to tell you that's going to muddy things up a bit from Meg's angle."

Chapter 21

Meg woke to an empty bed and an empty stomach. The sheets where Ryan had been were cool, and she sat up. The clock said it was just after noon. Her body felt battered and sore from the inside out, but she welcomed the delicious satisfaction. She realized now that she had never made love before. She'd had sex. Good sex, even. But no one had ever taken her like Ryan had. She already craved their next encounter.

After donning the T-shirt and shorts Ryan had helped her shed the night before, she went in search of him.

She found him above deck. Kelsey Sumner sat across from him, gripping a glass of iced tea, her face turned to the sun. "Ah, Ryan, I envy your life on this yacht. You know how to live."

"You didn't used to think so," he said.

"I didn't know what was important then." She gave him a significant look, one brow arched. "I think I'm learning."

Ryan, as if sensing Meg's presence even though she had not made a sound, shifted in his chair and saw her. "Good afternoon, you." Going to her, he pulled her into his arms without an ounce of self-consciousness. His kiss was so thorough that she forgot they weren't alone. When he pulled back, he tucked hair behind her ear and smiled into her eyes. "You've been sleeping for fourteen hours. Doing okay?"

She returned his smile, delighting in the flutter in her stomach. She couldn't recall ever feeling so calm, so certain that what was happening was right. "Guess I needed it."

His thumb grazed the skin under her eyes that was still bruised with exhaustion. "You need more."

"We're being rude," Meg said.

He gave her a puzzled look. "What?"

"We have a guest."

"Oh." Ryan turned back to Kelsey. "Sorry about that, Kelsey."

The lawyer rose and crossed to them, smiling. "Looks like you two are getting along better. Meg, you look stunning. The sun, or something, agrees with you."

"Kelsey called earlier and asked to drop by to check up on you," Ryan said. "I told her you were doing fine, but she had to see for herself."

"Yes," Kelsey said. "I know what an ogre this man can be when you spend too much time alone with him."

Meg laughed. "Oh, he's definitely an ogre."

"If you two are done tarnishing my reputation, I'm going to throw some grouper on the grill for lunch," Ryan said. "Care to join us, Kelsey?"

"I'm afraid I can't," she said. "I have a full slate this afternoon, and I'm already running behind. I really just wanted to check in on Meg." She grasped Meg's hand. "From what Ryan tells me, I'm thinking we'll cross paths again."

"Thanks for everything," Meg said. "I appreciate what you did for me."

"Oh, I brought you some clothes. Ryan put them somewhere for you." She gave a quick, easy smile. "Not that you're going to need them."

As soon as Kelsey was gone, Ryan turned Meg into his arms and nuzzled her neck. He would tell her later, when she was stronger and more rested, what Nick had told him last night. For now, he wanted to enjoy her and her to enjoy him. "You smell incredible," he murmured.

She dropped her head back on a sigh. "She's still in love with you."

The quick flick of his tongue on her skin raised goose bumps. "Who?"

She smiled. "Good answer."

His lips curved against her throat as he felt the rapid beat of her pulse under his lips. "If you're talking about Kelsey, it's been over between us for more than a year."

"What happened?"

Slipping his arms around her, he pulled her close. "We had a scheduling conflict. She didn't have the time or the energy for me. She always had one more case to take care of, one more commitment, before we could get away for a few days, a long weekend, whatever. It never happened."

She clasped his face between her palms. "She was stupid."

He chuckled. "The things you do to my insides. You can't imagine how much I want you right now."

Sliding her hand to the back of his neck, she brought his mouth to hers. When they parted, breathless, she said, "Then take me."

"Come with me."

He led her below deck. Beside the bed, he lifted the T-shirt over her head and watched strands of curls tumble over her shoulders. Pressing his lips to the curve of her neck, he felt her sigh against his shoulder, then lightly nip his flesh.

His mouth moved against her throat and downward. She let her hands slide over his body, digging her fingers into him as he found and played her pleasure spots. Tumbling her back onto the bed, he seared kisses from the tops of her thighs down to her ankles and back up, planted damp caresses across her belly, his tongue dancing around the pink pucker of flesh on her lower abdomen where the bullet had struck her.

Meg squirmed on the sheets, caught in a whirl of sensation that was wonderful—and frightening. God, he'd just begun, and she was already writhing. Sinking her fingers into his hair, she urged him up until their mouths fused together. They rolled across the bed, Ryan trying to fumble out of his shorts without breaking the embrace.

When her tongue flicked his nipple, his hands tightened in her hair. He pulled her head back to the pillow and watched her face as his fingers stroked down her stomach, smiled as her eyes slid out of focus and her head arched back on an intake of breath. Her fingers sank into his shoulders, her body tensing.

"Please," she whispered.

"Not yet." He paused when he knew she was on the edge. She clutched at his wrist, pushing at his hand, desperate for release. When he allowed her to leap off the edge, he put his mouth on hers, his tongue imitating the intimate caress of his fingers. For a long moment, she wasn't aware of anything but the pleasure that shuddered through her.

When reason returned, she pinned his shoulders to the bed and straddled him. He reached up to caress her breasts, but she captured his hands. "No, it's my turn."

She made love to him with her mouth and hands until he was groaning beneath her, straining toward the edge of the abyss that she wouldn't allow him to dive into. Each time she felt his body tense to steel-hardness, she stopped and smiled at him, her hands braced on his shoulders, her legs tangled around his as her hair swayed above him.

He was gasping for breath, and it seemed that every move she made snatched from him the air, and control, he needed. He concentrated to hold himself in check, certain that he would hurt her if he took what he wanted as violently as he wanted to take it. Instead, he let her set the pace and hoped he could keep track of his wits long enough to make her pay for it later.

When she allowed him the pleasure, her own body tensed with spasms that left her breathless against his chest. His hands played against the slippery skin of her back, his heart hammering under her ear.

Nothing could have been more perfect than this moment so close to him.

"I can't move," she said, laughing.

He loved the sound of her laugh and vowed to hear it often in the years ahead. "We'll kill each other if we keep this up."

"Definitely, if we don't have food very soon," she said.

"Good God, you haven't eaten since—"

She grinned down at him.

"What?"

"You're so cute when you worry," she said.

"Cute. I suppose there are worse things."

"Oh, would you prefer devastatingly handsome?"

"Hmm. Yes, that would be most flattering," he said.

"Well, you're that, too. Unfortunately, I'm starving, and at the moment food is far more important to me than—" She broke off on a hitch of breath. Her eyes slid closed as a fresh wave of sensation swept her up. "Except that. How did you—" The thought was driven away. "God."

Shifting their positions, Ryan smiled as she arched her head back into the pillow. "Open your eyes, Meg. I want to watch you."

Her hands clutched at his shoulders as if she had to hang

onto him or fall into oblivion. "What? Oh, Ryan." Gasping, she buried her face in his neck and clung to him.

He didn't mind that she kept her eyes closed.

Later, while he showered, Meg rummaged through the cupboards in the galley. She found chicken noodle soup, a box of crackers and a bag of pretzel rods. Ripping into the pretzels, she munched and searched drawers until she unearthed a can opener and went to work on the soup.

Hearing herself humming, she paused. She was humming, smiling like a goof and feeling better than she had in months. Because of a man. That was something new.

She went back to opening the can and humming. The lid popped up. For a moment, she thought the can was defective because there was no soup inside. Instead, black velvet lined the aluminum, and a ring lay in the bottom. She dumped it into her palm.

Ryan ambled into the kitchen, buttoning a clean shirt. She looked damned sexy in just his T-shirt, her long legs tan and firm. He had to tamp down the instant desire, ordered himself to wait until she ate something first. "Find anything good?"

Turning, she held up the ring. "How's chicken noodle and emerald soup?"

He didn't laugh as she had expected. He reached for the ring. "I forgot to warn you about that."

"About the ring?"

"No, the fake soup can." He stared at the ring grasped between his fingers, his face serious.

"I'm afraid I used the opener on it."

He didn't respond, and she started to worry about who the ring belonged to. Perhaps there was someone in his life. Perhaps it had been meant for Kelsey. Damn it, she'd started humming too soon. "Whose is it?"

He blinked at her. "What?"

"The ring. Who's it for?"

"Beau had it made for Margot with one of the Kama emeralds."

Relief made her feel lightheaded. "The ones she stole?"

He gave her a humorless smile. "He never got a chance to give it to her before she helped herself to the other eleven."

"How did you get it?"

"It was in his pocket the night he was found dead. I didn't know what to do with it, so I put it in here until I could decide."

"It's gorgeous. I've never seen anything like it. May I?"

He handed it to her. "He loved her. I hope he never knew what she really wanted from him."

"The stone, the setting, is fabulous. There's an inscription. 'Happy twenty-eighth birthday. Love you always. October fifteenth—' " She broke off.

Ryan, caught by memories, wasn't paying attention until she put a hand on the counter as if for balance. He saw that the blood had drained from her face. "Meg?"

She shook her head, trying to think rationally. She'd suspected it after she'd seen the security tapes. They'd looked so much alike. But to actually know . . .

"What's wrong?" Ryan asked. "Are you sick?"

"We have the same birthday."

Her voice was so low that he didn't hear her. "Come sit down." He led her into the bedroom where he sat beside her on the bed and took her hands into his. "Your hands are like ice. Tell me what's wrong."

She pulled her hands free, unable to think with him touching her. "We have the same birthday. We're the same age." Her heart was slamming against her ribs.

Ryan rubbed his hands over his face. Too soon. He had wanted her to have more time to heal. "Damn it. I was going to tell you—"

"You knew?"

"Nick said the FBI profile mentioned Margot's adoption, and you told him about yours. He cross-referenced your personal information, and the birth dates came up a match."

Pushing herself off the bed, she began to pace. She focused on the anger. That was easier to deal with at the moment. The larger, more important, issue was too overwhelming. "You knew, and you didn't tell me?"

"Nick told me last night while you were sleeping. I wasn't going to drag you out of a sound sleep that you desperately needed to turn your world upside down all over again."

Facing him, her eyes snapped with green fire. "When were you going to tell me, Ryan?"

"Today. I was going to tell you today." He went to her, put his hands on her shoulders, felt her shaking. There wasn't a hint of color in her cheeks. "I was going to tell you. You have to believe that."

She shrugged away from him, holding her hands up to keep him back. "Margot is my twin."

The questions tumbled faster than her brain could process them. Had her parents known she had a sister? Was that why they hadn't told her she was adopted? Had they not wanted her to know they had separated twins? Were they that selfish? Certainly they could have afforded to adopt twins. So why hadn't they? She would never know. Never.

And *Margot Rhinehart* was her sister. A thief. An accomplice to murder. And not just any murder, but Ryan's brother's. What was the irony in that? A long-lost sibling on a one-way road to prison for helping slay the brother of the only man she had ever felt passion for. And if that wasn't enough,

Margot was also indirectly responsible for whatever had happened to Dayle.

Ryan watched the emotions lurch across her face. Disbelief and a grief so tangible he could almost taste the tears she wasn't shedding. He wanted to hold her until the pain in her eyes faded, until he could recapture the laughter they had shared for so short a time. But he kept his distance because that's what she wanted. The helplessness made him ache. "I'm sorry, Meg. God, I'm so sorry."

She knew he was. She heard it in his voice, saw it in the gray eyes that begged her to lean on him. But she couldn't. If she allowed him to touch her now, she'd crack. Pulling in a long breath, she forced the shock away. "This changes everything."

She was too calm, and that worried him. Especially when he saw the way her hand trembled when she dragged it through her hair. "How do you mean?" he asked.

"How can you ask that?" She choked down the hysterical edge that crept into her voice. "She's my sister. My *twin* sister. Your brother loved her."

"And look where it got him," he said.

"It's not so cut and dried anymore."

"What are you saying?" he asked. "She's forgiven for what she's done because she's the sister you never knew you had?"

Sinking onto the bed, she drew a pillow onto her lap and hugged it to her. And grappled for a reason to believe that somewhere along the way she and Ryan had misjudged Margot, perhaps had misinterpreted her actions. "We don't know her side of it."

"Like hell we don't. She works for Slater Nielsen, and one of her jobs was to set up my brother. Whether killing him was part of the deal or not doesn't change the final result. Beau is just as dead. Because of Margot. Maybe she didn't kill him

197

herself, but she is responsible. You can't argue with that."

She couldn't. A dull ache began to pound in her temples, and she rubbed at them. There was too much to think about. And she was still so tired.

Ryan stared at the top of her bent head. He understood her well enough to know what she'd meant when she'd said, "This changes everything." She wouldn't turn her back. It wasn't her nature. Not when Margot needed help. Not when Meg would see their blood as a moral obligation to be the one to do the helping, regardless of Margot's guilt. That's what family was about. He had used the same logic when he searched for Beau's killers.

Looking up at him, Meg blinked back tears. The grip she had was tenuous, and she didn't want him there when it slipped. He would be kind and soothing, and that would only make it more devastating. "I need some time alone."

His face hardened, first with anger, then with hurt. "You're not going to shut me out."

"I just need—"

"Me," he cut in. "You need me."

"Ryan, Jesus—" She pressed the heels of her hands to her forehead where the headache was raging. "I can't do this."

"You can't do what?"

She squeezed her eyes shut. "Please."

Kneeling in front of her, he tugged her wrists down from her face. "Why are you hiding from me?"

She tried to pull away, but he held on. "I'm not hiding," she said. "Let go."

He released her and stood. "I want you to go home."

She glanced up at him, surprised. "What?"

"You heard me." He saw the temper flare in her eyes, watched with relief as it seared away the shock. "Until I can handle it," he said.

"I just found out for sure that Margot is my twin, and you want me to go away so *you* can *handle* it? Of all the arrogant, chauvinistic, selfish—"

"Wait a minute—"

"No, *you* wait a minute." She bounced off the bed, forcing him back a step and kicking a pillow out of her way that tumbled to the floor. Pacing at the foot of the bed, she struggled to control her anger. It was as if she was a puppet on a string, and he was her master. She had been the puppet most of her life. Her father had pulled the strings, repeatedly had done the very thing that Ryan was trying to do now. She'd be damned if anyone ever controlled her again—

The inner tirade broke off when Ryan whirled her around. She was startled at first, then pushed at his chest. "Back off."

Seizing the wrist she flung out at him, he jerked her toward him. "Listen to me, Meg. I'm asking this of you because I care, all right? I couldn't stand it if something happened to you. Something did happen, and it was ugly. What I felt was ugly. I couldn't live with it if you . . ." He trailed off, his cheeks paling. "God help me, I can't even say it."

The breath left her as if he had tossed a light punch to her stomach. He cared. A lot. She knocked a loosely clenched fist against his chest, appalled when tears began spilling down her cheeks. "Bastard," she whispered, covering her face with her hands.

Pulling her against him, he stroked a hand over her back, feeling the shudders that shook her. His own eyes welled up, and he blinked the emotion back. "It's okay," he murmured against her hair. "We'll work through it."

The soothing words and the gentle hand on her back were foreign to her. Even when she'd been a child, comfort had not been offered with so little effort. The kindness shredded her defenses. And when she was defenseless against the emotion she had been holding in since her parents, and then Dayle, had been taken from her, she broke.

Ryan felt her body convulse against him. Concerned, he pulled back, but she curled her fingers into the front of his shirt. "Don't leave me."

The ragged pain in her voice tore at him, and he swept her up in his arms, frightened by how she wept, startled to see such raw emotion in a woman so strong.

Sitting on the bed, he cradled her on his lap, soothing her in a low voice, until she lay curled against him, spent.

Sniffling, she wiped at her face. "As a general rule, I'm not normally weepy. In case you're wondering."

He caught her chin and angled her head back so their gazes met. "Your world has been turned upside down more than once. I'd be worried if you weren't emotional."

He knew the right things to say. She turned her attention to a button on his shirt to avoid becoming a blubbering idiot again. "You made me mad on purpose."

"You give me too much credit."

"What are we going to do?"

She'd said "we." The tightness in his chest loosened. "We can't do anything right now. The FBI hasn't found Margot."

"But eventually they will."

"I'm certain of it. And I'm also certain that we're not going to figure it out all at once. You're tired, Meg. You need sleep."

"I sleep best with your help."

Smiling, he eased her back on the bed. "If you get the urge to drift off, let me know."

She curved her arms around his neck and pulled him down for a long kiss. As he trailed his lips down her throat, she caught her hands in his hair. "I don't think drifting off is an option."

Chapter 22

Margot sank her toes into sand that held the morning sun's heat. It felt good, and she allowed herself to enjoy it. She didn't expect that there'd be many more mornings like this—sitting in a faded wooden chair outside the cabin of a Captiva resort on the shore of the Gulf—before she was forced to do what had to be done.

Kill Slater Nielsen.

She wondered what it would be like, how it would feel. Would she be relieved when it was done? Or sad? What would happen afterward?

The best-case scenario: She would walk away, physically unscathed, to create a new life with a new name, a new past. She would do her damnedest to raise Beau's child to know the difference between right and wrong. She would be an exemplary mother, honest and caring, an upstanding citizen.

However, she wasn't naïve enough to think that she would actually get away with killing Slater. Perhaps, if she was caught, she could claim self-defense. Perhaps she could say she had been forced, threatened, terrorized. Perhaps a jury would take pity on her.

Closing her eyes, she acknowledged that if she were caught, Beau's child would most likely be taken from her, to be raised by strangers. She might never know him, might never hold him. The thought was horrifying, but she accepted the risk because she had no other choice. Turning herself into the police now would make her an easy target. She would have no control, no protection. At the very least, she had to stay alive long enough to bring Beau's child into the world, and the only way to do that was to eliminate the biggest threat.

It occurred to her now that if she did get caught, then perhaps her sister could take in Beau's baby.

"Come here often?"

She looked up with a sharp intake of breath. The sun was shining directly into her eyes, and she raised a hand to shield them. He wasn't a Slater thug. No man who worked for Slater would wear a Milwaukee Brewers baseball cap, khaki shorts, red polo and sandals. His smile was friendly, the skin around his dark eyes crinkling as if that smile was his most frequent facial expression.

Undaunted by her lack of response, he said, "I'm in the cabin next door. Just checked in for the week." He extended his hand. "I guess we're neighbors. For a while anyway."

Staring at his hand, Margot was unsure of how to respond, so she didn't. She didn't have time for a new friend anyway.

He let his hand drop to his side. "Well, it was nice meeting you." He started to turn away, but paused. "If you change your mind, get lonely, or whatever, I'm next door. I, uh, I'm alone, too."

An alarm went off in her head. "How do you know I'm alone?"

He seemed surprised that she spoke but recovered quickly. "The guy at the check-in desk mentioned it."

"Why would he do that?"

A broad smile curved his lips. "Hell if I know. Maybe he

thought I'm a great-looking guy and I'm alone, and you're a beautiful woman and you're alone, perhaps . . . you know."

For an unguarded moment, she smiled, liking him in spite of herself. "The guy at the check-in desk is playing match-maker?"

"Well, he's right, after all. Are you vacationing?"

"Not really. You?"

"Naples resident," he said. "Just like to get away every once in a while, and this is a good spot for it. Where are you from?"

"Doesn't matter."

"No problem." He helped himself to the chair next to hers. "Mystery appeals to me."

"Don't get comfortable."

"Wouldn't dream of it," he said.

"You look like you're getting comfortable."

"Would that be so terrible?" Tipping his cap back, he grinned. "Want me to leave?"

"Yes."

He didn't look the least bit disappointed. "But I just got here."

"Look, I'm not interested in—"

He held up his hands in a placating gesture. "Neither am I. Just making conversation."

"Whatever." She stood to go, brushing at the sand that clung to her shorts. She hesitated before turning her back on him. "Good-bye."

"If you change your mind, just holler. I'll be just next door. Name's Nick Costello."

Chapter 23

Meg couldn't resist stretching like a cat on the towel spread across the deck. Sails snapped in the wind. Through slitted eyes, she saw clouds lining up along the horizon like mountain peaks. It was almost too cool, but the sun warming her skin kept the goose bumps at bay.

"Morning."

She smiled, arching her back in the white bathing suit that Kelsey had included in the clothing she had brought for her. She had only to turn her head to see Ryan idly rubbing his tummy, his shorts unbuttoned at the top.

"It's about time," she said, reaching for the sunglasses that lay nearby. Sitting up, she considered the ripple of his stomach muscles as he lowered himself to the end of a chaise. His eyes were sleepy and soft as he yawned.

"How're you feeling? Did we overdo it last night?" he asked.

She smiled, touched by his concern. "I'm okay."

"Just okay?"

"Pretty okay. You know, sometimes it's a little hard to tell at first." She closed her eyes, suppressing a smile when his cool shadow fell across her body.

"Hard to tell at first, huh?" he asked, lifting the sunglasses from her face.

He swooped down, his mouth muffling her laugh. She wrapped arms damp with moisture and tanning oil around his neck, releasing a moan as his lips left her mouth and explored the place where her pulse throbbed in her throat. His hands catching in her hair, he nibble-kissed his way across her face, neck and shoulders. When his mouth came back to hers, he tasted of oil and salt and passion, while his fingers tugged loose the knot that secured her swimsuit at the back of her neck.

"Is this *all* you can think about?" she asked, laughing.

"At the moment." He pressed his mouth to her breast and closed his teeth around the nipple through the cloth.

Air lodged in her throat at the erotic sensation. "Shouldn't we go below?"

"There isn't a soul around. Just you and me."

He lowered his head to kiss her, but she held him off. "What about low-flying helicopters?"

His chuckle vibrated against her body as he ran his hands back up into her hair.

"And hot air balloons," she added.

His mouth settled on hers with an urgency that dragged her into aching awareness. Winding her arms around his neck, she pressed against him, already frantic for him. But he braceleted her wrists and pinned them to the deck. "This time, you're just going to take it."

She released a shuddery laugh. "What?"

"I'm going to love you, and you're not going to do anything but let go."

She started to protest, but he drew her arms over her head where he captured both wrists in one hand.

Panicking at the thought of what he intended, she tried to wiggle free. "Ryan—"

He silenced her with his lips, and with one methodical

hand, removed the barrier of her swimsuit. He lavished sweet, throbbing attention on each body part as it was freed from the constraints of the suit, his hand gentle one moment, ruthless the next, until every caress wrung a long moan from her.

When he held her on the edge, he released her wrists and used both his hands and his mouth, setting a slow, drugging pace that had her moving restlessly, desperate as his tongue moved over her, and into her. The air seemed to thicken around her, and she sucked at it, clutching at the towel under her as if she had to hang on to something to keep from tumbling into a pool of sensation that would rob her of self-control.

It was too much. She couldn't take it anymore. Arching up, she reached for him, but he restrained her hands. "No. Let me." And he brought her ever closer.

"I can't . . . Ryan . . ."

He clenched his teeth, ready to explode, and she hadn't even touched him. Just having her bucking under him, sighing his name, was enough to push him over the edge. "Yes, you can."

She fought to hang on, fought to drag in air that seemed too hot, too moist. "Oh, God, please."

Ignoring her plea, he moved up her body, shedding his shorts along the way. Pinning her hands on either side of her head, he wanted to plunge into her and cut loose. The need was turning to pain. "Say you want me."

His voice in her ear, low and husky, sent her spiraling. She gulped in air. "You know I do."

"Say it."

"Ah, God, I want you. I want you inside me. Now, damn it. Now."

He smiled, kissed her temple. "You're so eloquent when you're crazy with need."

He let go of her wrists, and she shoved at his shoulders. As he rolled onto his back, she straddled him and took what he'd been holding back. Almost the instant she had him inside her, she peaked so hard she cried out. The climax left her limp and shuddering against his chest, struggling to remember how to breathe.

"Meg?"

She couldn't lift her head. "I'm sure my sanity is somewhere nearby," she murmured. "I only lost it in the past few seconds."

"I'm not done yet."

"Wha—"

He arched his hips, and she released a surprised breath. "It seems neither of us is done yet," he said with a grin, switching their positions in one swift move.

Wrapping her legs around him, she answered him thrust for thrust, meeting the next plateau with another cry. Her arms slipped from his shoulders, and her legs around him went slack. He stopped moving, schooled his breathing, waited for her.

She shoved a hand through sweat-wet hair, her brain short-circuiting. "No more."

"Again," he rasped, resuming a crawling pace, grinning when she turned her head to the side, her nails digging into his back. The cords in her neck stood out, her skin slick with moisture.

She couldn't hold a thought. She could only feel him moving inside her, building another intense wave. They exploded at the same time this time, and he buried his mouth on hers, swallowing her scream and giving her his.

For a long time, they lay gasping for breath, Ryan too limp to even shift his weight away from her. Meg didn't mind. She liked his weight, liked having him still inside her. Liked everything about him. Perhaps loved everything about him.

He raised his head with some effort, trying not to look too pleased that she had trusted him enough to lose control. "You okay?"

She smiled. "I've never been there before."

"Glad we could go together the first time."

"What's that noise?"

"What noise?"

"My ears are ringing."

"Oh, it's the cell phone. Don't move." She gasped as he withdrew, and he patted her arm. "Sorry about that. I'll just be a sec."

She lay with her eyes closed, feeling the warmth of the sun bearing down. She didn't think, just let her mind drift like the clouds overhead.

Ryan returned to find her still naked, curled on her side, her hair tangled and damp as it fell across her face. She looked peaceful, calm as she dozed. He hated that what he was about to say would take that away from her.

Opening her eyes, she smiled at him. "Who was it?"

He swallowed the lump in his throat. "Nick found Margot."

Meg sat up, wrapping the towel beneath her around herself. "Where is she?"

"A resort on Captiva. Cabin eighteen."

So close. Only an hour from Fort Myers. "All this time?"

"He thinks at least a week. She's alone."

"How'd he find her?"

He retrieved his shorts from the deck and pulled them on. "Partly luck. Mostly ingenuity. In a nutshell, she's created a new identity for herself. She made a visit to a Captiva urgent-care facility, and he tracked her from there to the resort."

"Urgent care? Is she sick?"

"He didn't say." He watched Meg squint against the sun, saw her start to shiver. When she said nothing more, he went on. "Nick followed her today. She picked up a gun from a street thug in Fort Myers."

Meg closed her eyes. *Her sister, the goon.* "Damn."

"Nick said no one's gone near her. Feds included."

"Then let's go see her."

"And do what?" He already wished he'd asked Nick to tip off the feds and been done with it. He hadn't because he didn't want to make that decision without first consulting Meg.

"I don't know," she said. "Ask her what the hell she's doing. Ask her what happened in October, find out her side of it. She's been on the run for some reason. Maybe Nielsen forced her to set up Beau. Maybe she really did love him. In fact, the FBI agent who questioned me—Loomis—said a woman called nine-one-one that night. That was probably Margot. Why would she do that if she knew Beau was going to be killed?"

Ryan clenched his jaw. "We need to turn this information over to the FBI and let them deal with it."

"But what's wrong with waiting a day? Nick said she's been there a week. No one else knows where she is. I could meet my sister."

"What do you think's going to happen when you see her? Do you think you'll connect somehow?"

"I don't know. I just—"

"Do you think you'll remember her? You were infants when you were separated."

Rising, Meg secured the towel around herself. "I want to try to help my sister, Ryan."

"Maybe she doesn't deserve your help."

"Well, I can't really know that until I talk to her, can I?"

"Meg, you're ignoring the facts. Margot stole the emeralds. Why would she do that if she loved my brother? Hell, Beau loved her so much that he would have given them to her if she'd asked. But, no. She *stole* them. And after she found him dead, she bolted. What does that tell you?" He didn't give her a chance to respond before plunging on. "I'll tell you what it tells me. She didn't love him. She duped him so she could take the emeralds. She's guilty."

"But where did she run, Ryan? She didn't run to Nielsen, the man she worked for, a man powerful enough to protect her forever. She ran away."

"You don't know that."

"Of course I do," she said. "We both know it. How many of Nielsen's henchmen have tried to persuade me to return to him? How many of them have threatened my life when I refused? Margot ran *away* from him."

"Regardless, she's a thief and accomplice to murder," he said. "She'll never be the woman you want her to be."

"But she's my sister. I can't just walk away. And that's what you want, isn't it? After everything we've been through."

"Yes," he snapped. Then, seeing her flinch, he repeated, "Yes." He went to her, his palms damp as he cupped her face. "I almost lost you once, Meg. I'm not eager to repeat the experience."

She smiled, touched by his tenderness. "You're not going to lose me."

"You can't guarantee that."

She retreated to a deck chair and sat, wrapping her arms tight around her middle. The sun had gone behind a cloud, leaving the air cool. But that was only part of the reason she was shivering. Peering at Ryan, she asked, "What about Beau? I thought you wanted justice."

"Justice is the FBI's job. I lost sight of that for a while, but I can accept it now."

"Well, maybe I can't. Slater Nielsen took my best friend from me. I want him to pay. Margot can help me with that. This isn't just about helping my twin sister."

"I understand what you're feeling. Believe me, I do. It's got you so tangled up you can't think straight. But revenge is not the answer."

"What is the answer? Tell me what's going to make this knot in my stomach go away. And don't tell me time will heal it, because so far time isn't doing the job." Choking on the last words, she lowered her head and hugged herself tight. She couldn't stop shaking.

"I love you."

She didn't move, didn't breathe. She was afraid to look at him, afraid that she'd imagined what he'd said.

"I love you," he said again. "Nothing else matters."

He drew her up, and she buried her face against his bare chest and held on, overcome by emotion. She didn't know what to say, how to respond. It was all too much.

He held her close, his heart breaking. Not so long ago, he hadn't been able to imagine anything that could eclipse his driving need for vengeance. But love did it. His love for Meg. Unfortunately, what she felt for him, if anything, wasn't substantial enough to convince her that the only answer was to turn her back on Margot Rhinehart and Slater Nielsen and walk away with the man who loved her. Perhaps the only way she would realize that was if she met Margot and saw for herself that the woman wasn't worth the effort. Besides, he had a few things he wanted to say to Margot himself.

"Ryan, please, I need this," Meg whispered. "What's one more day?"

He pressed a kiss to her forehead before setting her away from him.

"Where are you going?" she asked.

"To fire up the engines. We should be off Captiva sometime tonight."

Chapter 24

Margot stared down at the gun in her hand. It was black and heavy. She ran her thumb over the safety lever. Next time, she wouldn't forget to flip it off.

Clenching her eyes shut, she imagined holding the gun to Slater's head and squeezing the trigger. She imagined looking into his eyes and watching them go dead. And wondered whether she should worry that the thought of it didn't repulse her. She was planning to take another life. Shouldn't she feel something? Sorrow? Anger? Anticipation?

But the truth was, she felt nothing. Not even fear.

Maybe that meant she was ready.

Setting aside the gun, she rested her palm on her stomach and breathed deeply. "You're going to be okay, baby," she whispered.

Rising, she went into the bedroom and changed into the new black jeans and dark sweatshirt she'd bought earlier in the week. Stealth clothes, she used to call them. It seemed like a lifetime ago. She took a moment to imagine what life would have been like if she had never met Beau. Empty. But would she have realized it? She had thought she was happy with Slater, had thought her life was pretty damned good. She hadn't missed what she had never known.

Walking back into the living room, she retrieved the gun and pushed it into her purse on the table by the door. Then she stopped to gaze at a vase of roses. They were red and fragrant, every bloom almost perfect. She had picked them up that afternoon, hoping they would be a happy reminder of Beau, who had often showered her with roses.

She reached for the vase, weighed it in her hand, then heaved it. The vase shattered against the wall, water and flowers splattering the carpet. Closing her eyes, Margot let herself enjoy the rush of satisfaction. There it is, she thought. Anticipation.

She reached for the lamp.

As Meg slipped out of bed, Ryan mumbled in his sleep, reaching for her. She gave his arm a reassuring pat. "I'll be right back."

They'd dropped anchor two hours ago off the shore of Captiva and within sight of the island resort where Nick had found Margot. Ryan had persuaded Meg to wait until morning to confront her sister. The morning would bring a clear head, he said. And they both needed the rest. Meg hadn't agreed, but it wasn't because she thought he was wrong. She just had other plans.

Now, in the bathroom, she slipped on jeans and a T-shirt from the clothing Kelsey had provided. It felt odd to push her feet into her worn Nikes, odder still to think that she was so close to meeting her twin sister. As she slipped the watch Nick had given her onto her wrist—it seemed that months had passed since that night—she wondered what Margot would say when they stood face to face. Would she be happy to meet the sister she'd never known?

Shoving away her apprehension, Meg stared at herself in the bathroom mirror. She hoped Ryan would understand why she wanted to meet her sister alone. He was convinced of Margot's guilt, and Meg was certain her twin wouldn't respond to anger and accusatory glares. Few people would. At least alone, she and Margot might be able to talk candidly. Perhaps alone, their first meeting could be a reunion rather than a confrontation.

An hour before, Ryan had made love to her. Reverently. With murmurs and sighs of love. She swallowed against the lump of emotion that formed in her throat. He loved her.

And she was about to seriously piss him off.

Ryan wasn't sure what awakened him. Realizing that Meg was not beside him, he shifted so he could see the bathroom door. It was closed, a thin stream of light visible along its bottom edge. Relaxing, he made plans for her return to bed and drifted off again.

Chapter 25

Meg stood before the door to cabin eighteen. Not allowing a moment to second-guess herself, she delivered three light taps.

The door opened a crack. A woman with short black hair and green eyes peered through it. Meg took an involuntary step back as the door swung open.

She had already reasoned that a surge of affection would be unrealistic. She had also anticipated the loss for words. She hadn't expected, however, that Margot's face, so like her own, would be so void of expression that she may well have been looking at a piece of furniture she neither liked nor disliked. Meg saw no kindness in the eyes that were identical to her own, and their flat expression was as jarring as a slap. "I made a mistake," Meg said, and turned to go.

"Wait."

Meg thought about ignoring her and walking away anyway. She didn't need another reason to be disappointed in family ties. But she reminded herself that there were things she needed—wanted—to know, and only Margot had the answers. Pausing, Meg noticed that Margot's eyes were red and puffy. She'd been crying.

Margot leaned a shoulder against the door, casually so as

not to give away the panic that had gripped her when her sister had started to go. When the knock had come at the door, her twin was the last person she had expected to be standing there. At least now she knew that Slater hadn't gotten to her. Maybe there was a reason to feel hope after all.

"Well," Margot said, taking a moment to check her sister out. She remembered having hair that long and disordered, and her twin's body was leaner and more muscled than her own. Her twin was also not all that happy to meet Margot. That was obvious in the way she met Margot's gaze. A direct hit, not a hint of mercy.

Meg refused to shift even though Margot's scrutiny was unnerving. It was eerie to gaze at a woman who looked different from her only because of the cut of her hair or a slight variation in their weight. She wondered whether her own forehead wrinkled in the spot just above the bridge of her nose when she scrutinized another person. She wondered whether lines etched by stress on either side of Margot's nose were as prominent on her own face.

Margot stepped back from the door. "Come in."

Meg moved past her, ever more certain she was making a mistake when she saw that the cabin had been trashed: lamps shattered, chairs upended, sofa cushions tossed about. Several red roses were strewn across the floor amid water stains and shards of glass. "What happened?"

"I'm having a bad day," Margot said, righting a rattan chair and patting a cushion into it. "Have a seat. You look like you could use a drink."

Instead of sitting, Meg watched her sister go into the kitchen nook. She moved gracefully as she dropped ice cubes into a glass then poured cranberry juice and vodka from the minibar. Her clothing—dark jeans and a sweatshirt—was inconsistent with an evening at a beach resort.

Margot forced a smile as she brought the glass to her sister.

"I'm drinking alone?" Meg asked.

Margot gave a negligent shrug. "Not thirsty."

Meg sipped the drink, hoping for a quick, calming effect.

Unable to stand still, Margot said, "I could use a cigarette." She crossed to the desk in the corner and rummaged through a drawer until she came up with a pack of cigarettes and a lighter. Damn it, she was so unsettled by her sister's presence that her hands were shaking. "I managed to quit smoking last year," she said, cursing herself for being so rattled. "Some habits you just can't cut loose. Do you mind?"

Meg shook her head.

As she lit up, Margot squinted at her through the smoke. "Megan, right?"

"Meg."

Taking a long drag, Margot held the smoke in her lungs, then exhaled, telling herself that as soon as Slater was taken care of, she'd quit. For the baby. Feeling calmer now, she was able to look at her sister and not flinch at what she imagined Meg saw when looking back at her. "I've known about you since I was sixteen."

Meg couldn't fathom waiting twelve years for this moment. "How did you find out?"

Margot blew out a thin stream of smoke. "Dad was mad at me for being a bad girl and said he was glad I wasn't his daughter. Even forked over the papers to prove it." Pausing, she stared down at the cigarette clenched between two fingers. The dragging sensation in her chest as she remembered was not new, but she hadn't felt it in years. Not even when she and Holly had talked about what had happened. "I ran away from home right afterward," Margot went on. "I was on a mission to find my real parents . . . and you."

Meg gripped the glass tighter. "You found them?"

Margot arched a brow. "You don't know?"

"Nothing."

"They're dead. Plane crash." Margot empathized with the disappointment that darkened Meg's eyes. "The way they died made it easy to find out more about them. Plane crashes are big news. Much bigger than car wrecks and stuff like that. Our parents were the only Fort Myers couple on a small plane out of Tampa to Milwaukee. The papers around here covered the hell out of it." She paused to take a deep pull on the cigarette and sent smoke swirling. "Dad was a computer analyst, Mom a programmer for the same company. They were relocating to Wisconsin. You and I—we were only a couple months old—were already there with friends of the family while Mom and Dad tied up loose ends in Florida. They had no siblings, and both sets of grandparents passed on a long time ago."

Meg's head started to pound. *Everybody is dead. There's no one. Only Margot, a jewel thief and accomplice to murder.*

Snagging an ashtray from a table by the chair, Margot tapped ashes into it. She didn't like it that when Meg's forehead creased as if in great emotional pain, her own throat constricted. "I was adopted first," Margot said. "In case you're wondering who split us up. Hell, it's possible your parents didn't even know about me."

Relief expanded in Meg's chest. She'd needed to know that, to believe it. It was *something.*

"So how'd you find me?" Margot asked.

"Looked you up on the Internet."

Margot's smile was hard. "Ha ha."

"Some of your associates came after me."

Margot reached for Meg's empty glass. "Another drink?"

Meg withheld it. "Did you set up Beau Kama?"

Margot stared at her. Meg knew much more than she had expected. "No."

"His brother thinks you did. So do a number of law enforcement officials."

Well, that answered the question of whether the police were looking for her, Margot thought. "Do you think I set him up?"

"Tell me what to think."

Margot sank onto a chair, her mouth dry. She clenched her teeth against the grief that struggled to the surface. She told herself she wouldn't break down, not in front of a stranger. "A hit man killed him to punish me for believing in happy endings. I learned my lesson."

She was being flip about it. A man was dead. And Margot was flip. Anger shimmered through Meg. "You're taking it rather well."

The contempt in her twin's eyes surprised Margot. "You came here to judge me?"

"I came here to help you."

"I don't need anyone's help."

"Don't be stupid," Meg said.

Wincing, Margot looked away. It had always mattered to her what Meg would think of her, how Meg would perceive her. It was why she had not asked Slater to try to find her until last year. She'd always planned to be a different person, a better person, by the time she met her twin. But that hadn't happened, and now, in Meg's eyes, Margot was a fool who had to be saved from the consequences of her own actions. The truth hurt.

Retreating to the kitchen nook, Margot put the breakfast bar between them. The physical barrier made her feel less vulnerable. Taking a drag on her cigarette, she glared at her sibling through the smoke and let defensive anger take root.

"You may think you have all the answers to turn my life around, but it's not that easy."

"I suppose if it were that easy, you would have turned it around by now. Mags."

Margot started at the use of the nickname, and for a moment, her mind went blank. A stinging in her fingers snapped her out of it, and she put the cigarette out in the stainless steel sink. She said the only thing that came to mind. "Get out."

Meg looked surprised. "What?"

"You heard me. I don't want your help. I may need it, but I'll be damned if I'll take it."

"If this is a pride thing—"

Margot's eyes blazed. "It has nothing to do with pride."

"Then what? What could be so important that you would turn down an offer of help from someone who might actually care about you?"

"How could you care about me?" Margot asked. "You don't even know me."

"You know what? Maybe I don't want to know you. Maybe I didn't want to be involved in any of this. But I didn't get to make that choice. I was dragged into it by force. I've been punched, held against my will, nearly strangled to death, arrested and shot. My best friend is probably dead because of you. Even if I wanted to walk away and never look back, I can't because your friends are too stupid to see that I'm not you."

Margot braced a hand on the counter, shaken. "How did you get shot?"

Meg passed a hand over her eyes. This wasn't going the way she had hoped, and she was beginning to realize that she'd been naïve to think that it could have gone any other way. "It doesn't matter. My best friend wasn't so lucky."

Margot edged around the counter, thinking of Holly. "What happened to her?"

"Two men tried to grab me and got her instead. The cops think she's dead." Her energy gone, Meg eased onto a stool, a jittery weakness in her knees.

"I'm sorry," Margot said.

"They thought I was you."

"That's what Slater told them. But he knew who he was really getting."

Meg watched her sister. "What does he want?"

Misery almost overtook Margot. "I betrayed him. I fell in love with another man, and he didn't like it."

"All of this has been about jealousy?"

"Revenge mostly. Slater would never admit that he was jealous."

Meg shook her head, disgusted. "Dayle was a good person." Her voice cracked. "She didn't deserve what happened to her."

"I'm sorry," Margot whispered. And she was, but she knew that would never be enough. "I don't know what else to say."

Meg didn't know what else she wanted to hear. Words weren't going to make it okay anyway. "Did you love Beau?"

Margot closed her eyes a moment, then opened them wide to hold off welling tears. "Yes. I loved him very much."

"What about the emeralds?"

The question surprised Margot. "What about them?"

"I know you stole them. I saw the tape."

"There's a tape?"

"Recorded by a camera made especially for thieves like you," Meg said.

"I'll be damned. I never even saw it."

"So where are they?"

"It hardly matters now, does it?" Margot said.

"It might."

"They're on Beau's yacht."

Meg almost smiled. "You returned them."

"Yeah, big deal," Margot said.

"So you have a guilty conscience that needs to be unloaded."

Margot nodded with a short laugh. "And while I play witness for the prosecution, who's going to protect me from Slater?"

"There are ways to stop him."

"I could testify until I'm blue in the face, and it won't save me," Margot said. "He has people everywhere."

"There are witness protection programs. I'll help you."

"I told you I don't want your help. I'll handle this my way."

"Your way is to buy a gun," Meg said.

Margot narrowed her eyes, irritated. "Is there anything you don't know about me?"

"There's plenty."

But what she did know was too much, Margot realized. And the more she knew, the more dangerous it was for her. Being here now was too dangerous for her. Who knew if Slater's thugs were about to knock down the door? She doubted they were, but she'd already taken too many chances with the lives of the few people she cared about. She was determined that Meg not get caught in any more crossfire.

Resolute, Margot crossed to her sister, who stood only a few feet from the cabin's door. "You have no idea what I'm dealing with," Margot said. "Buying a gun is the only way I know how to handle this problem. It may not be the way you would handle it, but I'm not you. I'm not anything like you. We may look alike, but we're not alike. You've made the right choices in your life, and I haven't. It's as simple as that."

"It's *not* that simple—"

"Let's get something straight," Margot cut in. She stepped closer, forcing Meg back a pace. "I don't want you here. I don't want your help. I don't want to know you. And if you don't leave now, I'll call security and tell them you barged in here and trashed the place. You'll sit in jail while I finish this. It's your choice." Reaching around Meg, she opened the door at her sister's back.

But Meg wasn't about to walk away now. "I'm sure we can work—"

"You have thirty seconds."

"Margot—"

"Twenty."

"I'm not leaving," Meg said.

"Don't make me count down from ten."

"What am I supposed to do, Margot? Tell me."

"Go home. Five."

Meg crossed her arms and locked her knees. "Forget it."

"Your determination is touching, but I'm a desperate woman who has something important to take care of, and you're in my way. Four."

"What are you going to do?" Meg asked. "Hit me?"

Margot reached past her and pulled the gun from her purse on the table by the door. "Three."

Meg laughed incredulously. "You wouldn't."

Margot pointed it at Meg's chest, resisting the need to check the safety. She knew it was on because she'd double-checked it before putting the weapon away. "You don't know me, Meg. Not at all." She cocked the gun. "Two."

"I'm not stupid enough to believe you'd shoot me."

Margot stepped toward her, and Meg backed away involuntarily. She didn't realize what she'd done until Margot smiled and lowered the gun. "One."

She slammed the door in Meg's face and flipped the lock.

Chapter 26

Ryan sensed Meg was gone the instant he woke. Scrambling out of bed, he threw open the bathroom door. Empty.

He dragged on jeans, shoes and a shirt before going above deck where he saw that she had taken the inflatable raft to shore.

"Damn it!"

Instead of driving his fist into the wall, he called Nick. "Meg's gone."

"I just saw her," Nick said. "She came to see Margot."

"Where is she now?"

"I thought she was headed back to you. She looked upset, so I didn't bother her. Everything looked fine otherwise. No one's hanging around Margot. No one followed Meg."

"How long ago?"

"Fifteen minutes."

"She should have been back here by now."

"Damn, Ryan. I didn't think to—"

"Just keep an eye on Margot until I get there."

Throwing the phone aside, he whipped the life raft out of its compartment and pulled the cord to inflate it.

Within minutes, he was pounding on the door to cabin eighteen.

Margot yanked open the door and froze.

Ryan stared at her, the words stuck in his throat. She looked so much like Meg that it stole his breath. Brushing past her, he scanned the room. "Where is she?"

Margot knew who he meant but was too stunned by his appearance—and his resemblance to Beau—to respond right away.

He stalked up to her. "Where the hell is she?"

"You're Ryan."

"You're the bitch who got my brother killed. Where's Meg?"

"I didn't know Slater was going to kill him."

He jerked her forward by the front of her sweatshirt. "I don't give a fuck at the moment. Just tell me where she is."

"I don't know. I suggested she go home and forget about all of this."

"If anything happens to her, I'll break your neck before Slater Nielsen can get anywhere near you." He stormed out.

Margot watched him go, a pang of envy shooting through her. Oh, to still be loved like that.

Nick stood at the end of the walk, waiting, his baseball cap in his hands.

Ryan said, "Call the feds and tell them where Margot is."

Meg didn't think about Margot or Ryan or anything but climbing the steps to her front door. Her brain was too muddled to sort through it. All she wanted was to sleep.

When she stood before the door, realizing she didn't have her key, she saw that it didn't matter. The door was ajar. She pushed it open to destruction.

Plants had been dumped out of their pots, the dirt spread out as if someone had sifted through it. The bookcase had been tipped, books and pictures scattered, the television

226

dumped on the floor. Even her mother's dollhouse had been smashed. Next to it, MOMS KRAFT BOCKS had been reduced to sticks.

A low moan came from deep in her throat as she sank to her knees. Rocking forward, she dug her fingers into the carpet, closed her eyes against the sorrow. How had everything gotten so messed up? What had gone so wrong?

"Meg."

She raised her head to see Ryan standing just inside the front door, his forehead creased with concern. Rage clouded her vision. She was surrounded by the debris of her life. Control had been stripped from her. And he had helped.

Going to her, he reached down to help her up, but as she rose, she pushed him away and swung at him with an open hand. Her palm struck his cheek with a crack.

He flinched back but made no other move.

She hit him again, a dry sob catching in her throat. When she blindly struck out a third time, he caught her wrist, his fingers gentle but firm.

She jerked free. "This is my life," she said. "Take a good look."

"I'm sorry."

She turned her back on the apology, swiping at the moisture in her eyes. Her cheeks burned with shame for striking out at him when he had done nothing more than try to love her. She fought off the need to scream. "There's nothing left," she whispered. "Nothing."

"It can be replaced," Ryan said.

She whirled on him, seizing on the anger to hold back the grief. "The TV can be replaced. The microwave can be replaced. The pictures even. My peace of mind can't be replaced. Losing your best friend and getting shot kind of messes with that after a while. And what's it all been for,

Ryan? We haven't accomplished anything but lose the people we love."

She kicked at the remains of a picture frame, dissatisfied when it merely disintegrated into more pieces. A pace away, she picked up a jagged chair leg and swung it at the remains of the television. Glass shattered. She spun for something more to batter.

Before she found it, Ryan snatched her into his arms. He hung on, his arms strong around her until she melted into him. Her breath hitched as he stroked a hand through her hair.

"Margot didn't want me," she said, beating a loose fist against his shoulder. "She didn't want me."

He tightened his arms around her. "I'm sorry, Meg. God, I'm so sorry."

She broke the embrace before the precarious grip she had on her self-control shattered.

He let go, hurt by the rejection. He needed her so much, but she didn't seem to need, or want, him. "Meg, please."

"She didn't keep the emeralds. I know where they are."

He rubbed both hands over his face. "That doesn't change—"

"I love you. You're the only one I've ever loved so much I can't think." Crying now, she said it again. "I love you." It came out easily, and she repeated it a third time, realizing that she had never spoken the words aloud to anyone before him.

He buried his face in her hair. "Thank God." It was all he could manage.

Meg curled her fingers against his back. "I'm sorry I keep pushing you away. What I feel for you scares me. I'm so afraid something will happen to tear it away from me like everything else—"

"This is all very touching."

They sprang apart. The man they each knew as Turner Scott gave them a toothy grin. "Unfortunately, I have work to do," he said, and lunged.

Ryan wasted any advantage he would have had over Turner by thrusting Meg out of the way. She caught herself against the wall as Ryan took a stunning blow to the jaw. He went down with a thud, and Turner towered over him, plunging a hand into his jacket.

Throwing herself at his back, Meg hooked her arms around his neck. He jabbed an elbow into her ribs. She fell back and was scrambling to her knees, groping for a weapon, when Ryan wobbled to his feet. Turner slugged him in the midsection, and Ryan doubled over. The thug karate-chopped him across the back of the neck before slamming a knee into his kidneys.

Grasping the splintered chair leg that she had used on the television, she swung it at Turner's head. It connected with a jarring crack, and he pivoted toward her.

She swung again. He caught the makeshift weapon with one hand, grinning, and walked her backward until her back hit the wall. Panic stuck in her throat.

Turner twisted the weapon in a direction her wrist would not bend. One final jerk, and she released it with a grimace. He trapped her against the wall with his shoulder and pulled out a gun. "This will be fun."

Over his shoulder, Meg saw Ryan staggering to his feet. She went for Turner's eyes, but he grabbed her wrist, yanked her around so that she faced Ryan, and locked a forearm across her throat. He pressed the gun into her back, where Ryan wouldn't be able to see it.

Meg saw blood trickling from the corner of Ryan's mouth, saw a red welt at his temple. Black spots floated across her vision at the sight of the blood on him, but she blinked them away. "He has a—"

Turned jerked her head back, choking off the warning, and her air.

Ryan's eyes went black with rage, his hands clenching into fists at his sides. "Let her go." He took a menacing step forward.

Meg dug her fingers into the arm against her throat, sought to catch Ryan's eye. But he had focused his hatred on Turner, as if he knew that seeing her struggle for air would undo him.

She felt Turner flex his gun hand behind her back, heard the slight but distinct click of the hammer being pulled back. She gasped out a desperate attempt to say the word "gun."

Too late. Ryan lunged.

Meg didn't hear the gunshot.

She just saw Ryan reel back. He hit the wall and slid down it, his eyes wide with shock. When he hit the floor, his head flopped forward. A broad streak of blood defined the path that his body had taken down the wall.

Suddenly free, Meg staggered forward, a black curtain closing in at the edges of the world. "Oh, God. Oh, God."

Dropping to her knees at his side, she gripped his arm with a shaking hand. Blood had stained his shirt from his shoulder across the front of his chest, had spattered his neck and face with bright red droplets. There was so much of it she couldn't tell where he'd been hit. "Oh God, *no*."

Turner hooked a hand under her arm and hauled her up. Choking out a protest, she tried to get away from him, slapping, kicking and screaming at him. Ryan needed help. Ryan was bleeding. *Dying*.

Shoving her against the wall with one hand, Turner pinned her there with a hand on her throat. He pointed the gun at her nose, and she froze, comprehending that if she was dead, Ryan would most certainly die, too.

"What's going on here?"

Turner turned at the sound of his partner's voice, and Meg shoved at him with a strength born of desperation and fury. He stumbled back, and she shoved again. Off-balance already, Turner went down on one knee and ducked his head as Meg fell on him and rammed a fist at his face. She punched him again and again until strong hands seized her by the arms and lifted her away.

She saw blond hair and a scar as she writhed against this new assailant, screamed in frustration when he wrestled her to the floor and pinned her on her stomach, a knee in her back. With her cheek smashed against the carpet, she saw Ryan propped against the wall, blood pooling under him. She squirmed desperately under the weight on her back.

"Help me, asshole," Dillon shouted at his partner. "Get the cord from the blinds."

He let up with the knee, but before she could take advantage, he wrenched her arms behind her back. "Tie her. Hurry, damn it."

Turner wrapped the cord around her wrists and jerked it tight. Meg released a sharp gasp of pain, her head arching up off the floor.

"Not so tight. Jesus," Dillon snapped.

The cord loosened slightly.

"Gag her, too."

Turner stuffed something, a dishcloth from the texture of it, in her mouth and secured it with a bandanna.

Bound and gagged, Meg let her cheek fall to the carpet and lay still. She focused on Ryan, on his chest. She couldn't tell if he was breathing. Hair fell across his forehead and into his eyes, but he showed no signs of awareness.

The knee in her back disappeared as Dillon got to his feet. "What the hell were you thinking, Turner?"

"The guy was threatening me," Turner said.

"He doesn't even have a weapon, dickhead. Just get her out of here."

Hands caught at Meg's shoulders, wrenched her to her feet. Turner tossed her over his shoulder and headed for the door.

Away from Ryan.

She bucked on his shoulder, beat her head against his back. Even when his shoulder ground into the tender part of her abdomen, she continued to squirm. Unfazed, Turner carried her down the steps and to a dark blue van parked in the driveway. He pitched her carelessly into the back of it.

Meg rolled, gained her knees and lunged for the doors as he climbed in. Hooking his hands around one of her elbows, he dragged her farther into the van, then, gripping her shoulder, forced her forward and down. "On your stomach," he ordered.

She was no match for him, even if her hands had been free. But lying still was too much like giving up. As he turned to shut the doors, she flopped onto her back and kicked at his butt with both feet. He stumbled forward, smacking his head on the door. Calmly, he closed the doors, but when he faced her, his cheeks were bright red. Blood streamed from a split in his lip where she had struck him earlier.

"Big mistake, bitch," he said, and backhanded her.

Her head snapped to one side, but she clung to consciousness by a thread. If she let go, Ryan would die.

Dillon got into the van and started it. He glanced back as he steered the van into traffic. "Get rid of the gag. I have some questions."

Her brain worked sluggishly as Turner loosened the bandanna and removed the gag. The moment it was gone, she started bargaining. "I have money. Tons of it. It's all yours if you—"

"Shut up," Dillon said.

"All you have to do is call help for him. We don't have to go back. Please, he's going to bleed to—"

"Turner?"

Turner leveled a gun at her head.

"See Turner's gun?" Dillon asked.

Meg steeled herself. If Ryan died, she had nothing to lose anyway. "Use a pay phone. It could never be traced to you."

Turner raised the gun as if to strike her and Meg braced for the blow.

"No!" Dillon shouted. "We need her conscious if we're going to get our hands on those fucking emeralds. Sit down. When I'm done, you can play."

Turner obediently sat on the wheel well and grinned down at her, his tongue flicking over his lips.

She watched him, aware of the way her shirt had bunched up to reveal bare skin. A sick new dread crawled through her.

Dillon said, "Where are the stones?"

She kept her gaze on Turner. "I'll tell you if you go back and help Ryan."

"It's too late," Dillon said.

Her senses sharpened, and she shifted on an elbow so she could see the back of his head, Turner's threat forgotten. "What do you mean it's too late?"

"Just what I said. It's too damn late."

"No." A crushing pain paralyzed her, as if a steel pole had been driven through her chest. Closing her eyes, Meg's muscles went slack.

Ryan was dead.

Chapter 27

"Looking for me?"

Margot whirled, her breath jamming in her chest when she saw Slater Nielsen standing before her in the hallway outside his study. "How did you—"

"Did you honestly think I wouldn't adjust my security systems after training you to evade them all these years? You were tripping silent alarms all over the place. Very sloppy." He let his gaze rove over her, as if he had missed her. Then, smiling, he gestured toward his office door. "Please, be my guest."

She entered his office, feeling him watch her every move. Its décor—a heavy mahogany desk, dark brown leather sofa and chairs, gleaming hardwood floor and a mural of a sailboat on a glass-like lake—was the same yet seemed different. She had never entered this room with the conviction that she would not leave it alive.

Behind her, Slater put a hand on her shoulder to stop her. "If you wouldn't mind."

His hands were brisk and thorough as they moved over her arms, down one jean-clad leg and up the other. He discovered the gun she had tucked into the waistband at her back and took it. "Have a seat."

Calm washed over her as she lowered herself to the sofa. It was out of her hands now, and she was relieved. She no longer had to worry about whether she would be able to pull the trigger when it was time.

"Welcome home, Margot," Slater said.

He had changed slightly. The wrinkles at his eyes seemed more pronounced, and his thick, dark hair had more gray in it. His body, however, looked trimmer than it had three months ago, more toned. The designer suit he wore fit more snug in the shoulders, looser at the waist. His blue eyes, a startling icy hue enhanced by the tan he maintained year-round, were framed by long, black lashes that Margot had often envied. He had a tiny dark mole on his cheek where women preferred a beauty mark. Her gun looked small and ineffective in his large hands.

"I trust you had an uneventful trip here," Slater said.

"Can we cut the bullshit?"

He arched a salt-and-pepper eyebrow. "I never considered our relationship bullshit, Margot."

She glanced away, long enough to get her nerve back. "Is it the emeralds you want?"

"You think all this has been about emeralds? I thought you had outgrown your naïveté."

"Then what? What do you want from me?"

"Margot, honey, I never wanted anything from you that you weren't willing to give. Twelve years ago, I gave you choices, and you made them."

She rose, intending to confront him face to face. But when she stood in front of him, dwarfed by his superior height, she retreated to a pair of French doors that opened into a flower garden. She gazed through the panes at carefully tended red roses, protected from the harsh sun by large shade trees. "You gave me a lot, Slater, but you never gave me choices.

You told me what you wanted and I did it."

"I don't recall you ever questioning what I was asking you to do, my dear. How did you get a conscience?"

She turned. "You sent me after the wrong set of emeralds."

Some satisfaction nudged her at his frown. He put his hands, along with her gun, into his pockets and rocked back on his heels. "Well, that brings us to what happens now, doesn't it? We both know that resuming the relationship we had before Mr. Kama is impossible." He pursed his lips. "You once asked me why I chose Beau Kama, and now I'll tell you. He was a test."

"What do you mean?"

"I suspected that your heart wasn't in the game anymore, that perhaps you were growing tired of me. So I tested you with a rich, handsome man who was also, of all things, a nice guy. You were right when you questioned my choice of target. Mr. Kama didn't fit the profile, and you fell for him the moment you met him. You can't imagine how angry that made me, Margot."

His smile didn't touch his eyes as he crossed to her. Withdrawing a pack of cigarettes from an inside jacket pocket, he shook one out. "Cigarette?"

Margot started to refuse, then accepted it. She needed something to distract her from the realization that she had stumbled into his trap, killing the man she loved along the way.

Slater produced a lighter that he had once told her was solid gold and lit the cigarette for her. She sucked the air into her lungs, narrowing her eyes as she focused on the buzz and its accompanying calm.

Slater watched her, waiting for her to exhale. After the smoke swirled through the air between them, he said, "Now, the options are somewhat muddied. You've been flirting with death for a while now. Defying Mr. Bloodhound was not a bright move and unlike you. He's still in jail, in case you're wondering."

"I hope he rots there."

"He just might." He waved a dismissive hand. "But we were talking about you. Coming out of hiding concerns me, Margot. I had no idea where you were. Did you know that?"

"I figured as much since none of your thugs were pounding on my door."

"Yet here you are, trying to sneak into my home with a gun." He paused as he sauntered to a bar stocked with ice and the finest Scotch. "Drink?"

She shook her head.

"My conclusion," he went on, "is that you've resigned yourself to your fate. You know I can't let anyone get away with double-crossing me because then my other employees might be tempted to be less loyal." He splashed liquor into a glass and swirled it before sipping. "What it boils down to is this: How do I deal with you when what you expect is for me to kill you? We both know how much I like to behave in unexpected ways." He smiled as warmly as he was capable, showing perfect white teeth.

Margot had felt those teeth gently nibbling at her bottom lip and even at her breasts, but now they looked like they could rip open her jugular.

"Why don't you sit down, Margot? You look a bit pale."

"I'll stand."

His smile widened. "Do I need to tell you how much I'm enjoying this, Margot?"

The way he kept using her name aggravated her.

"The key, naturally, would be to take something from you that you care about," he went on. "Mr. Kama filled that bill nicely, but I didn't get to see your face when you found him, so I feel a bit cheated. Would you like to know the alternative I have in mind?"

Margot held her breath, cigarette forgotten.

"I've found her, Margot. Just like you asked me to. About the same time that Mr. Bloodhound tracked you down in Wisconsin, I sent Turner and Dillon to Fort Myers Beach to collect your sister. Of course, I let them think they were collecting you. Why bother to explain the finer points to a couple of half-wits? Unfortunately, your sister proved to be a bit slippery. There also was a nasty shooting incident in which one of my associates got a bit overzealous, but luckily for all of us, she pulled through that. Overall, I've expended quite a bit of manpower keeping track of her for you."

She couldn't respond, rooted to the floor. *Meg is safe. He's bluffing.*

Slater went to his desk, picked up an ashtray and crossed to her. He waited while she stubbed out the cigarette, so close she heard him breathing. "Now," he said, "the logical thing would be to bring her here so the two of you can meet. Would you like that?"

A bluff. Please, God, let it be a bluff.

He chuckled. "You're not answering, but your face is saying no." He leaned in. "Doesn't that defeat the purpose of me spending my hard-earned money to have your sister found for you?" His lips were poised less than an inch above the curve of her cheekbone. "I'm not getting much feedback here."

"What did you do?" she asked in a husky voice.

"What did *I* do? This is about what *you* did, Margot." His lips brushed her cheek.

She flinched back. "She doesn't have anything to do with this."

He nodded, thoughtful. "True. She's an innocent. But you're not. And you care about her."

"I don't even know her."

"But you asked me to find her. You planned to care. And anyone you care about has everything to do with this. Death would be too easy for you."

"You're . . . you're—"

"At a loss for words?" he asked. "See? You do care."

The telephone rang. He moved to answer it, and Margot had only a moment to be relieved he was on the other side of the room before he fastened an intense stare on her.

"I see," he said into the phone. Watching her, he opened the top drawer of his desk, placed her gun inside and closed it with his hip. "I'll have someone meet you at the dock." He hung up. "Turner tells me he and Dillon will be making a special delivery very soon."

Chapter 28

Ryan regained consciousness in the emergency room. Disoriented and weak from loss of blood, it took him several tries to communicate to the medical staff that he didn't give a damn that a bullet was still lodged in his shoulder, that what he wanted more than a painkiller was to know who brought him in.

"An ambulance, sir," the nurse said, a picture of patience.

"Was there a woman with me? Dark hair, green eyes—"

"No one was with you, sir. A neighbor called in the emergency. I'm going to give you something to calm you down."

"No. Get me a phone."

"Sir—"

"I need a phone, damn it." He grabbed her wrist before she could shove a needle into his arm. "Get. Me. A. Phone."

Another nurse thrust a cell phone into his free hand, and he released the one with the needle. "Thank you."

He dialed Nick's number with one hand while both women went to work cleaning up his shoulder. Once his friend answered, Ryan barked his name into the phone and choked on a hiss of breath when one of the nurses poured antiseptic into his bullet wound.

"Ryan? Is that you? Jesus, where are you? I lost Margot. I

couldn't get a decent signal on my cell phone, so I went back to my cabin to call the feds on a land line. She slipped out while I was gone. I'm sorry, man. I feel terrible."

Ryan finally got his breath. "Nick, I'm at the ER. Come get me."

"What happened?"

"The bastards got Meg."

Meg fought them again when they transferred her from the van to a midsize boat, but her struggles must have seemed pathetic because they didn't acknowledge them. After reapplying the gag, they locked her in an empty storage compartment below deck.

In the dark, she began working at her bonds, wincing every time the band of Margot's watch dug into her flesh. She had no idea what she would do if she got free. She only knew that if she could do it before the boat left shore, she might, just might, have a chance of getting to Ryan.

She refused to believe he was dead. The thug had just been playing with her head, she reasoned. He'd been trying to frighten her into telling him what he wanted to know.

Only a few short minutes passed before the boat's engines roared to life. Meg fought frantically against the cord wrapped around her wrists. She didn't feel it biting into her flesh as she twisted and pulled. She didn't feel the intense heat. Didn't know that sweat raced down the sides of her face.

The boat took off and bumped through some rough waves before leveling off.

The fight drained out of her by slow degrees. She went limp, her wrists awash in her own blood, and closed her eyes.

"What do you remember?" Nick asked.

Ryan winced as he steered with one hand and tried to adjust his arm in the sling. A doctor had removed the bullet and given him painkillers, but the discomfort was still intense. "The son of a bitch shot me. The next thing I knew I was in the ER. He took her." *Please let her still be alive.* He glared at the notebook computer on Nick's lap. "What's taking it so long?"

"It has to boot up. You're sure she's still wearing the watch?"

"Yes. I think so." Damn it, he couldn't remember. His head was killing him.

"Okay, here we go," Nick said. He tapped keys, manipulated the button that controlled the mouse. "It's working. Holy shit, there she is." His voice rose with excitement.

Ryan strained to see the computer screen, almost driving off the road in the process.

Nick grabbed the dashboard. "Watch where you're going."

Ryan focused on the street, blinking back the moisture that had blurred his vision. "Where is she?"

Nick squinted at the screen, his fingers flying over the keyboard. "Let me check the coordinates."

"Come on, damn it. Hurry."

"She's moving. Looks like she's in the Gulf."

"In the Gulf?" Ryan asked. "How can that be?"

"They must be transporting her by boat."

"Nielsen's got an island. Didn't you say he's got an island?"

"Yeah, it's private," Nick said. "The feds have been trying to locate it for months."

"That must be where he's taking her," Ryan said. "We need a boat. A fast one."

"We can take mine. It's at the marina." Yanking out his cell phone, Nick flipped it open.

"What are you doing?"

"I'm calling Delilah at the FBI," Nick said. "She can call out the troops, meet us there."

"No, that's too risky. I don't want—"

"We can't take on Nielsen and his henchmen by ourselves, Ryan. We need help."

Meg gauged that half an hour passed before the boat slowed and she heard the hull thump against what she assumed was a dock. She didn't move when the compartment door opened and Turner ducked into the area. His cowboy boots clunked hollowly on the wooden floor before he flipped on a light.

Meg blinked against the brightness as he moved, wolf-like, to stand at her feet. Curling his fingers into the front of her shirt, he pulled her, almost gently, to her feet and removed the gag. "How are you at begging, baby?" he asked.

Meg showed no reaction when he grabbed her breast. His grip was strong, bringing tears to her eyes, but she waited. Waited even as a grin spread across his mouth, and his eyes narrowed with desire. "Damn, you're going to be a sweet piece," he said.

He locked his arms around her and drew her flush up against him. Stiffening, Meg almost panicked before she felt his fingers working at the knot in the cord that bound her wrists. "You're going to need your hands for this," he said, his breath hot on her neck.

At the same moment that her hands, slack from lack of circulation, fell free, she seized Turner's shoulders and drove a knee into his crotch. He dropped to the floor with a howl and curved his body around the pain. One side of his jacket flopped open, revealing the butt of a gun.

In two scrambling strides, she was on him, her hands inside his jacket. Her fingers closed on the gun, and she yanked it free, triumphant for only an instant before a shadow came at her from the side.

She fumbled with the gun with hands that were numb and clumsy. Too late. Strong hands snatched her around the waist and heaved her against the wall.

She broke the fall to the floor with a hand that bent unnaturally back. Agony shot up her arm and into her shoulder, and the compartment took a slow, sickening spin. Seeing Dillon barreling at her, she raised the gun and jerked the trigger. Nothing happened. *Damn it, damn it, damn it.* It wasn't cocked.

Dillon grabbed her by the collar and savagely slammed her against the wall. Her back cracked with the impact, and when he let go, she landed hard on her butt, pain zipping up her spine. She held onto the gun by sheer luck. As he bent down to grab her again, she aimed it at his face and cocked it.

His eyes crossed when he focused on the weapon. "Shit."

Meg would have smiled, but her head was spinning, little firecrackers of pain exploding in her back and wrist. She cradled her injured wrist in her lap, fighting to recover the wind he had knocked from her. "Back off."

He obeyed, raising his hands palms out. "Easy, easy," he said.

Turner groaned as he got to his knees.

"Tell him to be still," Meg said, scrunching up one shoulder to stop the sweat running down the side of her neck. She was soaked with it.

"Stay where you are, man," Dillon said.

Turner lurched to his feet on the other side of the room.

Meg leaned her head back against the wall to catch her breath. "Tell him."

"Don't do anything stupid, Turner," Dillon said. "The lady's got your gun."

"Fuck me," Turner said.

"We're both screwed if you don't behave," Dillon said.

Meg braced an elbow on the wall behind her and used it to help her get to her feet. Her legs were weak, as if she had just ridden a bicycle up a steep hill. Pain was bursting in her side and back. The son of a bitch had probably busted some ribs when he'd thrown her into the wall. She shoved the weakness back. "Get your hands up."

Dillon obeyed as sweat tracked his scar to the corner of his mouth.

"Where are we?" Meg asked.

"Island in the Gulf."

"Slater Nielsen lives on the island?"

"He owns it." Dillon shot a nervous glance at Turner, who was dancing from one foot to the other in agitation. "Be still, you idiot. You're making her nervous."

"What happened to my friend?" Meg asked.

Dillon gave her a baffled look. "Turner shot him."

She bit back the grief that surged to the surface, forced herself to focus. "The woman you kidnapped. Her name is Dayle. Where is she?"

Dillon wet his lips. "I had orders."

"Is she dead?"

"Listen, lady, the boss told us to get rid of her," Dillon said.

"Give me a straight fucking answer. Is she dead?"

He swallowed. "Yes."

She took a moment to absorb that, tempted to pull the

trigger and find solace in vengeance. Both men watched her in trepidation.

Gesturing with the gun, she said, "Turn around."

Dillon hesitated.

"Slowly. Any fast move I'll consider a threat. I'm not kidding. I have nothing to lose."

"All right, all right," he said. "Just take it easy."

He lunged for the gun.

She jerked back from him in shock and felt his hands clamp around hers. They both hit the wall, and the gun went off. His body twitched once before he dragged her to the floor under him. Squirming violently, feeling the warm rush of blood, she was mindless to anything but getting out from under him. Blood was everywhere. On him. On her. She pushed at his chest but couldn't budge it. She saw his eyes open and staring.

Her body arched like a bow, and she screamed. Kept screaming even as Turner pulled Dillon's body off. He tried to grasp her arm to pull her up, but she hit him in the face. He reeled back, then came at her again. Raising the gun over his head, he swung it down at her.

A blinding flash of pain at her temple lit up the inside of her head. The light went out.

"How close are we?" Ryan shouted over the roar of the speedboat's engine. Visibility in the dark was minimum, but a moon that was almost full provided some relief. The wind against his face was cold, but his shoulder was on fire. His stomach burned hotter, however, with fear for Meg.

"Maybe a mile," Nick shouted back. He was standing next to Ryan, hunched over the computer balanced near the boat's controls. "Keep heading west."

Ryan gritted his teeth as the boat plowed through a large

wave, jarring his shoulder.

"Are you sure you're up for this?" Nick asked.

"If he touches her, I'll kill him."

"Jesus, Ryan, don't say that."

"I'm saying it because I'd go through you or anyone else to do it, so don't get in my way."

Chapter 29

Margot paced the bedroom. Slater had told her to go to bed, as if his brutes were not about to deliver her sister for one express purpose. To die.

She paused in her pacing as nausea rolled through her. When the sickness passed, she sat on the edge of the bed, a fist curled against her stomach, aware of the pink satin comforter that wrinkled under her. She hated everything about this room. Its pinkness was a joke. She had only wanted what she had not had as a child—pretty, girl things. Dolls and dollhouses, frilly dresses and real china tea sets.

The door slammed inward as if it had been kicked in, and she jolted to her feet. Turner Scott stood there, staring at her in shock. Her sister hung limp as a rag doll in his arms, her head fallen back over his forearm, one arm dangling. She was covered with blood.

"Oh my God," Margot breathed.

Turner carried Meg into the room, his gaze fixed on Margot's face. "What the fuck?"

"What did you do to her?" Margot demanded.

"I didn't do shit to her," he said, dropping Meg on the pink satin comforter. She didn't react to the rough handling.

"Is she breathing?" Gingerly touching her fingers to Meg's

throat, Margot felt a strong but erratic pulse. Then her gaze fell on the raw skin circling both of her sister's wrists. She'd been tied up. Margot whirled, ready to take a swing at Turner, but he had retreated to the door.

"Who is she?" he asked.

"She's an innocent woman," Margot said. "You brought an innocent woman here to die."

"If she's related to you, she's hardly innocent."

"That's warped and you know it."

"The bitch killed Dillon. If Slater hadn't wanted her so bad, she'd already be dead." He walked out, slamming the door behind him.

Behind her, Meg stirred, a low moan escaping her lips.

The sight of the blood brought Margot's nausea storming back, and she put a hand on the bedpost to steady herself. When she had her stomach under control, she bent over her sister and tried to locate the source of the blood. It took her several moments to realize it wasn't Meg's.

Her knees weak with relief, she went into the bathroom and wet a towel. Then, sitting on the edge of the bed, she wiped blood from Meg's face. At her temple, she discovered a nasty bump. "Oh, baby, this is not good," she said.

Meg's eyes fluttered open, and she stared up at the ceiling, disoriented.

Margot touched a knuckle to her sister's cheek. "Hey." Meg's gaze shifted to her, and Margot tried to give her a reassuring smile. "You're okay. Everything's okay."

A long moment passed before Margot realized that the stare Meg had fixed on her was vacant. "Meg?"

"They're both dead."

Margot flinched, and the knot in her stomach tightened. "Who?"

"Dayle and Ryan." Meg braced herself on her elbows.

"They killed Dayle and Ryan," she said. A shudder shook her, and she sagged back to the bed. Rolling her head away from Margot, she curled her fingers around the corner of the pillow. "They're gone."

Margot was back in Beau's house, stumbling around with his blood on her hands, so racked by grief she could barely walk. The grief she had felt then was just as intense as what she felt now, but another emotion accompanied it. This one had teeth. Vengeance.

"We're going to get even," Margot said, leaving the bed. She paced to the foot of it and back again. "I don't know how, but we're going to rip his fucking heart out. That *bastard.*"

Meg's eyes slid closed. "It won't matter."

Margot leaned over her sister. "Did you hear what I said? We're going to make him pay." Her voice rose. "Are you listening, damn it?"

Meg didn't move.

"Don't do this to me." Margot glared into her sister's pale face. "I want you to get up. Get up right now."

Nothing. Not even a twitch.

Margot went to the dresser and found a pack of cigarettes and a lighter. Her fingers were clumsy as she put a cigarette between trembling lips and lit it. "You're next, you know," she said in a shaking voice. "He's going to put a gun to your head and make me watch while he pulls the trigger. He might even torture you a little first. It's all about payback. Is that what you want? Is it? Answer me, damn you." She put the cigarette out. "Damn it, I'm not going to let you give up. You're all my kid has going for it."

Grasping Meg by the shoulders, she hauled her into a sitting position. Then, locking her hands under Meg's arms, Margot half-carried, half-dragged her across the room and into the bathroom.

"You're not broken," Margot said as she maneuvered her sister into the shower stall. Pinning her against the wall, she grasped Meg's cheeks with one hand. "Do you hear me? I refuse to let you retreat this way. Catatonic will not cut it, Meg." She waited for a response but got none.

"*Goddamn it.*" She fumbled with the cold water.

When the water struck her, Meg jerked. But Margot held her and directed the water onto her. She felt her sister begin to shudder, felt her own shaking. Felt everything start to come apart inside her. First, Beau. Then, Holly. And now . . . when would it end? When would it be over? Would her child ultimately become a victim as well?

"Do you think this is what I wanted?" she asked on a hitching breath. "All I ever wanted was for someone to treat me right." She clamped her eyes shut against the tears. Damn it, she couldn't afford to cry. "Before Beau, Slater was the only one in my whole pathetic life who tried to make me happy. I didn't want to see that it was bad because I desperately wanted for it to be real. God, I was a stupid, *stupid* kid."

Opening her eyes, she looked at Meg, whose teeth had begun to chatter. Sorrow tore through her. "I can't get through this without you," Margot said. "Are you hearing me? I can't get through this without you."

It took her a moment to realize that Meg had focused on her. Easing her weight back, Margot was suddenly self-conscious as Meg leaned her head against the tile. Margot touched her sister's hair, tried to offer comfort, but Meg lifted her shoulder against the contact. She pushed weakly at her until Margot released her.

Covering her face with trembling hands, Meg slid down the wall. At Margot's feet, she rested her forehead on her knees and took several deep, gasping breaths.

Margot shut off the water. Silence filled the bathroom,

marred only by the trickle of water down the drain. She reached out to touch her sister but paused with her fingers an inch above her shoulder. Her throat tightened, and she pulled her hand back. "I'm sorry. I know it doesn't help."

When Meg raised her head, her eyes were dry. The dull pain in them seemed to Margot far worse than hysteria, far more volatile.

"What are we going to do to make him pay?" Meg asked.

"It's the partner of Turner Scott," Ryan said, nudging the dead man's arm with the toe of his shoe. He and Nick had stumbled over the body tossed onto the beach a few paces from where they had slogged through shallow water to shore. They'd left the boat, dark and silent, anchored several yards out.

"Shot in the chest," Nick said.

Ryan choked back the need to be sick and lowered his head.

"You all right?" Nick asked.

"Damn it."

"Want to rest a minute?"

Ryan clenched his jaw against the terror that they would come across Meg's body disposed in a similar manner. His stomach heaved, and he threw up in the weeds.

"Let's rest," Nick said.

"No! I'm fine."

"Ryan, you're about to collapse."

"I'm fine," he repeated, and took a deep breath. "Let's find the house."

But Nick was pivoting away from the path leading inland. "What's that?" he said, pointing. "Out there on the water."

Ryan squinted against the dark. "Lights."

"A shitload of lights. It's got to be the feds."

"Excellent. Let's go."

"Hell, no. We're waiting for them," Nick said.

"I'm not waiting," Ryan wheezed. "Meg doesn't have time for this."

"I'll coldcock you if I have to, pal. We don't even have a decent weapon."

Ryan jerked his chin at the stun gun Nick clutched in one hand. "What do you call that?"

"I sure as hell don't call it decent."

"Keep it handy anyway," Ryan said, plowing into the underbrush.

Nick, whose only other choice was to abandon his friend, followed.

Chapter 30

After the shower, Margot forced Meg to stand still for an inventory of her injuries. Myriad bruises and welts flared in red, black and blue along her arms, legs and back, and Margot worried about cracked ribs and internal injuries.

"How's your wrist feel?" Margot asked as she removed Meg's watch and examined where its silver band had made shallow cuts in her flesh. "Do you think it's broken?"

Meg focused on the watch in Margot's hand. "That's yours."

Margot frowned as she flipped it over in her hand. She'd never seen it before. "No, it's not." Setting it aside, she went back to her examination. The knot on her sister's head troubled her more than anything, and she could tell it hurt like a son of a bitch every time Meg moved her head.

As Meg secured her robe, Margot told her to sit on the bed while she fetched aspirin and water from the bathroom. "You probably have a concussion," she said, handing them over.

Meg swallowed the pills and didn't respond.

Margot looked into her twin's shell-shocked eyes and felt hatred for Slater, ugly and potent, slide through her stomach. It was bad enough what he'd done to Beau. But this . . . "The bastard won't know what hit him," Margot said.

Meg left the bed in favor of the window. It was dark outside, the grounds illuminated by several spotlights. A healthy wind blew through the trees that dotted the yard, and she watched them bend, snap straight, then bend again as another gust struck them.

Taking jeans and a green polo shirt from the closet, Margot dropped them on the bed. "Why don't you get dressed?"

Meg nodded but didn't move.

Margot retreated to an easy chair in the corner and lit a cigarette with hands that had steadied. She'd changed into black leggings and a snug, white T-shirt.

Meg watched her sister brush at a piece of tobacco that clung to the hem of her shirt and felt fury begin to build. She latched onto it, used it to slap back the grief. "How can you just sit there and smoke?"

Margot straightened her back. Putting the cigarette out, she was careful not to be as fierce about it as she wanted to be. "You don't know me very well," she said. "Please don't make snap judgments about the way I handle a situation."

Meg could have hit her. The desire almost propelled her across the room at her sister, but she turned her back to clamp down on the violent urge. It wasn't Margot's fault that Slater Nielsen was a murderous bastard. She had made bad choices, and now she was paying for them. They both were.

Bracing on the sill, Meg pulled in a shaky breath. Fatigue hummed through her system. It was difficult just to hold her head up.

"I don't blame you if you hate me," Margot said.

Meg let her breath out, closed her eyes.

"I mean, I've made a mess of things," she went on. "I guess I got stupid for a moment, thinking I could be happy, thinking Beau and I could—" She choked.

In the reflection of the window, Meg saw Margot press impatient fingers against her eyes.

"Christ, I'm pathetic," Margot said.

Meg gripped the windowsill so hard her knuckles ached. "What do you want me to say, Margot? That it's okay that you were so easily manipulated? It's not okay. People are dead. Good people." Unlocking the window, she jammed it open, and a chill wind rushed into the room. "How far is the drop?"

When she got no response, Meg turned to see that her twin's emotional moment had ebbed. In its wake was the toughness that Margot had let slip.

"I'm only human," Margot said, crossing to her. "I didn't have the opportunities that you had. I know you don't think that's a good enough excuse, but I didn't steal the food out of a starving kid's mouth or snatch a little old lady's purse. I stole from rich, insured people. I know it's not right, but you act like every time I emptied a safe, I slashed someone's throat. Well, *I* didn't *kill* anybody. I did what I did to survive. If I hadn't started working for Slater, I probably would have become a prostitute. And maybe in your eyes, I am a whore, because I slept with Slater and he gave me things, not in return like you think, but because he wanted to."

Elbowing Meg out of the way, she slammed the window shut. "It's three floors, so don't even think about jumping."

She paced back to the bed, still furious, her fists clenched at her sides. "Damn it, I'm a decent person." She rounded on Meg and jabbed a finger at her chest. "*You* might not think so, and, twenty years from now, my kid might not think so, but damn it, I don't deserve what's happened to me any more than you do. The only crime I committed that cost anyone anything more than cold hard cash was trusting someone who I thought cared for me. And not caring for him as much as I cared for someone else. So get off my back."

Margot headed for the dresser and the pack of cigarettes. She lit one with jerky movements, meeting her sister's green eyes as smoke curled around her head. Meg was giving her a strange look.

"What?" Margot snapped.

"Your kid?"

Her eyes teared up. "Yeah, I'm pregnant. Ain't that the pits."

Bracing a hand on the wall, Meg rubbed the tips of her fingers under the knot at her temple. Ryan would have enjoyed being an uncle. He would have been a good one. Attentive and encouraging. Supportive. Her head swam, and she closed her eyes until the dizziness passed. Then she went to the bed and began pulling on the jeans and polo. They had to do something. They couldn't just sit and wait until Slater Nielsen got ready to kill them.

"Did Slater give you a weapon?" Meg asked, sitting down to tug on her Nikes, which were still wet.

"No."

"All those times you played jewel thief for him, and he never gave you anything for protection?"

"I didn't need protection," Margot said. "I was a thief, not a killer." Her face softened as Meg stood and seemed to grow more pale. "Why don't you sit down? You don't look good."

Meg sank back onto the bed. "We have to get out of here," she said more to herself than to Margot.

"The door is unlocked. Slater never locked me in."

Meg, disbelieving, went to the door and tried the knob. It turned without resistance. Facing Margot, she asked, "Does your former boss keep a gun in the house?"

Ryan and Nick crouched in the weeds just beyond the

landscaped grounds of Slater Nielsen's palatial home. Gun-shots sounded from the direction they had just come.

"Feds made land," Nick said.

"Good," Ryan said. "Hopefully, all the guards are on the beach trying to hold them off."

There didn't appear to be any activity outside the house, though harsh lights seemed to illuminate every inch of the yard. Ryan focused on the windows, trying to detect activity beyond them. "Let's go in."

"Ryan, wait—"

Ryan rounded on his friend. "Look, Nick, you can sit here on your ass and wait for the FBI to do their thing or you can help me get Meg the hell out of there. We have no clue how much time she has or if she's not already dead. So which is it going to be?"

Nick swallowed hard and nodded. "We're going in."

"We'll go through the back. And watch for guards. They might be trying to secure the house."

Slater Nielsen was in his office, and when Meg and Margot stood in the doorway, side by side, he smiled at them from beside his desk. Margot had told Meg moments before where he had stashed her gun.

He gestured them in. Meg felt Margot close behind her as she moved into the office. Meg's gaze never left his face. Even as she charted the various routes to the middle drawer of his desk, she registered that he wasn't quite what she had imagined. He wasn't young and dark and brooding. She had not expected salt-and-pepper hair, bushy eyebrows and startling blue eyes.

He indicated a leather sofa. "Have a seat," he said.

Meg would have preferred to stand. The battered state of her body was going to slow her down enough without having to waste precious time propelling herself off the furniture first. Her knees didn't give her much choice, however. Margot stayed behind the sofa.

"I trust you're well?" Slater asked Meg.

She wanted to kill him, just smash his head against a wall until it was mush, until she could squeeze its contents through her fingers. The desire didn't surprise her, but it disgusted her that she had sunk to his level, that she was allowing herself to be so ruled by emotion that right and wrong no longer seemed to matter. All that mattered was that Ryan and Dayle were dead and this man was responsible.

"Slater—"

He had only to look at Margot to silence her, then returned his attention to Meg. "I've been looking forward to meeting you, Ms. Grant. Whatever you need, just ask. I'm sure your sister can tell you I'm a gracious host. Can't you, Margot?"

Margot didn't respond.

Walking behind his desk, he settled onto the leather chair, which creaked under his weight. Meg began calculating the odds of getting him away from the desk. "Sit down, Margot. Next to your sister," Slater said.

Margot hesitated.

"Do it, or I'll make you regret it, and you know how good I am at that."

She obeyed, casting a sideways glance at Meg, who didn't acknowledge that she had heard the subtle threat. Her gaze, hard as stone, was fixed on Slater.

"Twins indeed. Striking." Opening the middle drawer, he rummaged through it. "We're going to play a game, ladies."

"Slater—"

"Shut up, Margot." He said it without a trace of hostility. "It's a simple game. Few rules. I'm going to set you both free.

259

If you can make it to the outer rim of the island without getting caught, you're free. I will be your hunter." He smiled at Meg. "See how reasonable, how accommodating I can be, Ms. Grant?"

"What's the catch?" Margot asked.

"It's minor. Very minor." He spread manacles connected by a two-foot chain on the desk. Next to them, he placed the gun he had taken from Margot's purse earlier.

Margot's breath hissed between her teeth. "You're fucking kidding me."

His cold blue gaze didn't stray from Meg, who stared at him with hatred in her eyes as she adjusted her plan for Margot's gun. "You'd think your sister would know me better, Ms. Grant. She's known me for twelve years, and she has no idea that I'm deadly serious."

He picked up the manacles, the chain rattling, and tossed them. "Do the honors, Margot."

Margot caught them as if he had thrown a dead animal at her.

"Just to let you know how reasonable I am, I'm giving you a head start," Slater said.

"He'll wait until we're almost to the edge of the grounds," Margot said, her voice shaking. She'd heard of this particular game of his but had not believed it until now. "Then he'll shoot one of us. He'll use the trail of blood to hunt us down."

He glared at Margot. "I'm getting impatient with you, Margot."

Margot fumbled with the handcuffs, wrapping one around her slim wrist and snapping it shut. The metallic zipper-click was sharp in the silence. She held the other end out to Meg.

Meg didn't take it.

Margot, searching Meg's face with a worried frown, sensed Slater's impatience and feared what he would do if either of them defied him. She slipped a cuff around the raw flesh of Meg's left wrist.

Meg met her twin's gaze, saw the fear raging in her eyes.

Slater cleared his throat, a broad smile curving his lips when they looked at him. "I would say, 'Let the games begin,' but this has been nothing more than a game from the start." He grinned at Margot. "And you lost."

"Not yet I haven't," she said.

"Even if you get out of here alive, you won't have the one thing that you cared enough about to fight for—Beau Kama. Even if you survive, I win." His smile was hard. "But then, you've known since I had your lover killed that your chances of surviving are slim. And yet, you insisted on running. Just look at the cost." Holding up a hand, he ticked off fingers as he spoke. "Your lover. Your friend in Green Bay. Your sister's friend. They're all dead. And why? Because of you, Margot. Because you're too weak to face up to your mistakes and take your punishment like a good child. Stand up."

Margot stood, then looked down at Meg when she didn't do the same. Meg was staring at Slater Nielsen. "Your sister's friend," he'd said. *Dayle. Or did he mean Ryan?* Her vision blurred, wavered, turned white. She closed her eyes, thought that her brain was shutting down again in self-defense. But when she opened her eyes, Slater Nielsen's smiling image was clear.

Meg rose next to Margot. The chain linking them rattled, and she heard a clock chime somewhere in the house. With each chime, the pressure in her chest made her lungs feel like they were in spasm. She had nothing to lose. Not one thing.

Slater smiled. Happy. The man was happy. "Well, I suppose this is it—"

Meg lunged across the desk, dragging a surprised Margot along with her. Slater didn't have the time to blink before she smashed a fist between his eyes. He reeled back. Margot shouted her name.

Meg scrambled to her knees on the desk, fumbled for the gun. She felt Margot yank on the chain at her wrist.

Meg leaned sideways, bracing all of her weight against Margot's. The metal cuff bit into the abraded flesh of her wrist, strained against abused tendons, but she ignored it as the fingers of her free hand grazed metal.

Slater drove a fist into her shoulder, knocking her back, toward the edge of the desk. Meg clung to the chain for support, her balance precarious at the desk's edge. She saw a flash of his manicured nails as he clasped the butt of the gun. She kicked at his hand, but he jerked it back, then aimed it at her chest.

Out of the corner of her eye, Meg saw Margot freeze, both hands wrapped around the chain. Meg's own fingers were slippery on the taut links that kept her from toppling backward off the desk. She didn't breathe as Slater's finger twitched on the trigger.

"Don't," Margot said between clenched teeth.

Slater's gaze slid from Meg to Margot. "Watch me."

"I'll tell you where the emeralds are," Margot said.

"Too late." He closed one eye as if to take careful aim.

"I'll do anything. Whatever you want. Forever."

"This isn't about what I want, Margot. It's about making you pay in a way that will haunt you for the rest of your pitiful life." He wet his lips, narrowed his eyes. "I know you care for your sister."

"You're wrong."

"You're shaking with it. I've never seen you tremble, Margot. Not like you are now."

"Then what are you waiting for? Do it."

He glanced at her in surprise.

Margot let go of her end of the chain.

Meg fell backward off the desk and landed on her back on the hardwood floor. Rockets of pain went off in her head. She lay stunned for a moment, then pushed herself to her knees. Fire flashed through her chest, stealing her breath. If a rib had been cracked, it was broken now.

Slater Nielsen hauled her to her feet, and she staggered against him. She noticed that there was no resistance on the other end of the chain and that double doors leading into a dark garden stood open.

Ryan and Nick hugged the wall as they crept down a hall at the back of the house, exchanging winces every time a floorboard creaked. The guards already knew they were in the house. Ryan had faced one down right after he'd eased into the kitchen through the window he'd broken. He'd used a long shard of glass to defend himself, felt the gush of the man's warm blood over his hand. Now, he tossed aside the dishcloth he'd used to wipe away the blood as he rounded a corner onto the next landing of stairs, Nick just behind him.

"Watch it!"

Ryan pivoted at Nick's warning, but it was too late. A second guard slammed him back against the wall, sending knives of pain into his shoulder. Aiming a gun at Ryan's temple, the thug growled, "Don't move."

Before he could do more than that, Nick jumped him from behind, nailing him in the neck with the stun gun. After the thug dropped, Nick gave Ryan a sick smile. "Think we're doing okay without a decent weapon, don't you?"

Ryan scowled, cradling his throbbing arm. So much for painkillers. "Let's just find Meg and get the hell out of here."

A shout sounded from another part of the house.

"I'm afraid I taught your sister how to pick locks a little too well, Ms. Grant," Slater said, sounding more amused than angry as he maneuvered Meg through the French doors and into the garden.

The cool night air turned the sweat on her face clammy. Or perhaps it was the knowledge that Margot had freed herself and run, had left her behind to deal with Slater alone.

"Margot!" Slater called as he scanned the garden. "Are you watching?"

He rested the cold barrel of the gun against Meg's head. Her effort to jerk away was feeble. "Stay with me now, Ms. Grant," he said, then raised his voice. "I'm going to kill your sister, Margot, unless you show yourself."

Only the wind moved.

Lowering the gun, he uncocked it. "I guess she wasn't bluffing when she said she didn't care." He smiled at Meg. "It's rather chilly out here, isn't it?"

Meg would have smashed her fist into his face again if she'd had the strength. "Fuck you."

His brows arched. "I'm shocked. You seem like such a refined woman. Principled, too, I learned from my very thorough research. Did you really refuse to take your father's money once you got to college?"

She didn't answer as she considered her chances of wresting the gun away from him.

"Don't even think about it, Ms. Grant. You're hurting, and I could kill you before you got anywhere near it." He steered her back into the house, the chain dragging on the floor.

Inside, he released her to pull the doors closed. "Tell me something. What will become of your father's hard-earned money, the apparent bane of your existence, once you're dead?"

"Go to hell."

"Feisty. Like Margot." He gave her a melancholy look. "For twelve years, I was everything to her. Did you know that? I gave her whatever she wanted. And she betrayed me."

She tried to take a deep breath, but agony sawed through her chest, cutting it off. "You betrayed her first when you tested her."

"Oh, I see. I should have trusted her, and she never would have cheated on me. I find that hard to believe. Whoops." He caught her arm as her knees buckled.

Meg shook him off, forcing strength back into her legs. The chain hung heavy from her wrist, and she began to rotate her hand, tangling the links around her fingers. She needed to keep him talking. "You should have let her make her own decisions. You don't have the right to manipulate people."

"Your father manipulated you, didn't he?"

"Don't compare yourself to my father. There's no resemblance."

"Are you sure about that?"

She raised her chin, aware of an eerie thump-thump-thump in her ears. "Positive. He was a decent man, and you're a monster."

He cracked a smile. "A monster. I like that. I'm protecting my interests, and that makes me a monster." He glanced upward, his eyes narrowed. "Interesting. We have uninvited company arriving in a helicopter." Still holding her with one hand, he fished a cell phone out of his jacket and pressed a button. "What's going on?" he snapped. He listened a moment, his fingers tightening on Meg's arm. "Why didn't someone call me? . . . How long ago? . . . I don't care what you do. Just take care of it." He flipped the phone closed, put it away. "Idiots. I suppose I don't have any choice now but to get this over with."

Meg swung the chain at him like a whip. It lashed across his face, and he threw a hand up in surprise and pain. As she turned to bolt, he dove after her, caught a hand in the back of her shirt, and jerked her off her feet.

She landed on her back on the Persian rug. Through a red haze of agony, she saw him aim the gun at her chest. She kicked out at his legs, incensed that this was how she was going to die. Alone. Betrayed by her only flesh and blood. Helpless.

And then his face exploded in a bloody cloud.

He collapsed and shuddered, a moan gurgling up through his throat before he lay still.

Meg twisted away, choking back a wave of nausea. Staggering to her feet, she grabbed at the back of the sofa when her knees refused to support her. She heard a voice and saw Margot standing in the doorway, a shotgun braced on her shoulder.

"I asked if you're all right," Margot repeated.

Meg sank to her knees, almost blacking out.

Margot walked to where Slater lay in a dark red pool of blood that was soaking into the rug.

"Is he dead?" Meg rasped, pressing a hand to the fire in her side.

Margot felt for his pulse, then straightened to stare dispassionately down at him. "He's dead." She dropped the shotgun. "I would have been here sooner, but I couldn't get back into the house until I found a broken window in the kitchen. Sorry I didn't tell you about the shotgun earlier—didn't think about it until about three minutes ago." She gave Meg a sick smile that faded to concern when she saw her sister curled on the floor. "Christ, you're hurt." She knelt beside her. "Can you get up?"

"In a minute." Meg lowered her head to the floor, trying to fight the weakness back. It would have been easy to just let go. "The handcuffs . . . how did you—"

Margot dipped into the collar of her shirt and withdrew a paper clip. "Old habit."

"What's that noise?"

"Helicopter."

"Nobody moves!"

Margot jerked her head up as Turner Scott stepped into the room, both hands gripping a revolver. His gaze took in Slater's body, then darted around the room as if he expected them not to be alone. "Cops are here," he said, flicking the gun from one woman to the other. "One of you is my ticket out of here."

"I'm your ticket," Margot said, rising.

Meg pushed herself up until she could lean against the back of the sofa. Her head wouldn't stop whirling. "Don't."

Turner fastened his gaze on Meg, but Margot said, "She's hurt. She'd only slow you down."

"Yeah, but they won't shoot her," Turner said. "You're one of us." He gestured at Margot with the gun. "Help her up."

Meg smiled, thinking reality had slipped away because she could swear she saw Ryan, his arm in a sling, his face sweaty and pale, creeping through the French doors behind Turner. That was impossible, of course. Ryan was dead.

But Margot saw him, too, and as she looked at him, she knew she'd given him away.

Turner spun and started firing. Ryan hit the floor and rolled, no longer conscious of the pain in his shoulder, bullets tearing holes in the rug in his wake.

With a snarl, Margot launched herself at Turner, but

someone tackled her from behind and rolled with her up against the wall. She recognized him in an instant as her cabin neighbor. Confusion paralyzed her.

Turner fired again, his shots wild, and Meg, seeing Ryan vulnerable as he staggered to his feet, forced herself up. Turner didn't see her lurching toward him, or if he did, he didn't consider her a threat. She managed to grab his shooting arm and thrust it up. He shoved her away, and she stumbled. Catching the back of the sofa, she somehow stayed on her feet. He swung the gun toward her.

Ryan roared as he drove into Turner and took him out with one punch. Then, wobbling to his feet, he took two long strides to Meg, dragged her against him and hugged her close. "Thank Christ," he breathed against her neck.

Meg was too stunned to put her arms around him. She could smell him—wind and soap—but she couldn't believe it.

He eased back far enough to kiss her, his lips urgent and trembling, then gathered her to him again.

"I thought you were dead," Meg gasped against his throat. Her fingers sank into the front of his shirt, felt the warm body underneath. "You're here."

Setting her back from him, he searched her eyes. They were glazed with shock, and his stomach rolled with concern. He heard Nick and Margot getting to their feet as he started looking Meg over. Rage nearly blinded him when he saw the knot at her temple. "Who did this to you?"

She gave him a goofy smile, happier than she had ever been. He was here. Alive and holding her. "I can't feel my knees."

Her eyes rolled back, and she fainted.

Chapter 31

Meg opened her eyes reluctantly. Feeling no pain or fear, she seemed to be drifting on a soft cloud. She let her lids drop again.

Ryan, perched on the edge of the bed, his hand covering hers on top of the white sheet, saw her eyes flutter and leaned in. "Hey," he said.

Hearing his voice, she forced herself to blink some of the muzziness away and try to focus on him. "Hi." She frowned at the sight of his arm in a sling and brushed the tips of her fingers over it. "Your arm. Are you okay?"

He grinned, reveling in her concern. "I'm terrific. What about you?"

She returned the smile. "Great." She floated for a moment, realizing that they were not on his yacht as she had assumed. Feeling his palm against her cheek, she turned her head into it, sighed. "Where are we?"

"Hospital. You're a mess, but you're okay." Brushing hair off her forehead, he rolled with the emotions that tumbled through him. "Nick's okay. Margot's okay."

Tears began to roll back into her hair. "Dayle—"

He shushed her with gentle fingers against her lips. "I know. I'm sorry, Meg."

She gripped his hand, reluctant to let go. "I thought you were—"

"I'm not. I'm right here, and I'll be here when you wake up. Sleep now."

She drifted off.

The next time she surfaced, she came fully awake, conscious of aches and pains but clearheaded for what felt like the first time in days. She grimaced when Ryan helped her sit up.

"You've got a busted rib," he said. "But that's the worst of it now." On impulse, he kissed the top of her head. "The doctor worried that knot at your temple would give us some trouble, but apparently you have a very hard head."

"As if you didn't already know that."

Chuckling, he gave her a drink of water and waited while a nurse came in and checked her vitals. When they were alone, she smiled at him. "Guess I'm going to live."

"You about gave me a heart attack wondering after you fainted on me."

"Sorry about that." She had tons of questions but had no idea where to begin.

Ryan tangled his fingers with hers. "Think you're up for some visitors? Nick and Margot have been wearing down the tile pacing the hall."

The way he'd said their names had her arching a curious brow. "Nick and Margot?"

He grinned. "I'm no expert, but I think they like each other."

"Really? Exactly how long have I been out of it?"

He consulted his watch. "Since last night."

And he hadn't slept a wink from the fatigue she saw in his eyes. "You're not taking care of yourself," she said.

"I'll do better now, I promise." The truth was, he hadn't been able to function since the feds had airlifted her to the hospital in their helicopter.

The door opened, and Nick stuck his head in. "Hey, great, you're awake." He stepped into the room with Margot, his fingers curved around her forearm. And Margot didn't seem to mind.

Moving toward the bed, Margot smiled. "How're you doing?"

"Better now." Reaching out, Meg clasped Margot's fingers.

Margot looked down at the gesture that was at once warm and not the least bit self-conscious. Emotion welled into her throat.

Meg said, "Ryan? This is my sister Margot. She saved my life last night."

"I've already thanked her from the bottom of my heart," Ryan said.

Margot nodded, squeezing her sister's hand in return. "Everyone's been very generous." Her smile turned tremulous, and she swiped at a tear before it could embarrass her. She wasn't used to the kindness of relative strangers, but she'd take it any day.

Meg tilted her head, wondering what it was about her sister that looked different.

Ryan said, "Kelsey's working on a deal with the feds for Margot to testify against Jake Calhoun, the hit man who killed Beau. The details are still being worked out, and she's not off the hook entirely, but she earned big-time brownie points, of course, when she saved your pretty behind."

They laughed, and Meg realized what was different about her twin. She had never seen her smile, had never heard her laugh.

"We should go," Nick said. "Meg needs her rest."

"You'll come back in the morning?" Meg asked her sister.

Margot nodded. "If you'd like."

"I would."

Margot smiled again and let the tears drop unchecked down her cheeks. "Me, too."

When they were alone, Ryan crawled into bed with Meg. "Promise me something."

She slid her hand over his, loving the way his eyes darkened at the contact of skin on skin. "Anything."

"Don't scare me like that ever again. I mean it, honey. I can't take it."

She grinned. "Honey?"

He grinned back. "What would you prefer? Darling? Sweetie?" He kissed her forehead, a gesture so tender it made her chest ache. "How about Schnookums?"

Hugging him close, she inhaled his scent and closed her eyes. "You don't know what you're getting yourself into."

"I think I have an inkling."

"I can be difficult," she said.

"No way."

Her lips curved, and she pressed a kiss to his throat. "Stubborn."

"Really?"

Another kiss, along his jaw where a bruise smeared purple. "High-strung."

"You're kidding."

She kissed him on the mouth, pulling back when he tried to deepen the embrace. "Obstinate."

He caught his hands in her hair. "I don't care. Come here." He muffled her laugh with his lips.